Misty Manor

Linda Rawlins

Riverbench Publishing, I

Also by Linda Rawlins

Rocky Meadow Mystery Series:
The Bench
Fatal Breach
Sacred Gold

Misty Manor

Healthy Blessed Reading

Linda Rawlins

Misty Manor
By
Linda Rawlins

Dedicated to

Carol McGuire

Rest in peace, my dear friend.

I hear the library in Heaven is extraordinary!

And to

All hospice workers

You are truly a gift from above!

Acknowledgments

Although one name appears on a book cover, there are many invaluable people who help bring a book to life. I'd like to thank all of them for helping to bring Misty Manor to fruition!

My mom, Joyce, without whom I would probably not be writing, for initial editing and being a great cheerleader!

My children, Krista - for content review, grammar and line editing, fantastic suggestions and moral support. Matthew Liotti, the master producer for my fabulous book covers, bookmarks, websites, book trailers, social media, marketing and promotion. They are tough on me, but great cheerleaders! All mistakes, and I know I still missed some, are my own.

My husband, Joe, for quietly handling everything else to support and carry the family through while I am writing. Officer Paul Marinaccio, Top Shot Season 3, and his lovely wife Jenn for police procedural support and helping to make sure my BOLO's are correct.

My first circle of readers – Sandy, Anita, Ashley, Joyce, Joe, Krista, Claire – you rock!

To a very special writing group – Mekel, Steve, Melissa, Robert, Karen, Sally, Joe and Steve. The readings were phenomenal and Zack the chef was fabulous.

To all the readers, librarians, book sellers and others who are so enthusiastic and accepting of my words. I love hearing from you. My books could not live without you and I humbly thank you. I'll see you all at the beach!!!!

Happy Reading!

Chapter One

"Fired? Ed, look at me. What do you mean fired?" Megan asked, staring at her boss of six years for the Detroit Virtual News.

"Just what I said," Ed replied, chagrined as he shrugged his shoulders. "Fired, kaput, game over, end of the line."

"I can't believe you're saying this." Megan placed her hands on her hips as she shook her head in disbelief.

"Those are my orders, Meg. It wasn't my decision. I'm sorry."

"Did you fight for me? Did you explain everything?"

"I tried to, but they wouldn't listen. With today's economy, they're looking for reasons to get rid of people and you handed them an excuse on a silver platter."

"I handed them an excuse? Don't you mean, we handed them an excuse? I did exactly what you told me to do. Be aggressive, turn over rocks," Megan mocked.

"I'm sorry, there's nothing I can do. The complaint came in and they acted on it," Ed said gently. "Maybe this was one rock too many."

"Ed, I need my paycheck. I need to pay my rent. What am I supposed to do now?" Megan choked as tears formed in her eyes.

"I'm not sure. I don't know how it works because it's never happened before." Seeing her tears, Ed wanted to wrap his big bear arms around her, just the way he would his daughters, but knowing she would resent it, he stood next to her, hands in his pockets, uncomfortably shifting his feet.

"That's fine, but you tell them if they run one word of that story, they'll suffer the consequences. They can't tell me to dig dirt on someone and then fire me for it, while trying to reap the benefit." Megan picked up her purse and stormed out of the office, slamming the door in the process. She stopped at her shabby little desk and grabbed a dusty box from the floor near the wall. After packing her meager belongings, she picked up the box and headed toward the front of the building. Marge, the office manager, ran after her and judging from her facial expression, Megan realized Marge knew about the decision.

"Does everyone know?" Megan asked, with a sarcastic smile.

"Megan, I'm so sorry. I heard the news earlier today and I can't believe it. Not after all you've done for them." Marge gently placed her hand on Megan's shoulder.

"Believe me, no one's more shocked than I am."

"What'll you do now?" Marge asked, holding back tears.

"I don't know and I'm too angry to think about it." Megan shifted the box to her other arm as she juggled her purse strap over her shoulder.

"You have my cell," Marge said. "Text me and let me know what you decide. Maybe they'll change their minds when this all blows over."

"Screw them." Megan watched Marge's face drop. "Not you, just them."

"I feel so bad."

"I know you do," Megan said, managing a small smile. Still holding the box, she leaned into an awkward hug. Marge was a substitute mother to everyone who worked at the paper. She had always been a great source of comfort when Megan stressed over a column or needed help with research. Megan knew the decision had nothing to do with Marge and could sense she was torn between sympathizing with Megan and being loyal to the paper.

"Look, you better stay away from me before they accuse you of fraternizing with the enemy," Megan said, as she turned and walked out.

Standing at the door, wringing her hands in front of her, Marge looked paralyzed except for the tears streaming down her face, and her lower lip, which quivered as she tried to hold her emotions in check.

Megan hit the sidewalk and stopped. Turning back, she said, "I promise I'll call in a couple of weeks and let you know what I'm doing. You've been very nice and I'll miss you."

Chapter Two

Tossing the box holding her few work possessions into the back of her used SUV, Megan slammed the hatch and headed to the driver's seat. She slid behind the wheel and started to sob. Megan didn't know if she was angry, shocked or ashamed, but she was upset. Being fired was a new experience for her and one she was not ready to handle. She was a good journalist and had moved to the Midwest for this job. Michigan was a far cry from the New Jersey beach town where she had been raised and Detroit never would have been her first choice for permanent residence, but the job had made it worthwhile, up to now.

The chime from her cell phone had been incessant since she left the building. Convinced Ed was calling to let her know he would work things out, Megan pulled the phone out of her purse and checked the number. The display clearly indicated "Dean." Megan groaned as she recognized her father's name. Choking back the tears, she was tempted to pitch the phone out the car window. As if the day was not bad enough, what did he want? Her father had been in Europe with his "new" paramour for the past six months and Megan knew he would never call for pleasantries, so he clearly needed something. She pushed the "ignore" button and put the phone on the console.

Hands on the steering wheel, she stared into space as the tears continued. What was she going to do? She could not afford to be without a job and news traveled like wildfire in her profession. She would never be able to work for another paper in this town. Megan had followed orders. The physical paper had not been as popular since the advent of online media. Online news meant faster deadlines and sensational stories to grab the reader. They told her to dig up something newsworthy and she did. Instead of a reward, she was being fired.

Brushing the tears from her cheek, she glanced down as her phone started to chime again. Damn, her father. She was reasonably certain he did not know what happened but they were connected on social media. Megan did not want him to see something online before she got a chance to tell anyone. She would explode if she found a hint of her firing on the web, and even if her father knew, Megan was pretty sure he wouldn't care unless it personally affected him. Dean would either be sympathetic or start lecturing Megan as if she were nine years old. Might as well tell him now. With trembling fingers, Megan opened the phone and muttered a nasal greeting. "Hello?"

"Megan? Megan, honey, is that you?" Dean's eager voice asked over the phone.

"Yeah, Dad, it's me," Megan said, her stomach clenched in a knot. Speaking with her father was usually a drag and Megan was not in the mood to hear him go off on a rant about his life in Europe.

"I've been trying to get you all afternoon. Where have you been?"

Megan sighed, closed her eyes and stared out the window as she listened to her father's aggravated tone. "I was in a meeting," she said softly.

"Megan, you're crying. I can tell you're crying. Who told you? I purposely said I wanted to talk to you first. I swear I'm gonna wring someone's neck."

"Ed told me. Why would you tell me?"

"Ed? Who's Ed?"

"My boss," Megan replied, exasperated.

"How would Ed know?"

"Someone sent him a directive and he had to tell me."

"I know you work in media, but there really has to be some personal privacy."

"Dad, what are you talking about?" Megan said, annoyance creeping into her voice.

"I'm talking about your grandmother. What are you talking about?"

"What about Grandma?" Megan asked, suddenly shaking a little. Grandma Rose's health had been worsening for several months and the whole family was on pins and needles. "Is she okay?"

"Then you don't know?"

"Know what?" Megan yelled into the phone.

"The doctor called me this morning. Are you sitting down?"

Megan started crying again, because she knew what her father was going to say. "Is Grandma...?" Megan's voice trailed off as she couldn't finish the thought.

"Is Grandma what?" Dean asked, suddenly realizing Megan's concern. "Oh no, she's okay, for now."

"Then why did you ask if I was sitting down?"

"Because, I heard you crying and I didn't want you to get hysterical," Dean carped into the phone.

Megan choked on a big sob and wiped her face as tears dripped over her lips and onto her shirt once again. "Is she getting worse?"

"See, there you go getting upset. You know your grandmother has been sick, but, yes, it does look like she's getting worse." Megan cringed at her father's cold, uncaring attitude and began to rub her temples in response to the throbbing headache starting to form.

"Are you coming home?" Megan sighed. "You want to be with her, right?"

"Well, that's the problem. I really can't come home right now. Gigi has a big opening coming up and I have to be with her. Besides, we knew it was only a matter of time for your grandmother," Dean said evenly. "She's lived a good life but now she's confused at times. She might not even know me."

"Gigi? Are you serious? How long has she been around? Grandma's dying. Do you even care?"

"Megan, of course I care. She is my mother, after all."

"Yeah, your concern is overwhelming."

"I don't like your tone of voice, young lady."

"Whatever," Megan said, her emotions boiling inside her. She was thirty years old and her father was still calling her young lady when he was pissed, like she was nine.

"Anyway, there are some other issues which need to be taken care of," Dean continued. "Nothing has been done to the property since Hurricane Sandy hit the East Coast which has become a big issue. Megan, are you listening to me?"

"Yes, I'm here, Dad."

"Good, like I said, I can't come home right now. I need you to go back to New Jersey and handle a few things."

"What?" Megan asked, surprise evident in her voice. Her father took her hesitation for resistance and began to manipulate her as usual.

"I know, I know. Your job in Detroit is busy. But I'm not coming home from Europe. You're only twelve hours from Jersey.

The town is sending me legal papers and I need you to take a couple weeks off and handle this for me."

Megan wiped her eyes and nose with the heel of her hand as she grimaced and shook her head. "Wow."

"The other thing is the doctor said it's time for Grandma to go on hospice, so I need you to sign those papers too. Megan, are you listening? Megan? This is important. When it's all over and done with, I'll compensate you for your time."

"You are absolutely unbelievable," Megan steamed. "If I go back to Jersey, my first concern will be Grandma."

"Of course," Dean said, excitement creeping into his voice as he realized he would get his way, again. "Grandma would love to see you before she, you know."

"I really don't believe this. Yea Dad, I do know," Megan said, resignation in her voice. "A trip to the beach sounds exactly right at the moment."

"Oh Megan, I'm thrilled to hear you're going. Grandma will be too. After all, you're helping her, not me. It's still her house. You get the ball rolling. Once she passes, we can sell the property to a developer and be done with it."

"Are you kidding me? Grandma would have a stroke if you sold Misty Manor." Megan said as she started to tear up again.

"Misty Manor," Dean sighed with exasperation. "If I never hear that name again, I'll be more than thrilled."

"I can't talk to you anymore," Megan said. She hung up the phone and buried it inside her purse. Crying, she started the car, shifted into drive, and raced out of the parking lot.

Chapter Three

Megan turned off her music as she coasted into the driveway of the large Victorian home owned by her grandmother. According to the dashboard, it was ten o'clock in the morning. After leaving work, Megan spent the rest of her day packing bags, paying bills, and trying to explain to her landlady why she was leaving. The woman was kind and offered to hold her apartment until Megan had time to sort out her life, but she had to make a final decision within a month. After that, her furniture and belongings would be on the curb. Agreeing to the terms, Megan cleaned her apartment, packed her car, turned off the lights, left Detroit, and headed home to New Jersey. Megan had stopped twice for gas and fast-food. Munching on snacks during the quiet, dark night, the drive turned out to be meditative and she hoped this unexpected turn in her life would lead to the journey she was destined to travel.

Stepping out of the car, Megan stared at the house. The pebbled driveway crunched under her feet as she took a minute to stretch her back and look around. Her grandmother's house was a Grand Victorian mansion built in the early 1900's. The estate was named Misty Manor and sat on Ocean Ave, in Misty Point, NJ.

Megan remembered her grandmother telling her it was the first grand mansion, built in the town owned by her great grandfather, John Stanford. John had been a sea captain and was given land as a wedding present from a prominent Philadelphia philanthropist who was grateful John had braved the seas to deliver some very valuable resources to Europe.

John spent a few years redeveloping the land from a barren landscape into a small town named Misty Point. When John married his young bride, Mary, in 1915, he gifted her with the gorgeous mansion which they named Misty Manor. Directly in front of the house was a large unkempt lawn, which sloped down toward sand and surf. The house had been built on the Northern Cape and hosted a lighthouse near the water, which was still in use today. The back of the estate was adorned with a number of small cottages used by family and guests when visiting the shore. The southern side of the Manor had a large turn around driveway as well as a garage which held her grandfather's 1955 lime-green Studebaker. Growing up, she was not allowed to play in the garage or go near the car. Megan was not sure if it was still there or had survived the storm.

Misty Manor boasted wide open porches surrounding the house on two levels. Years ago, Megan loved to sit on the porch swing, while she read a book and enjoyed the breeze.

The house looked solid at first glance. Misty Manor could certainly use some fresh paint and new awnings but the foundation appeared intact. Normally, the estate would have been adorned with a cultured green lawn, complete with sculpted bushes and topiary, flowers in the garden and decorative pots on the front porch carefully placed between comfortable rocking chairs and tables.

Three years had passed since the coast of NJ was hit by Superstorm Sandy, a category three hurricane and one of the deadliest storms to hit the Atlantic Coast. Despite mandatory evacuation, many people died and destruction was estimated in the billions. Thousands of disaster workers were mobilized to help clear state roads and mitigate damage following the hurricane. Millions of people across the state were virtually paralyzed, forced to be without power, gas, and water for days. Thousands of first responders, with the help of hundreds of Canadian utility workers who traveled to NJ along with those from other states, helped to restore service. Life began again, but not without permanent scars to many families and residents.

Perhaps, because Misty Manor sat on a small hill, the mansion was able to brace the destructive winds, avoid flooding from large waves which crashed the shore, and survive with only moderate areas of damage to the estate. Unfortunately, the cottages were damaged beyond repair and the aftermath of the storm needed to be dealt with.

It was a testament to her grandmother's strength and determination that she insisted on going back to the mansion within weeks of the storm, despite food and power being severely limited. Now, at the tender age of ninety, Rose was ready for hospice. She had been slowing down before the storm and the threat of loss from the hurricane only added to her decline, but Rose would have her wish which was to spend the rest of her life at Misty Manor.

Megan reached into the hatch to retrieve her luggage. Piling her bags on the large circular driveway, she turned to look at the ocean. Megan loved the view of the water and the beach. In Detroit, Megan use to ride to Lake St. Claire, but the large lake did not begin to compare with the Atlantic Ocean. Staring at the surf, Megan remembered walking over the cool sand and swimming whenever she found free time. The ocean had always been meditative for her and a reminder her problems were small compared to its immense power.

Megan could feel the sun on her face, hear the surf, and smell the brine mingled with an occasional waft of sunscreen. The Misty Point boardwalk started at the edge of their property and continued for several miles south. Before the storm, she would pass benches and planters fixed with memorial plaques when she took her walk. Within a mile there were a series of buildings which housed gift shops, restaurants, an arcade and two hotels. Not sure if anything survived the storm, she was determined to check it out as soon as possible.

Megan took a deep breath and soaked it all in. She planned on getting settled and heading to the beach for a dip, even though the water was still cool in June. The venue was even more attractive in the evening, especially when the full moon reflected off the ocean and provided ample light for beach fires, late night charter boats and fisherman.

Picking up a few of her bags, she turned and walked toward the front of the house and the large set of steps leading up to the porch. Megan dropped the bags and ran down to retrieve the rest. As she climbed to the top, she imagined her family in the same spot, years ago, when Misty Manor was the grandest of all Victorian estates in the area. There was a butler who would have helped her collect her things, and escort her inside, but time and the expensive economy forced the Stanford family to relinquish their staff and sell part of their land to summer homeowners.

The porch had an inset, made of stone, with the name Misty Manor carved into it. Mansions and estates were not named much anymore. Dinner at Misty Manor had formally been held at seven o'clock, every evening, after an hour of hors d'oeuvre and festive libations on the veranda. Dinner guests dressed for the meal and held lively conversation after which they played card games in the parlor.

Once her belongings were on the porch, Megan fumbled in her purse until she found the key to the front door. After several attempts, she opened the door and was instantly rewarded with a waft of musty, cold air as she crossed the threshold. Opening a few of the windows, she turned on the lights and explored the main floor of the mansion.

"Hello? Grandma? It's Megan. Is anyone here?" As the silence enveloped her, Megan felt the back of her neck tingle. She had no clue if anyone was staying with Rose or helping her through her day and Megan felt ashamed she could not recall the last time she had spoken with her grandmother.

Racing up the grand staircase, Megan continued to call out. "Grandma, are you here? Hello?" She quickly crossed the balcony and headed toward her grandmother's bedroom. Not waiting to knock on the door, Megan turned the heavy glass knob and opened the door. Rose was lying in her bed, and appeared very small and still. She didn't move when Megan called her name. Holding her breath, Megan slowly walked over to the bed and peered down. After a minute, Megan thought she heard a small breath and reached out to touch her grandmother's cheek. The skin was smooth and cool, but not cold. Megan placed her hand near Rose's mouth and felt a small, warm puff of air as her grandmother exhaled. Taking a deep breath herself, Megan was relieved Rose had not passed. Anger welled up inside her. Had her father known what conditions his mother was living in? Who was taking care of Rose? Who was feeding her and helping her to the bathroom? Megan felt guilty she hadn't called more often and was determined to get answers. Her grandmother would not have to worry about being alone again.

Touching her grandmother, Megan softly called her name. "Grandma? Rose? Are you okay? It's Megan. I'm here to help you." Eyes filling with tears, Megan leaned toward her grandmother when she noticed the flutter of her eyelids. "Grandma? Are you awake?"

Rose slowly opened her eyes and turned her head. She was silent for a moment, then reached out with crippled fingers. Touching Megan's face, she said, "Megan, is that really you?"

"Yes, Grandma. I'm here now. I've come to take care of you."

"My precious baby. Why are you crying?"

"I'm so sorry. I didn't know you were alone. I would have come sooner, but I thought my father had someone here taking care of you."

Snorting, Grandmother Rose laughed and said, "Oh, your father. Yes, he did hire someone. She pops in on occasion and spends more time searching the house for items she plans to steal than with me." Rose chuckled, "But, she doesn't know where I've hidden the really good things."

"Grandma, what's her name? Trust me, I'll deal with her."

"Fran. Her name is Fran and she is a witch."

"Well, you won't have to worry about Fran anymore," Megan whispered. "Guess what? I'm moving back home to take care of you. We'll be together every day."

"Really? Megan, what about your job and why would you want to spend time with an old lady like me?"

"How about, because I love you? I'm so sorry, Grandma. If I had known, I would have been here sooner. I swear."

Smiling, Rose turned her head and placed her hand on Megan's cheek. "It's not your fault and taking care of me shouldn't be your responsibility. Please believe that. But now that you're here, how would you like to help me get up and go to the bathroom?"

Laughing, Megan extended her arm and said, "I can't think of anything else I would rather do at the moment."

Chapter Four

Covering Rose with a blanket, Megan settled her into a comfortable chair and turned to survey the bedroom. She walked over to the large windows and drew back the drapes. "Grandmother, it's a beautiful day. How about a little sunshine?"

"I haven't had those windows open in years. Is it breezy?" Rose asked while trying to pull the blanket up to her chin.

"It's nicer outside than it is inside the house," Megan said as she pushed the windows open. Getting some fresh air in the room would help the odor. Rose's bedroom had a sour smell after months of neglect, but a good day of cleaning and laundry would work wonders. Who knew the last time Rose or the bedclothes had been cleaned or laundered? Either Rose had gotten used to it or lost her sense of smell. "I have to bring my bags in from the porch and then I'll come back and start on your room."

"You'd better start on your old room," Rose said. "I'm sorry, honey, but I don't think it's been cleaned in years. You'll want a fresh place to sleep tonight, so start there."

Megan turned to look at her grandmother. The sad look on Rose's face broke Megan's heart.

"Okay, Grandma, I will. Are you comfortable for now?"

"Just grand, thank you, Megan. This is wonderful," Rose said through quivering lips.

"You rest. I'll be back in a little bit," Megan said as she adjusted the blanket.

Chapter Five

Pulling her luggage in from the porch, Megan made several trips to carry her bags up to the third floor, and into the room she used as a child. It was a beautiful ocean front room, but as Rose pointed out, it had been closed since the day she left, seven years ago. What a sad, memorable day that was. Her mother gone, her father angry, and Rose looking ill in the parlor, Megan had gathered a few belongings and left without looking back. She was eager to start her life and see the world.

Seven years later, she stood at the threshold of her room, enveloped with nostalgia. There had been some great times in this house, although mostly at the hands of her grandmother. She doubted her parents realized she was gone for the first month, but now Megan also realized she probably broke her grandmother's heart.

Megan opened the wide windows to allow the strong ocean breeze to enter the room. She pulled the sheets off the bed and aired out the mattress. She then went down to the second floor to do the same for Rose's room. She checked her grandmother and said, "I'll have your room tidied up in a jiffy, but I'll have to reintroduce myself to the washer and dryer first." When she did not receive a response, Megan turned back to look at Rose and noticed she was drifting back to sleep. Rose needed someone to help her stay clean, dry and comfortable, and the next time Megan spoke to her father, she would give him an earful for leaving Rose in this condition.

Listening to the surf pound the shore, Megan collected a variety of plates and glasses which appeared to have been in the bedroom for quite some time and made her way downstairs to the kitchen. Placing the dishes in the sink, she turned on the faucet and was rewarded with hot water. After searching the counter, Megan found some crusted dish soap. She plugged the sink, added a generous amount of dish detergent and let the water run. Using the few minutes she had, she walked to the side of the kitchen and checked the laundry room. The machines looked as if they had not been used in years. Megan opened the washer lid and pulled the knob. Water poured into the machine and Megan hoped a cleansing rinse with water and vinegar would dispel the odors. She then went back to turn off the kitchen faucet and let the dishes soak for a while.

Megan ran back upstairs and noticed Rose was snoring. She gathered the sheets and pillowcases and made her way down to the first floor, but stopped short when she heard a noise in the hall. Someone was in the house. Megan realized the sound was coming from her grandmother's study, off the hall. Squeezing the sheets tighter, she slowly approached the room, leaned forward and peeked around the doorframe. Inside, a woman with over bleached, chopped, short hair was pawing over papers on the desk. A small lamp cast pools of shadow and light across her craggy face. As stale cigarette odor greeted Megan's nose, the woman cursed when she could not find what she was looking for.

"What are you doing?" Megan asked loudly, her stomach clenched with anxiety. "Who are you?"

The woman jumped in surprise at Megan's question. Looking at the sheets clutched in Megan's hands, she screamed, "Who the hell are you?"

"I asked you first and you better talk fast because the police are on their way," Megan fibbed.

"What? You called the police?"

"That's generally what happens when I see a stranger rooting through my family's things," Megan said. "Who are you and why are you in my house?"

"Your house?"

"Correct, my house, and I'm still waiting for an answer." Megan frowned.

The woman crossed her arms. "Fran Stiles. I work here. Mr. Stanford hired me to watch after his mother."

"I see," Megan said as she shifted the sheets. "Well, Dean Stanford is my father and as you can clearly see, I've moved back home. He called and asked me to take care of Rose. Funny, he didn't mention you at the time."

"He didn't tell me he called anyone to help," Fran spat back. "But I'll find out."

"I'd like you to move away from my grandmother's desk. I don't know what you do here, but it sure doesn't look like you've done anything in a while."

"I bring food to the old woman," Fran said.

"Yes, I found the caked dishes upstairs," Megan shot back. "There's no food in this office, so I think you should leave, now. Don't bother ever coming back."

"I don't think Dean is going to take kindly to this," Fran said, as she dropped the paper she had in her hands and moved away from the desk.

"Well, feel free to discuss it with him, after you leave. Let me know if you find him, he's still in Europe," Megan said, as she dropped the laundry, planted a hand on her hip and watched Fran walk toward the hall. "I don't know what you were doing in here, but if I find any money or valuables missing, you'll be receiving more than a visit from the police."

Opening the front door, Fran turned, an evil expression planted on her face. "Oh honey, you haven't heard the last from me."

"I'm quivering," Megan said, as she pointed toward the porch. "Get out."

Fran left the house and slammed the door. Megan walked to the door and turned the lock as she rested her forehead on the frame. Obviously, the woman had a key. Megan fumbled through her purse to find her cell phone. She dialed 911, connected with a dispatcher and explained her situation. The officer kept Megan on the phone to get information until the officer arrived. Shaking, Megan ran to check on Rose.

Chapter Six

Rose was snoring softly, so Megan continued answering questions for the dispatcher until she heard someone knocking on the front door. Megan ran downstairs and pulled the front door open at which point the dispatcher promptly hung up with confirmation of arrival. Megan planned on filing the police report and then promptly calling a locksmith.

Standing in front of her was an attractive officer with broad shoulders, a sun kissed tan and sandy brown hair. He stared at her for a moment, grinned and said, "Please step out on the porch."

Megan kept looking at him, distant memories wiggling around her brain.

"Ma'am, please, step out on the porch."

Megan shook herself back to the present. "Why? She's gone and Rose is upstairs."

"You called about an intruder. Please step out on the porch until we secure the house."

Megan stepped out on the porch and noticed an older officer standing to the left. "Okay, give me a second."

The older officer pointed to the side. "Ma'am, please move to the end of the porch."

As she walked to the edge of the porch, she said, "Wow, I'm the one who called the police."

"We just want to be sure, Megan," the young officer said with a smile. "Mind if we take a look around inside?"

"No, of course not, but Rose, my grandmother is upstairs," Megan said, as she pointed toward the front door. "She's sleeping. I don't want to upset her." As she spoke, the older officer entered the house and began his search, checking each room.

"You called us, so let us do our job. Please stay on the porch," the young officer said, as he walked away to join his partner.

Megan stared after them, butterflies in her stomach. She looked around the porch and noticed two police cruisers parked in front. Strangers were starting to gather on the beach across the street. How did the officer know her name? She had given it to the dispatcher, but the officer would not have known she called in the report.

Ten minutes later, the cute officer appeared at the door. "Megan, would you please come inside?" Megan complied, concern written across her face as she stepped back into the house. The older office was coming down the steps, adjusting his shoulder radio and stopped in front of them.

"All is secure upstairs," he said as he looked at Megan. "Rose is upstairs and does appear to be sleeping comfortably."

"Yes, that's what I said, Officer Davis." Megan frowned as she stared at his name tag.

The officer's visage was one of being in a constant cantankerous mood. He stood with his hands on his hips and a frown across his brow. "Well, let's start from the beginning," he replied. "What happened here?"

"I was walking in the hall and found someone in my grandmother's study, pawing through her papers."

"Did you recognize her?" Officer Davis asked.

"No, I've never seen her before," Megan said, shaking her head. "But she said her name was Fran Stiles."

"Can I see some identification?" Officer Davis asked. "I've known Rose for quite a while but I can't say I recognize you."

"I don't believe this," Megan said. "I have to get my purse."

"That's fine, we'll wait," Davis said with a forced smile.

The young officer leaned toward his partner and whispered. "That's Megan Stanford. I went to high school with her. I even asked her to the prom, but she blew me off."

"Really? That's interesting," Officer Davis chuckled. "Who would she throw you over for?"

"Believe it or not, Jeff Davenport."

Davis turned toward him, right eyebrow raised. "Now I have another reason to question her character."

Officer Davis reached out for Megan's driver's license when she returned with her identification. "Thank you." He pulled out a pad and started to copy the information. "Your license says you're from Detroit. Back here on vacation, Miss Stanford?"

"No," Megan stammered. "I'm moving back. My grandmother needs help so I'm here to straighten things out."

Officer Davis looked up with another raised eyebrow. "Now that's real interesting to hear. Are you her legal guardian?"

"No, she doesn't have a legal guardian. At least, I don't think so. My father, Dean, asked me to take care of things."

"Yes, we've been looking for him," Officer Davis replied. "Is he expected to return soon?"

"I don't think so. He's in Europe. I thought I was making a report about an intruder. Why are you looking for him?" Megan asked, annoyance creeping into her voice.

"We have some legal papers for Rose, but she's been ill for a while and I didn't want to bother her," Officer Davis said. "I was looking for your father, hoping he would step up and handle things."

"What kind of legal papers?"

"Summons for the property. There was some damage to the cottages out back from Hurricane Sandy. It's been three years and nothing has been done. The town was getting concerned about the danger of someone getting hurt with all the visitors each summer."

"No one visits this house anymore," Megan said.

"So we've noticed," Officer Davis replied with a frown. "A lot of summer visitors cross your property to look at the lighthouse. At night, kids are hanging out by those cottages, drinking, smoking and doing who knows what. Plus, it's an eyesore. It's your property, but when it's not taken care of, the town has to step in. It's starting to pose a real danger to the community and the environment. We haven't been able to reach your father and Rose is too frail to get things done. If you have a way of reaching him, I'd suggest you place a phone call."

"Wow, I called you about an intruder and I'm getting the fifth degree," Megan said.

"Sorry about that, but things have been strained for a while at Misty Manor. We'd rather the homeowner take control, so it's good you're back. I'll be moving on now, but Officer Taylor will stay and take a complete statement about your intruder ma'am. We will be in touch." Officer Davis adjusted his hat, curtly nodded to his young partner and walked out the front door.

Chapter Seven

Megan turned and looked at Officer Taylor. "Wow, he's a bit cranky."

Nick smiled. "You don't remember me, do you?"

Megan took a second to rack her brain. "I can't remember your first name," she admitted sheepishly.

"It's Nick."

"Nick Taylor? From high school?" Megan said, looking at the tall, strong officer in front of her. "You look so different. I mean, you weren't so, so….."

"I know," Nick said, holding his hand up to stop her. "I was a skinny little kid in high school."

"There's nothing wrong with that, but you've definitely matured," Megan said, eyes opened wide.

"Late bloomer," Nick said laughing. "Time in the gym and a good diet helps too." Nick removed his pad and a pen from his left front pocket. "Now, let's get this report done."

The two spent several minutes going over the details of the woman who was going through Rose's personal things. They went into the small office and looked over the desk. "Does it look like anything is missing?"

Megan shook her head slightly. "I have no idea. I just arrived this morning and haven't been in this office for years, so I don't know what was on the desk to begin with."

"There's a checkbook in the corner," Nick pointed out.

Megan picked up the small plastic folder. "I hardly write checks anymore. It's so much easier to bank online," Megan said as she flipped through the check register. "There's nothing written down. I'll have to go to her bank and get statements. Once I see what checks were cashed, I'll have a better idea of what's going on and what kind of a financial situation Rose is in."

"In the meantime, you might want to put a new lock on the door."

"I'll be changing all the locks as soon as possible," Megan said. "I have to call my father to see who else he hired, but I'm sure he has no idea of what's been going on here."

"That's a great idea. You'd better let him know the town is looking into legal action over those cottages out back."

Megan felt her stomach tighten. "Thanks, I'll talk to him. Then I'll need some time to make arrangements before I can straighten things out."

"I'll talk to Davis and get you more breathing room," Nick said with a smile.

"Thanks," Megan said, smiling back. "I'm going to need to hire some help. Probably a contractor or a handyman."

"Once you've had time to organize things, I can give you names of some of the better businesses around here."

"I really appreciate your help, Nick. I still can't believe it's you. Hey, have you been keeping up with the school class? Any idea of who is still around?"

"I keep an eye on the town. Quite a few of us are still here. Some have great jobs but there are a few who are struggling," Nick said, his face impassive.

"Amber and Georgie are rarely on social media anymore. What are they up to?"

"They're here. Georgie is still a life guard, stationed around Tenth Avenue and Amber is dealing with corporate life."

"Really?" Megan said, laughing. "Did either ever get married? The three of us were so close back in high school."

"As far as I know, we're all still looking," Nick said, grinning. "How about you?"

Megan blushed, brushed her hair back and quickly looked down for a second. Looking back into Nick's face she said, "I was close once, but it didn't work out. Too busy with my job and all."

"Which is?"

"I was an investigative reporter for the Detroit Virtual News," Megan said, with a shrug. "I left Detroit and I'm here for as long as Rose needs me."

"Well, that's great to hear because Rose certainly needs someone to help her," Nick said, as he closed his small pad and placed it into his uniform pocket. "I'll file this report. You can pick up a copy from the police department in a couple of days."

"Thanks, Nick. I appreciate it," Megan said as they moved toward the front door.

"I'll see you around." He took a card from his pocket and handed it to her. "Call and let me know when you're settled. I'll get you that list of names if you need them."

"Sounds great," Megan said awkwardly.

"Try and get some beach time. You used to love that." Nick turned and ran down the porch steps with a back handed wave.

Backing into the house, Megan blushed again and shook her head in disbelief, embarrassed he remembered what she liked in high school. She cringed when she realized he had asked her to the prom. Megan did not remember much about that time. She hoped she had not acted like too much of a jerk during school, but she had her reasons for being standoffish. Megan was pulled out of her reverie when she heard a loud crash come from upstairs.

Chapter Eight

Megan raced upstairs to her grandmother's room. Flying through the doorway, she saw Rose sitting on the floor in front of her easy chair. The lamp which had sat on the table next to her was lying on the ground amongst several books and a small clock. "Grandma," Megan called out in alarm. "Are you all right?"

Rose looked up at Megan as if noticing her for the first time and smiled. "Megan, you're here?"

"Yes, I'm here and I'll be staying here. Are you okay? What happened?" Megan asked as she dropped to the floor to check her grandmother.

"I'm fine," Rose whispered. "I had a cramp in my leg. I was trying to shift forward and wound up sliding onto the floor."

"Are you hurt? Did you hit your head?"

"Megan, calm down. I'm okay. Nothing and everything hurts so who can tell?"

"Can you get up if I help you? Maybe we could get back on the chair for now?"

"I'll try," Rose said, as she pushed her bottom next to the chair. After a few moments of jostling, Rose turned to her right, got one knee under her and Megan helped lift her up on the easy chair. Rose leaned back in the chair, her chest heaving for breath while Megan fetched the blanket and covered her. Eventually, Rose started to relax and her breath and heart quieted.

"Feeling better?" Megan asked, as she smoothed her grandmother's hair away from her face.

"Yes," Rose said, as she nodded. "I'm sorry to be a burden. I keep asking God if he has an opening, but so far, he hasn't answered me."

"Grandma, don't say that."

"It's true," Rose said. "My time here is almost done."

Tears sprung to Megan's eyes as guilt wound its way around her heart. "Grandma, I promise, I'm here to help you now."

"I know Megan, I know." Rose squeezed her hand and smiled.

"Who is your doctor?"

Rose laughed. "Well, for years it was Ol' Doc Flanagan, but he needs more help than I do these days, so they sent a new young man. He's one of those house call doctors. He's very nice, but he wants me to get on a program."

"What program?"

"You know, where they take care of you at home."

"Do you want that?" Megan asked, her brown eyes wide.

Rose spent a moment looking at her granddaughter. "Megan, I'm old. My time is over. I don't want tests, but I don't want to suffer. If they can help me at home, that's fine."

"Grandma?"

"Listen, you call the doctor tomorrow and discuss it with him. Okay? His card should be in the kitchen. We'll talk about it again after that."

"Okay," Megan said. "Are you hungry? Do you want something to eat?"

"My appetite isn't good anymore."

"Well, how about I order us some soup? Try it, maybe you'll like it." Megan suggested.

"Ok, I'll try," Rose nodded.

"Good," Megan said, as she whipped her smart phone out of her pocket. "I'll call Antonio's. They're still open, right?"

Rose smiled and started to cough. After a few moments, she cleared her throat. "I think they're open. Everyone had such a hard time after the hurricane. Some of the stores were able to open. It's been years." Rose looked up at Megan. "Does that sound right?"

"Yes, it does, Grandma. Hurricane Sandy was a few years ago. I know a lot of people are still waiting to get back in their houses."

"Someone came by to look at the house after the hurricane. We've had some problems, but I haven't been able to check. As far as I know, the roof isn't leaking."

"It's okay Grandma," Megan soothed.

"I didn't want to talk to them. They would've made me leave the house. I didn't want to leave Misty Manor. I've been here most of my life and I'm going to die here."

"Grandma, please let's not talk about this," Megan pleaded.

Rose clamped down on Megan's wrist. "Megan, you have to check the property. Don't let anyone else look around until you check the property."

"I'll take care of it, I promise," Megan said, as she smiled at Rose.

"Megan, look at me," Rose pleaded, her eyes full of fear. "There's things here that aren't right. There are secrets, a couple of them are bad. Some wonderful things as well. If we're not careful, they'll take Misty Manor and the property. They'll put me in a nursing home to rot and die. Promise me you won't let that happen. I can't leave here without your grandfather," Rose squeezed Megan's arm tighter and whispered, "Promise me."

"Grandma, I promise." Megan's heart was pounding as she looked at her grandmother. What was going on here? She leaned toward her grandmother and said, "Nothing is going to happen to Misty Manor or you. I promise I'll handle things. I'm here to protect you now."

Rose sighed heavily and slumped back into the chair. Her forehead was beaded with perspiration and she looked very pale. "Thank goodness." She stared at her hands for a few minutes as if just discovering they were attached.

"Grandma, are you okay?" Megan asked, feeling shaky. She was worried about Rose and now realized she did not feel well herself. Megan hadn't slept since yesterday afternoon between closing her apartment in Detroit, driving to New Jersey and now discovering some disturbing things at home. Her only food had been snacks and turnpike chicken.

Rose looked at Megan, touched her hair and smiled. "You'd better call Antonio's. That's the only way we're going to know if they survived."

"I will," Megan said, remembering the phone in her hand. "I hope they did." Megan's hand shook as she searched for their phone number. "Here it is."

After a few moments, she tapped her phone and it began to dial the restaurant. Within five rings, a female picked up the call. "Antonio's, can I help you?"

"Joan, it that you?"

"This is Joan, who's this?"

"It's Megan Stanford."

"Megan? How are you? Are you in town?"

"Yes, I've come back to help my grandmother."

"I'd heard she wasn't doing well. I'm so glad you're here," Joan said excitedly. "Hey, a lot of us were worried. Who could forget all those great times playing in the lighthouse?"

Megan relaxed and chuckled into the phone. "Yes, I remember."

"Anything I can help you with?"

"Right now, I need food. I just got back into town and there's nothing in the house. I haven't eaten since yesterday and I'd love a real Jersey tomato pie and a great bowl of soup for Grandma."

"You got it, sweetie. We have a nice chicken vegetable tonight. Will that be all right?"

"My stomach is growling already," Megan said.

"You hang tight," Joan said. "I'll have someone over there right away."

"Can't wait," Megan said. "Thanks, I appreciate it."

"Anything for your grandma. When you get a chance, stop in and say hi. We have a lot to catch up on."

"Will do. I need a little time to get settled and then I'll be there," Megan said.

"Looking forward to it, sweetie," Joan said and then disconnected.

Chapter Nine

Weeks later, Megan stared out the kitchen window at the large expansive property in back of Misty Manor. Her eyes were directed to a bulldozer pushing down one of the homey white cottages. Megan had many fond memories of those cottages. Who else got to play house in an entire cottage while growing up?

Misty Manor was approximately one hundred years old and sat on five acres of land. The large Victorian home had three full floors with a walk in attic above those, which held several other hidden doors, one of which led to a storeroom and eventually out to a stairway and up to a widow's walk.

Megan had no idea how old the cottages were. She knew they were there when she was growing up and they had housed many guests her family had entertained early on. Some of the cottages were very old and others had been added as the housing demand from friends visiting the shore had grown. Rose had never turned away any friends who asked to stay at the estate. She had encouraged visitors and never charged. In return, they helped her with chores and maintenance of the property. Rose had been a single mother, raising a small son, in a coastal town and cleverly leveraged the family's love of the ocean for help.

How brave her grandmother must have been. Thinking over what little she knew of the family history, Megan remembered her great grandfather, John Stanford, was given a large expanse of property as a gift. He had married his sweetheart Mary and together they developed the town of Misty Point, on which they built their estate.

John and Mary had a son, named George, who was her grandfather. He married her grandmother Rose and together they had her father, Dean.

A short time after Dean was born, George disappeared without warning. From what Megan had been told, there had been a large search which covered the property as well as boats and the ocean, fearing an accident or foul play had occurred. Her grandfather was never seen or heard from again. The family waited anxiously for months, worried a body would wash ashore. Several did, but none of them were George.

Rose and her son Dean continued to live in Misty Manor with John and Mary. Rose became very close to Mary as the women kept company while John continued to join as many sea adventures as he could, partly because he had a vast love for the sea and partly to escape the pain of a lost son. When John and Mary passed away, they bequeathed the entire estate to Rose so she would be able to raise their grandson Dean near the ocean they loved. As time went on, and money became scarce, Rose sold pieces of the property to cover her finances.

"Excuse me, Megan?"

Megan turned to see the recently hired housekeeper, Marie, in the doorway of the kitchen.

"Yes?"

"I didn't mean to interrupt you, but Dr. Cameron's office just called. They wanted you to know someone from the hospice would be stopping by to talk to you soon," Marie said softly. Looking at the pain on Megan's face, Marie cocked her head and gave a small smile. "I know this is hard stuff, Megan. Your daddy left you in an awful position, but you're doing great and you have friends and family by your side."

"Thanks, Marie. I don't know what I'd do without you already." Megan crossed her arms and turned back toward the window. "It's been a crazy two weeks and I appreciate you helping me while we get everything settled."

"Nonsense, Megan. You're helping me. I need the work and I appreciate you thinking of me."

"C'mon, Marie. Once I called, I figured you'd be here, paid or not." Marie was a native of Misty Point and good friend of the Stanford family. She was the same age as Dean and occasionally worked at the pizzeria when Joan needed help. However, she recently needed more money to make ends meet and was eager to start when Megan called for help.

Marie laughed. "That's true. Rose is a beautiful woman and has been so kind over the years, I doubt there is anyone in Misty Point who wouldn't be willing to help her out."

Megan turned back toward Marie. "I believe that, but I don't understand why I came back to find her in such bad shape. If someone had called me, I would have been back here to take care of her."

Marie shifted uncomfortably and gazed down toward the floor. She lifted her head and looked back at Megan. "I don't want to speak ill of anyone, but truthfully, a lot of us have been out here trying to take care of Rose. We couldn't gain access to the house and we were concerned. We even called the police to help us."

"And what happened?" Megan asked, surprised to hear about their offer.

"We were told your dad had hired Fran Stiles. Unfortunately, no one could find your dad to confirm that fact. In the meantime, Fran had the only key and we were told to butt out. No visitors were allowed. We had no idea how Rose was being treated or Fran's intent toward the house."

Megan's heart weighed heavy hearing the news. "I don't understand why no one called me. Why didn't someone reach out?"

Marie shifted again as her face turned red. "Megan, we had discussed trying to call APS, adult protective services, and we turned to Dr. Cameron as well. Technically, your dad is the legal next of kin. No one really knew where you lived and we assumed if you were in touch with your grandmother and dad, you'd be here if you wanted."

Megan tuned back to look at the heavy machinery demolishing the cottage in the yard. Her face flushed red as she filled with guilt. Her job had kept her busy. She had been so busy trying to land a prominent byline, she lost track of things at home. She was guilty of not calling her grandmother, but realized the few times she had, no one answered and Megan did not call back. If she had any idea Rose was being held prisoner, she would have called the police herself. What had her obsession cost her? Her job and now her guilt over a beloved grandmother who was apparently neglected as a reward for all she had done for her family over the years. Megan silently kicked herself for not staying in touch.

Marie broke into her thoughts. "Megan, please go take a walk on the boardwalk. Go get some pizza or a soda. See if you can find your friends. You've barely left this house in two weeks."

Megan turned back, her eyes glistening. "I can't leave Rose alone."

"I understand, but now you have help. Take your phone and go for a walk. Officer Nick has been calling. Get some fresh air. I'll call or text if we need you."

Feeling suddenly overwhelmed, Megan welcomed the chance to get out. She used to love walking the boardwalk. "You're right, Marie." Megan left the window, blew her nose, gathered her phone and some money and walked to the front door. She turned back to Marie who was standing in the front hall watching her. "I have my phone." Megan knew Marie would call her if she was needed, but if she had known how quickly it would be, she would have run.

Chapter Ten

Megan walked along the boardwalk, the ocean breeze caressing her face. The sun was warm and she relaxed as she took some time to reflect. She gazed at the beach and enjoyed the mingled scent of suntan lotion, brine and cheeseburgers. Megan passed the boardwalk pizza shop, featuring sausage and pepper sandwiches and a variety of pizza. The food smelled great but she knew it did not compare to Antonio's on Main Street.

The last two weeks had been hectic. Megan had a long, aggravating talk with her father about Grandma Rose and Misty Manor. He clearly refused to leave Europe and pointedly told Megan to do whatever she liked as long as she kept the legal issues at bay and satisfied the town. Beyond that, he had little interest in the health of his mother or Misty Manor. Dean was kind enough to call his lawyer and have the necessary documents drawn up that would allow all responsibility to fall into Megan's lap. She was now Rose's power of attorney and health surrogate.

The first thing Megan did was have all the locks changed in the house. She had no idea who had been coming and going or who had keys to the old locks. Megan then arranged a meeting at the local bank to make sure her grandmother's accounts were secure. Rose had enough money to be cared for as long as it was managed appropriately. Megan then reached out to Dr. Cameron and scheduled an appointment for a realistic conversation about her grandmother's health. She was told her grandmother had chronic renal failure which explained her loss of appetite, excessive sleepiness and confusion. Dr. Cameron had suggested she seek out a nephrologist and consider dialysis but when Megan asked Rose, she flatly refused. Rose knew her condition was progressing slowly and told Dr. Cameron she was not afraid to die as long as she was not in pain. They had a long conversation about palliative care and hospice. Rose signed a POLST and listed Megan on the form. Megan agreed to an initial hospice consultation after she had a chance to speak to her grandmother about it once more. The palliative care nurses would continue to make house calls for Dr. Cameron as needed.

When she left the office, Megan called Nick to see if he knew anyone who could help as a caregiver for Rose. When he called her back with the phone number for Marie O'Sullivan, Megan and Rose were thrilled. Rose had known Marie for a long time and Megan trusted her.

Megan then made time to visit town hall in Misty Point and follow up on the legal notices Rose had received about the condemned cottages. The town wasted no time issuing permits so Megan could make arrangements to have the cottages demolished. Reaching out to Nick, she asked for names of contractors who could start work immediately. Nick was very happy to offer names and numbers as well as an invitation for dinner, which Megan politely refused stating she was not ready to leave Rose alone yet. Megan was surprised to find she was relieved when Nick told her he would ask again in a few weeks.

When time allowed, Megan placed several calls to the homeowner's insurance for Misty Manor, but was stalled or disconnected. After mentioning legal involvement, the company agreed to have a representative check the property. Megan was advised to take video of the cottages as well as provide a report of the damage before anything was touched. She complied but had no idea if the property had been inspected since the storm and whether she could prove any damage was related. Megan had heard horror stories of other homeowners who continued to live in temporary apartments since Hurricane Sandy, while waiting for their homes to be repaired. Some were denied coverage completely. However, she took the video and eventually an agent did come out to the property.

"Megan, hey Megan, back to earth." Megan looked up to realize her high school friend Georgie was leaning against the boardwalk rail. "I don't know what you were thinking about, but it didn't look like fun."

Megan laughed and turned to her friend. "Georgie, you look fantastic. I don't believe it, you haven't changed one bit."

"Now I know you're not on this planet," Georgie laughed and tossed her bleached blond hair back in the wind as she raced forward to hug her high school friend.

"I'm not kidding," Megan said, releasing the embrace. "The day I left Misty Point you were practically leaning against the same rail on the boardwalk, wearing the same red lifeguard bikini and tanned as always."

"Megan, it's been seven years. I've had a lot of lifeguard suits since then," Georgie smiled.

"You know what I mean," Megan laughed and hugged her best friend from high school again. "Are you still running the boardwalk every morning? It certainly looks like you are."

"You know it. I used to run with Amber but now she's corporate material, she's never available. Even when she does have time to run, she goes to the company gym." Georgie held up her hands and rolled her eyes

"I believe it," Megan chuckled. "Nothing but the finest and she was like that back in high school."

"So, what have you been up to? I was sorry to hear about Rose being ill. I'm glad you're back to take care of her."

"Yea, it's a mess right now," Megan said as she shrugged her shoulders. "I didn't realize things were so bad. Dad didn't call me until recently."

"No offense, but it doesn't look like you've gotten any sun or sleep for a while."

"That's for sure. Not in a real long time and that had nothing to do with coming back to Misty Point," Megan said, realizing for the first time how senselessly driven she had been at her job. "Hopefully, I'll be able to concentrate on my health, now that I'm off the crazy train. At least I think I'm off, although I'm not too sure. But first I have to take care of Grandma."

"I hear ya. You love the beach. We'll have to arrange some down time for you to relax. If we choose the right day, we may be able to get Amber to join us," Georgie said with a laugh. "Like old times, girl's night out on the beach."

A genuine smile appeared on Megan's face, yet she was suddenly overcome with sadness and nostalgia. She turned toward the ocean before Georgie could see her eyes become moist. "You don't know how good that sounds right now. I didn't realize how much I miss those times.

"You got it, girl," Georgie jumped up and offered a high five to Megan. "Just say the word. I'll call Amber today."

Megan felt herself begin to relax for the first time in weeks. Marie was right. The sun, the surf, the salty air were working until her cell phone started vibrating. Megan looked down to see the text.

There's big trouble. You'd better come fast.

"What's wrong?" Georgie asked, seeing the look on her friends face.

"I don't know. Marie says there's trouble so I have to go."

Georgie gave her friend a quick hug. "Call me when you can or if you need me. I have the same number. You know where I'll be."

"Definitely will do. Thanks Georgie," Megan said with a frown as she offered a quick hug, turned and starting trotting toward Misty Manor. As she made her way up the boardwalk, she could hear sirens in the distance.

Chapter Eleven

Megan noticed police vehicles lining the street as she neared Misty Manor. A lump formed in her throat and she feared Grandma Rose had passed. She would feel guilty forever if Rose died while she was away from the house.

Running into the house and then upstairs, Megan burst into Rose's room to find her comfortably asleep in her bed. Megan paused for several seconds to watch her breathe. Seeing Rose's ribcage rise and fall several times, Megan heaved a sigh of relief and backed out of the room.

Searching the house, Megan found Marie standing on the back porch, with tears in her eyes and wringing her hands. Officers were moving across the yard, carrying cases and taking photographs. The heavy machinery was now quiet and parked on the side of the property. Megan watched as one officer began to unroll yellow crime scene tape and wrap it around one of the cottages.

"Marie, what happened here?" Megan asked. She turned her head to take in the whole scene before her.

"Oh, it's not good, Megan. Not good."

"Okay, I believe you, but what is it?" Megan asked again as she watched more officers arrive, with special cases and equipment.

"I don't want to be the one to tell you. I'd rather the police did that, but they look pretty busy out there." Marie looked down and swallowed hard before facing Megan. "The contractors were knocking down a cottage and I think they found a dead body."

"What?" Megan asked louder than she intended.

"I think it's a corpse. They didn't tell me, but I was watching through the kitchen window, like you were this morning. The bulldozer was pushing on the cottage and suddenly the foreman was yelling at the workers to stop what they were doing. They were staring into the debris and the next thing I know, police cars were arriving and all the equipment was turned off."

"What makes you think it's a corpse?"

"I heard one of the men yell something to another about a corpse," Marie said, taking a deep breath and shrugging her shoulders.

Feeling a large knot in her stomach, Megan looked into the yard and saw Officer Davis storming around, shouting orders at everyone. Another officer was pushing construction workers away from the yellow crime scene tape while a third was talking to a foreman on the side. Megan turned toward the street in time to see Nick arrive in his cruiser. He stopped the car and raced over to Davis for instructions. Junior officers were placed in the street to control the crowd of curiosity seekers who had started to coalesce.

Several officials were kneeling by a pile of wreckage. They opened what looked like medical bags and pulled out wrapped packages of equipment to use at the crime scene. Working for the Detroit Virtual News, Megan had seen enough forensic crime scene teams to recognize the action. "That definitely doesn't look good," she murmured as she rubbed her arms, despite the heat of the day. She watched the officers in action until she noticed Davis speaking to Nick and then point to her on the deck. A sudden cold spot grabbed her in the stomach where the knot had been. She held her breath and watched as Nick turned and started towards the porch.

Chapter Twelve

"Hi Megan," Nick said as he climbed the back stairs.

"Hi, yourself," Megan whispered. "Nick, what the hell is going on?"

"Well, that's what I need to talk to you about," Nick said with a small grin. "How about we go inside?"

Megan, Nick and Marie went inside the house and Marie quickly excused herself to check on Rose. Nick pulled out a kitchen chair and gestured for Megan to sit down. "This is going to be shocking enough. I don't want you to get dizzy or anything."

"You're scaring me, Nick. What did you find?"

Nick took his notebook out of his pocket along with his pen. "The construction crew was piling all the debris from one of the cottages. They knocked down the walls and pulled up the concrete slab. Debris needs to be sorted and delivered to the proper area for processing or recycling."

Megan nodded her understanding as Nick continued.

"Apparently, they found body parts amongst the debris."

"Body parts?" Megan asked with widened eyes. "Like a bloody foot or something?"

"No, maybe, I should rephrase that," Nick said. "It was more like they found a few bones."

"Bones? You mean like a skeleton?"

"Yes, they're sorting through the debris now to see if there's an entire skeleton there," Nick answered as he watched her face register shock.

"That's awful. How would a skeleton get into one of the cottages," Megan asked as she watched her hands tremble. "How long was it in there?"

"That's certainly the question of the hour, isn't it?" Nick asked. "Megan, when was the last time you were in Misty Point?"

"Me? Why ask me?" Megan asked in alarm.

"Just trying to get a frame of reference, that's all," Nick said, continuing to watch her.

"This is my first time back since I went to Detroit," Megan said, rubbing her forearms.

"So that's how long?"

"About seven years," Megan answered.

"Do you remember there ever being a problem or issue with anyone before you left?"

Megan stared and laughed. "No, of course not. The only people living here at the time was Rose, my father, and me."

"Megan, forgive me for being intrusive, but where is your mom? When is the last time you saw her?"

"My mother?" Megan paused for a few moments. "I haven't seen her for a long time, but I stopped talking to her when she ran off with that boyfriend of hers."

"How long ago was that?" Nick asked patiently. "When was the last time you saw your mom or her boyfriend?"

"I don't know, years," Megan answered. "We don't discuss it, so we don't talk."

"Can you tell me a little about what you remember?" Nick asked, while jotting some notes.

The significance of his questions suddenly hit Megan. She blanched, steadied herself at the table and leaned toward Nick. "You think my mother's body could be out there?"

Nick tapped his pen on the pad while he looked at Megan. "You okay?"

"I am feeling a little dizzy to be honest," she said.

"Look, Davis let me come in and talk to you because he knows we're friends. Truth is, we have no idea who or how much of who is out there. If it is a skeleton, we'll have to wait until they can figure out how long it's been there. They have ways of doing that. The forensic examiner will be able to give us more information about whether it's a male or female and possible cause of death. Hell, it may not even be a real skeleton. In the meantime, Davis wants to get the ground work started. He'll have lots of questions, like who's lived here? Where are they now? Can we confirm who is alive or dead? He'll check missing persons' reports which have relevance as well."

"Nick, you're blowing me away, here," Megan said, feeling sick to her stomach. "Why do you think it's family?"

"We have to rule everything out. Maybe your dad has another reason to stay in Europe."

"Don't say that." Megan could feel her anger growing. "Dad's a skirt chaser, which was part of the reason my mother started seeing someone else, but a killer?"

"Megan, we have to consider every possibility. No one seems to remember exactly when your dad left for Europe, but we'll be able to check that out. Could a stranger have been living in the cottage without Rose knowing it? Maybe a drifter from after the storm?" Nick asked with a tilt to his head.

"Anything is possible. The only stranger I've seen since I came back was Fran Stiles," Megan said as she looked at Nick. "You're the one who told me kids were drinking and fooling around back there. Isn't that why the town was concerned to begin with?"

"Yes, but if there had been a fresh body rotting in one of those cottages, someone would have called if they stumbled over it or noticed the smell. Plus, if the body is skeletonized, it's been a number of years."

Megan had no answers and looked at Nick.

"Did you have the property inspected after Hurricane Sandy?" Nick asked as he prepared to write in his notebook again.

"I have no idea what they did," Megan said, shaking her head. "I asked Rose about the insurance company before I arranged the demolition, but I didn't get anywhere. I don't know if they came out and inspected after the storm. I assume the town must have walked the grounds if they were concerned about a hazard. Is there a town report?"

"I'll have to ask Davis."

Megan looked up sheepishly. "But I did have an inspector here recently and I went out and videotaped the whole area, just in case I needed it for the insurance company. I don't remember if I got the inside of every cottage."

"Well, we're going to need that video. Like I said, we'll have to check for missing persons for the last several years as well."

"What if they're not missing from here?" Megan asked.

"Hopefully, the coroner can give a general description of gender, age and condition. Then we make it available to other agencies," Nick pointed out. "Bodies decompose at different rates under different conditions, so it's not an exact science."

"I think I'm getting nauseous," Megan said.

"To be honest, there are more people missing than you think. We're constantly on the watch for bodies or skeletons washing up from the ocean, or the bay. The marsh is a big area as well."

"Nick, please stop. Is it possible a body washed up in the cottage and has been out there for a while?"

"That's what we're going to find out," Nick said. "But I can't imagine a fresh body would have been there for years without someone noticing it."

"Could someone have dumped it back there?"

"Like you said, anything is possible. We need to check your video to see if that cottage was clear a week ago. Also, we're not sure if the body was above or below the concrete at this point." Nick put his pad and pen away and took Megan's hand in his. "I'm going to need your help. I know Davis wants to talk to Rose, but I don't want the poor woman to have a heart attack on our watch. Think about how we can make an interview as easy as possible while we're waiting for the coroner to finish his investigation."

"Do you have to speak to Rose? She's so confused at times, she may not help at all." Megan's face flushed as she remembered Rose's warning from two weeks ago. Megan could not bear to think the family was involved with something as heinous as dead bodies.

"We have to try, Megan. It's part of the process," Nick said. "Your hands are cold. Have some coffee and we'll talk again soon." Nick got up from the table and returned to the back yard.

"This day just keeps getting worse," Megan said in disbelief as Marie poked her worried face around the corner.

Chapter Thirteen

Megan took several deep breaths as she looked down at her hands resting on the kitchen table. A body in the cottage was simply unreal. She reached into her pocket, found her cell phone and quickly punched in her passcode to reach the home screen. Hitting the contacts button, she typed her mother's name into the search bar. Megan looked at the last number she had stored for Donna Stanford and bristled about how much her mother must care about her daughter. Her father was not any better.

Megan tapped the name to get more information and hit the call button. She sighed as she listened to the phone trying to connect. After a click, Megan called out, "Mom, is that you?"

Two seconds went by before Megan heard a response. "The number you have reached has been disconnected." After listening to an annoying repetitive tone for a minute, Megan disconnected the call and dropped the cell phone on the table. She could not recall when she had last talked to her mother and she would not have used her current phone even if she had. As a journalist, Megan kept all contact information on file and simply kept downloading her contacts to the next device. Many of the numbers were obsolete but they helped her keep track of timelines when it was important. Megan knew her mother never tried to call her so any number would have been third party, but it was worth a try.

"I didn't mean to eavesdrop, but I couldn't help hearing some of your discussion with Officer Nick," Marie said as she slipped into the kitchen. She dropped into a seat at the table and leaned closer to Megan. "Truth be told, if he was asking me those questions, I would have passed out."

Megan looked at Marie for a few seconds. "You were a good friend of my parents, weren't you?"

Marie blanched at her question. "Yes, long ago. We went to high school together. Your mother and I were in the same class, and your dad graduated one year ahead of us."

"Were you all close?" Megan watched Marie turn pink as she fidgeted in her chair. "Marie, please answer me."

"What does that information have to do with a dead body in the cottage?"

"You heard what Nick said." Megan reached out and placed a hand on Marie's arm. "The police think the body may be my mother or her boyfriend. Mom and dad weren't friendly when I left, but I can't imagine my father a killer. On the other hand, I was barely out of college. I'm sure I didn't grasp a lot of what was happening back then."

Marie shifted in her chair to face Megan. "When was the last time you spoke to your mother?"

"Believe it or not, I can't remember," Megan said, tears welling up in her eyes. "I've been gone from Misty Manor for seven years. Mom had already left and never looked back. She didn't call, she didn't write. How could she leave me like that?"

"Megan, it's not that simple," Marie whispered. "Your mother loves you."

"Loves? As in present tense?" Megan reached for a napkin and wiped her tears. "When was the last time you spoke to my mother?"

Marie took a deep breath and blew out a heavy sigh. "Truth be told, a year or two. She was here in Misty Point. She said she had legal business with your father. I tried to call her two weeks ago and tell her you moved back, but the number was disconnected. I also tried to call her when Fran Stiles wouldn't let us into the house."

"Did you reach her?"

"No. The call didn't go through."

"Are you sure she ever left? A year or two is still enough time for a body to decompose if it were her."

"Actually, no, I never saw her leave. We said goodbye on the boardwalk. I left to work a shift at Antonio's and she went back to the house to pack."

"So you don't know for sure if she ever left Misty Point?"

"No, I just assumed," Marie stammered.

"What about a car? Did she drive herself here?"

"No, your mother never liked to drive. She would have called a taxi to take her to the train station."

Megan paused for thought and chewed the inside of her cheek. "I need to call my father again, but it's evening in Europe, so he'll not want to be disturbed or he'll be in a club and won't be able to hear his phone."

"I'm sorry, Megan," Marie said. "This is all so terrible."

"You've got that right." Megan got up from her chair and headed to the sink. She turned on the hot water and added dish detergent.

"Let me do those," Marie said. "You've got enough on your mind."

"No, I'm fine. I need something to keep me busy right now. This is one of those rare times I'm happy we didn't modernize the house with a dishwasher." Megan picked up a sponge and shifted the dishes. "At least the kitchen and refrigerator are clean and sterile now." After a small pause, Megan turned and asked, "How long do you think a taxi company keeps records of their fares?"

"I have no idea," Marie said with a shrug. Both women jumped at the sound of the telephone from the hall. "Your hands are wet. I'll go get it."

Megan continued washing dishes and tried to remember the names of the cab services in town. She smiled at memories of her and her friends being picked up and taken to a nearby club for drinks. The transport service was a mother's best friend when Megan first graduated high school. All the bars were close and transport was available at all times. The kids would call a van, and ten friends would pile in together and split the fare. As each friend reached legal drinking age, they would all go celebrate, even those who were only allowed a soft drink. At some point the van would pick them all up and bring them home safe and sound. The drivers were local and knew most of the residents of Misty Point. Transport drivers had a tight network and would frequently talk or warn others of dangerous situations, even competing companies. One of the drivers was a relative of a student and would often be called by a mom tracking down her child. If the driver didn't know where the student was, she'd get on the radio and find out. Now that everyone had a cell phone, the dynamic was probably different, but maybe not as good. Warm thoughts flooded Megan as she realized the kids were allowed their independence back then but were still watched out for.

Two years had gone by since her mother was last seen in Misty Point, but Megan hoped to track down the taxi who collected her mother so she could prove she was not the body in the cottage.

Chapter Fourteen

Megan was drying her hands when Marie returned to the kitchen.

"That was the hospice service," Marie said, looking at the notes she had taken while on the phone. "Apparently, the social worker and intake nurse were here earlier, but the police wouldn't let them near the house."

"Well, that's awkward," Megan said, placing the dish towel on the drain.

"Yes, they made another appointment for tomorrow. I told them I would check with you and call back if you couldn't make it."

"Thanks, Marie. I appreciate it. Tomorrow should be fine." Megan turned to face Marie and reddened. "Did they happen to say if they knew what was happening?"

"No, they didn't. I don't think they're aware because it sounded like the girl was fishing for information." Marie picked up the dish towel and started to dry dishes. "I assured them Rose was stable. With all the police cars, they thought we might have been shipping her to the hospital. I explained the situation had nothing to do with Rose, but I didn't say anything else." Marie made a gesture to indicate her lips were zipped.

Megan chuckled as she watched Marie in action. "Marie, I want to take another look in the yard to see what the police are doing and then maybe talk to Rose."

"I understand. You go do what you have to do," Marie said. "It's hot. I'll make a pitcher of lemonade so no one passes out back there. After that, I'll start on dinner. I'd rather be busy in here than watching what they're doing out there."

"You and me both, Marie. You and me both."

Two hours later, Megan was standing in the back yard with Nick and Officer Davis. The corpse had been fully excavated and two technicians were carrying a black body bag toward a medical examiner's van in the street. Megan turned to see another officer with a big role of yellow tape near the street. "What is he doing?"

"He's surrounding the area with crime scene tape," Davis muttered as he wiped sweat from his brow. Putting his hands to his mouth, he shouted, "Peters, take it all the way down to the far tree. Close off the garage, too."

"Is that really necessary?" Megan asked, turning to face Davis.

"Yes, the crime scene boys will be back tomorrow to collect more samples of dirt and debris. Ms. Stanford, do we have your permission to search the garage? It's only a short way from the cottages. There may be important evidence inside."

Megan paused, not sure what to say. She realized she had not so much as peeked inside the structure since she had returned to Misty Manor. It was a natural response since she was never allowed there as a child.

"Either you grant permission or I'll return with a warrant," Davis pressured.

"Sure," Megan shrugged. Her stomach clenched as she remembered her grandmother's words, but it was too late to stop them now.

"Thank you for your cooperation. We'll be back tomorrow and I don't need anyone trampling the ground in the meantime. That includes you, Ms. Stanford," Davis said as he turned to face her. "Stay away from the back yard and the cottages until I tell you everything is clear. The tape will keep everyone away from the lighthouse too."

Megan cringed as she realized the whole town must be talking about Misty Manor by now. "I can't believe this is happening," Megan said as she shook her head.

"Everyone is at a loss at the moment, but we'll keep at it until we know exactly what happened here." Squaring his hat on his balding head, Davis scowled and strode off toward his cruiser.

Chapter Fifteen

Cuddled in a blanket, Megan watched the dark sky from the window seat in her bedroom. The window was open and a strong ocean breeze made the sheer curtains dance with the wind. Megan cradled a strong cup of coffee in her hands and listened to the surf pound the shore. She had not slept well, anticipating questions about Misty Manor and Grandma Rose from the police. Was it possible Grandma knew something about the skeleton? Megan was determined to discuss the body with her this morning, before the police got around to asking questions. Megan was anxious Grandma Rose would say something which would incriminate her without realizing what she had done. Should she have her lawyer present? She was ill and facing end of life, she should not have to endure an interrogation.

Staring out the window, Megan flashed to her childhood. She had always been an early riser and watched many a sunrise from her window seat. The best times had been when she and Grandma Rose made warm drinks and snuck up to the widow's walk with blankets. They would huddle against the strong, salty, ocean breeze and watch spectacular sunrises while sipping their drinks. Her parents never knew they went up there, which was not surprising. Her parents were in the habit of staying out late and sleeping until noon. The views from the top of the house were phenomenal and the widow's walk had been a great hiding place when her parents were fighting. Her parents never found her secret place, but Rose was always aware of her whereabouts.

Feeling melancholy, Megan wished she could revisit some of those mornings with her grandmother and fully appreciate the time they spent together.

As the sun rose, Megan felt the heat through the glass and left the window seat. She dressed for the day and went downstairs to the kitchen. Placing her mug in the sink, she made a breakfast tray for her grandmother, complete with eggs, toast, orange juice, and coffee and made her way back upstairs.

As was their custom, the door was slightly ajar and Megan pushed the door completely open with her shoulder while balancing the tray. Several steps into the room, she placed the tray on the bedside table and checked her grandmother. Rose was lying in bed, eyes open, staring at the ceiling. Megan felt her cheek, which was warm to touch and was rewarded when Grandma Rose turned her head toward her.

"Megan, you're up early," Grandma Rose said, her voice weak.

"Not really. I was watching the sunrise, the way we use to when I was a child," Megan said with a smile.

"Did you go through the attic? Up to the widow's walk?"

"No, I curled up on my window seat," Megan said as she arranged the tray. "It wouldn't be the same without you."

"Good, that's good," Grandma Rose said as she let out a heavy sigh and looked up at Megan. "You mustn't let anyone go through the attic. No one should be in there except you."

"Why? Is there something hidden there?" Megan felt her hand shake as she set the utensils on the tray. *Please Lord, don't let it be another body.*

"There are things from the past, Megan. Some wonderful and some not. There are secret things. I don't remember what some of the secrets are anymore, but no one must go there except you. I keep it locked. Remember, always turn to your Bible for answers, Megan."

Megan stopped working with the breakfast tray and fell to her knees at the side of the bed. Her grandmother looked so frail. Taking Grandma Rose's hand, she said, "Something happened yesterday. Something bad. The police were here and they're coming back today. They want to talk to you and see if you have any information to help them."

"Did they find something?"

"Yes." Megan stopped and cleared her throat. "In one of the cottages."

"Well, what was it?" Grandma Rose trembled as she looked at Megan. Her ashen face held worried eyes.

"It was a body, Grandma. A dead body," Megan said as she squeezed her grandmother's cold hand. She could feel the arthritic fingers grab hold of her wrist.

"Oh, my stars," Grandma Rose said as she covered her mouth. "Do they know who it is?"

"No, not yet. That's why the police want to talk to you. They want to know if you know anything."

"What would I know about a dead body?"

"Well, they want to talk to you about the family. They'll ask if there were ever any fights in the past or if someone went missing." Megan cringed as the words flew past her lips.

"Of course, your grandfather went missing. We looked for months, years even, and he was never found. But he wasn't missing, he was dead."

Megan's hand flew to her grandmother's shoulder as her stomach clenched. "Grandma, how do you know that?"

Grandma Rose looked at Megan's face for a second and smiled. In a frail voice she said, "Because he came to me in a dream. He does that you know. Every now and again. He's waiting for me on the other side."

"Oh Grandma, you scared me," Megan said, breathing heavily at the bedside.

"There's nothing to be afraid of," Grandma Rose chuckled. "I want to go, but the good Lord doesn't see fit to take me yet. He better do something soon, because I'm getting tired of waiting."

"Please don't say that to the police," Megan begged.

"Don't you worry, honey. I know what to say to the police." Grandma Rose squeezed Megan's hand. "Listen to me. You watch who you talk to in this town. Don't trust anyone except Billy."

"Billy who?" Megan asked.

"Billy Conklin. You know, the crusty guy who lives in the lighthouse. He's lived there all these years. He was a good friend to your grandpa. They grew up together."

"Wow, is he still alive?" Megan had dim memories of the man who lived in the lighthouse. He had been kind when they were near, but made an effort to keep his distance whenever he could and was near the same age as Rose.

"Far as I know," Grandmother Rose said. "He told me he promised your grandpa he would stay around and watch over me if anything were to happen to him. Then your grandfather disappeared and Billy has always been here. He seldom talked to me directly, you understand? He kept to himself at the lighthouse, but I've seen him watching and checking the property."

"Are you sure he's still there?" Megan asked. "Did anyone check on him after Hurricane Sandy?"

Rose yawned as her face drooped to the side. She patted Megan's hand and said, "Trust me, he's there. I don't think Billy would ever leave, storm or no storm."

Megan held Rose's hand until her grandmother fell asleep several minutes later. "I trust you. I love you, Grandma," Megan said softly as she moved Rose's arm to the bed and covered her grandmother with her favorite quilt. Leaning over, Megan placed a kiss on her grandmother's cheek. "Sleep tight."

Chapter Sixteen

Megan stood up and covered the breakfast tray on the table. Marie was scheduled to arrive at any minute and could spend time feeding Grandma Rose when she woke up.

Leaving the bedroom, Megan was more confused than ever. Speaking to her grandmother raised more questions than answers. She remembered Bill Conklin from when she was a child and he was cranky. Megan did not speak to him much when she was young. She had been afraid of him. Bill was a loner, a pariah of sorts, but she did remember him looking out for her grandmother. Megan often remembered odd little jobs which needed to be done around the house. Her father was not a handyman. Her mother never seemed focused enough to arrange for work to be done. Yet, the jobs were completed. Megan was too young to question who was responsible, but she would see Bill putting tools in the garage or cleaning his hands with a garden hose.

Megan was full of questions as she descended the large staircase in the foyer. She had not seen Bill since returning to Misty Point. Could he be the body in the cottage? No one knew what happened to her grandfather. Could his body have possibly been in the cottage for all these years? Who would have put him there? Was Bill involved and salving his guilt by watching out for Rose? Megan needed to talk to her father and find her mother or at least confirm she and her boyfriend were alive. She needed to talk to the taxi service as soon as possible. Someone must have remembered picking her mother up two years ago. The possibilities were multiplying rapidly. What if the body was a stranger, trespassing in the wrong place when disaster stuck? No one would have looked for a missing person at Misty Manor if they weren't expected to be there. It could be a stranger. Megan sighed heavily and headed for her grandmother's office. She needed to start researching right away and find the keys for the attic. Grandma Rose was too worried someone else would go in there.

Two hours later, Megan yawned, rolled back the desk chair, reached toward the ceiling and stretched her back. Searching the desk, she found an old phone book and started calling every taxi service listed. Most would not give her any information, but asked plenty of questions instead. Was she the police? Why did she want information? Did she have written permission? Megan would patiently answer all questions and explain she was looking for her missing mother. After more questions, she was told fare records were protected and kept confidential unless requested by police or subpoena.

On her seventh call, Megan got a hit. She called the Misty Island Taxi Service and as luck would have it, the dispatcher was a woman who attended the local high school two years before Megan. Her name was Maureen Forsythe and she remembered much of the island gossip from years gone by. She knew Megan had left for Detroit and was also aware of Dean's reputation and resulting difficulty with marriage. Maureen was very sympathetic and told Megan she vaguely remembered some talk about her mother being here two years ago. Maureen had also heard rumors about a body being found at Misty Manor and after trying to pry some additional information from Megan, she was more than eager to do her part to help locate Megan's mom. Maureen realized it was only a matter of time until the police requested the same information. With a promise to search the records, and get back to Megan as soon as possible, they disconnected.

"Why don't you take a break and have something to eat?" Marie said as she popped into the small office with a tray which held a fresh salad, lemonade and a chicken sandwich. "You look tired and lunch is ready."

Glancing at the food, Megan cleared a space on the desk. "That looks delicious."

"Having any luck?" Marie asked. A cloud of anxiety passed over her face as she set down the tray.

"Hopefully." Megan shook out the napkin and placed it on her lap. "One service is doing a little research and will get back to me."

"Good, that's good. We'll find your mother soon. I'm sure of it." Marie bent forward and picked up the crumpled paper Megan had thrown to the side of the desk.

"How is Grandma Rose?" Megan asked as she sipped her lemonade.

"She's fine, but very sleepy today," Marie said with a shake of her head. "She kept mumbling about the attic. She looked upset as she mentioned it."

Megan looked up at Marie. She wanted to ask her many questions but reminded herself Marie had not been to Misty Manor in a long time. Megan did not want to reveal anything her grandmother told her earlier, so she kept silent.

After Marie returned to the kitchen, Megan searched her grandmother's desk thoroughly. Rose kept a set of keys which would unlock the doors to the attic and widow's walk, but Megan could not find them. She checked the attic earlier. Everything was locked tight as grandmother mentioned. Megan wanted to get in there as soon as possible. It had been one of her favorite spots when she was young but she might find something to help solve the mystery as well.

Megan continued to search for the keys when she was interrupted by the sound of a heavy knock at the front door.

Chapter Seventeen

"I'll get it," Marie called out as she ran past the office toward the front door. Megan had also made it out to the foyer by the time Marie opened the door to find several people waiting outside.

"Hi Nick," Megan said as she looked at him and took in the faces of several strangers on the front porch. "What's up?"

"Hey, Megan. I need to talk to you for a few minutes, but you may want to take care of your other guests first." Nick grinned and politely stepped aside.

Megan glanced at Nick in his freshly pressed uniform. Looking past him at two women, she realized they had not come with him to the house. Each one was wearing an identification badge attached to a lanyard around their neck. "Can I help you?"

The younger woman stepped forward, smiled brightly and stuck out her hand. "Hi, my name is Jessica Morgan. I'm a social worker with Cape Shore Hospice and this is Anastasia Gleeson, our chaplain," she said as she pointed to the woman to her right. "We have an appointment to meet with Megan and Rose Stanford today. Are you Megan?"

"Yes I am," Megan stammered as she shook the woman's hand. After a second or so, she stepped back. "Please come in. Everyone come on in."

"Thank you so much," Jessica said with a smile. "We stopped by yesterday, but had some difficulty reaching the house."

"Yes, so I was told," Megan said with a loud sigh.

"Is there somewhere we could all sit down and talk?" Jessica asked brightly.

Megan turned to Marie after eyeing the binders the women held, which would surely represent thousands of questions. "Marie, would you please show these two lovely women to the front parlor?"

She turned back and said, "I'll be with you shortly but I believe I need to speak to this officer first. Perhaps Marie can get you a drink while you're waiting? She's been doing a lot for Grandma Rose so she may be able to help you with some basic questions as well."

"Oh, of course," Jessica said, shifting her binder and purse. "Do what you need to do and we'll wait until you're ready."

"Thank you so much," Megan said as she plastered a thousand watt smile into place. When Marie had led the two women inside, Megan turned back to Nick. "What's going on?"

"Nothing worse than yesterday," Nick said. "How are you holding up? Did you get any sleep?"

"I tossed and turned most of the night. I can't believe this is happening. Do you have any information yet?"

"No, but there are a few things to check out today. The crime scene techs will be in the back yard most of the afternoon."

"Why?" Megan asked with a groan.

"Standard procedure. They need to sift through the dirt. They'll go through the garage and the debris to see what other evidence they can find. Anything that can link them to the identity of the victim or the killer would be helpful."

"How will they know what they find is related?"

"They won't right away so they'll collect everything and study it back at the lab," Nick explained kindly. "Speaking of samples, I have to ask you for a lock of your hair."

"What? Why do they want my hair?" Megan reflexively placed her hand on the back of her head.

"Part of the autopsy may involve DNA. The ME needs to see if he can find enough of a sample in the teeth or bone marrow of the body. If they do, they'll analyze it and compare it to yours. Then we'll know if you are related to the deceased in any way."

"Great," Megan said as she felt her stomach flop.

"Megan, I know it sounds strange, but if you don't voluntarily give a hair sample, they'll serve a warrant to do it later on."

"Okay Nick, I don't have anything to hide. It's plain creepy is all," Megan said as she looked up at him. His eyes seemed a more brilliant blue than the ocean. Megan looked down, swallowed hard and crossed her arms defensively. "How do we do this?"

Nick was amused at her defensive posturing, but kept his smile well hid. Using an official tone, he said, "The hair samples need to have roots attached so we can do this one of two ways. You can pull out some of your own hair or I can do it."

"Are you kidding me?"

"There is one other way we can get hairs. We'd have to backcomb your hair until we have some samples with roots attached."

"Can't we just cut a piece off?" Megan asked holding on to her head.

"We really need the root so it's better to pull." Nick said with a shrug as he pulled out a paper bag and tracking paperwork. "We should try to take it from the temple if we can."

Megan sighed in exasperation. "Let's get this over with. What do I need to do next?"

"Let me fill out the paperwork. I need some basic information. Can you spell your name? What's your birthdate?"

Megan answered his questions with her head cocked to the side, clearly not happy with the procedure. "Now what?"

"I, ah, need your hair color and I need to know if it's been treated. Dye, permed, etc."

"My hair color is auburn or light brown and I haven't had time or the mental space to treat my hair in a long while," Megan said uncomfortably as she blushed.

"Well, I think it looks great," Nick said. "I like it better than when you had those blond streaks before the prom."

Megan blushed all the way up to her temples. She stammered as she attempted to apologize. "Nick, I'm sorry I don't remember everything that happened in high school. It was such a blur for me. You know there were family problems and I was kind of messed up."

"You were the most beautiful girl in the class. Every guy wanted to go to the prom with you."

"Nick, please let's not go there," Megan said tersely.

"I'm not. I'm simply trying to explain why I remember those things so clearly. Hey, I understand why you went with Jeff," Nick said shrugging his shoulders. "You two were the A list. The most popular students in school."

Megan began to fume. "Forget the A list. I'm sure you don't understand. Despite the A list, I didn't like Jeff. To be honest, he was a jerk. Especially after the prom when he felt he was entitled to whatever he wanted."

Nick's mouth dropped open until he understood her message. "Megan, I'm sorry. I had no idea," Nick said, clearly embarrassed.

"Trust me, he didn't get what he wanted which is why he never talked to me again. Not that I cared."

"So why did you agree to go with him?"

Megan smiled as tears formed in her eyes. "Because he asked me and because every other girl wanted to go with him. Nick, my parents were so messed up. My self-esteem was in the gutter. So when the mayor's son asked the town founder's great granddaughter to the prom, it seemed like a natural pairing. Let's leave it at the fact I survived with my reputation intact, but I still want to slug him every time I see him."

"I don't know what to say," Nick said softly.

"Say nothing. Forget high school and please forget the prom. Let's get this hair thing over with," Megan said. "I have to talk to the hospice people, too."

"Of course." Nick took hold of the paper bag. "Okay, ready when you are. Try to grab a few hairs and put them directly in this bag. Let's hope the roots are attached."

Megan did as she was told with a grimace. She was able to pull five hairs from her right temple and at least four of them had roots. Megan dropped them in the special paper evidence bag which Nick quickly folded and sealed. They followed instructions and carefully marked the time, date, site and manner of sampling.

"Let me get this back to the lab," Nick said. "Thanks for giving us the sample. I'm sorry it got so awkward."

"It's okay, Nick. Like I said, I have nothing to hide and the sooner we find out whose body it is, the better. What happens next?" Megan asked as she walked Nick to the front door.

"Davis wanted to come by today and talk to Rose, but I'm going to tell him it's not a good idea," Nick said as he looked into the dining room toward the hospice staff. "I think you'll both be exhausted before long."

"Bless you, Nick," Megan said, visibly upset.

"I know this has to be difficult for you, but hang in there. I'll try and keep Davis reigned in as much as possible around you, but he's tough."

"I would appreciate that," Megan said with a small smile.

Nick smiled back and squeezed Megan's arm. "I'll call you later to see how you're doing."

"Thanks." Megan waved as Nick walked down the porch steps. She closed the door and acknowledged the weight in her chest as she prepared to talk to strangers about putting her grandmother on hospice.

Chapter Eighteen

Megan yawned and let her head fall back on the cool pillow. She spent the last two hours speaking with representatives from Cape Shore Hospice. They were lovely, nice people, but Megan had a hard time signing the papers. Yet, she was doing what Grandma Rose asked her to do. After confirming the initial information for admission into the program and making sure all the scripts were signed by Dr. Cameron, the group went upstairs to talk with Grandma Rose. Megan, with the help of Marie, had done a wonderful job taking care of Grandma Rose who promptly declared she no longer wanted medical testing or complicated treatment. Megan was conflicted about starting hospice but was relieved to have the extra help because she needed it.

Once hospice started, Rose would be cared for by a group of professionals whose focus was to make the patient comfortable. Rose would have a whole team including an RN, social worker, aide, chaplain, medical director, volunteer coordinator and even a dietician. The hospice would neither delay nor hasten her disease state, but definitely make sure she was comfortable and well cared for at home.

Megan turned on her side and faced the front windows. The air conditioning was on, but Megan had partially opened her window. She loved to feel the breeze and hear the surf pound the shore, especially on days such as this. It had been a long time since she felt the weight of the world on her shoulders, which was common when she was a teenager. The conversation with Nick had dredged up all the negative feelings from high school as well as memories of her parents fighting in the next room. As a teen, Megan would run down to the beach at night and lay on the sand, very close to the water's edge. Megan would let her senses be overwhelmed with the salty scent of the sea, the coolness of the sand and the wind in her face to fight feeling defeated. She had not had time to lie on the beach since she returned to Jersey, but she was starting to feel the need to run to the water's edge once more. For now, her cool pillow, the breeze and sound of the surf would have to suffice.

Stomach rumbling, Megan woke an hour later. She did not plan to fall asleep but emotional fatigue won out. Jumping out of bed, she pushed her hair back and was amazed to find it was past seven at night. She straightened her cloths and peeked in on Grandma Rose, who was back in bed, sound asleep, her covers tucked neatly around her. Although failing, Rose now looked well cared for, clean and comfortable, compared to when Megan first returned to Misty Point. Marie had been a great help and now she would have more support when the hospice aide started in a day or two.

Megan went downstairs to the kitchen and found Marie drying the dishes. At the sound of her name, Marie turned and smiled. "Megan, I'm glad you're up. I was trying to decide if I should leave a special plate for you in the microwave or put everything back in the fridge."

"I don't know what you made but it smells delicious," Megan said, her stomach grumbling.

"Nothing fancy. A simple meatloaf with mashed potatoes and green beans. I have extra gravy here for you as well."

Megan took a seat at the table while Marie quickly rearranged the food platters. Within minutes, Megan's plate was full with food as well as a steaming chunk of homemade bread with butter. Megan quickly ladled gravy over the meatloaf and potatoes and dug in. "I didn't realize how hungry I was until now. Marie, this is delicious."

"It's no wonder you're starving. You certainly didn't have lunch and I'm not sure you had a decent breakfast."

Megan looked up at Marie. "It was one crazy day, wasn't it?"

"It sure was. Those men in the backyard collected a couple bags of dirt and other stuff. Lord knows if they found anything, but they were out there for hours. Did Nick have any more information today?"

"None to speak of. I'm waiting to hear from him. Davis still wants to come speak to Grandma Rose."

Marie pulled out a chair and sat at the table with Megan. "Why don't they leave the poor woman alone? I'm sure she has never had part or parcel with any dead body."

"I guess they're doing their job, but she's going through so much right now," Megan said as she paused with her fork halfway up to her mouth. Megan put the fork down on the plate. "Marie, have you had any more thoughts of where my mother might be? Or how we could try to contact her?"

"No, I've been racking my brains," Marie said softly. "Have you talked to your father?"

"I placed a call to his Highness, but I haven't heard back," Megan said as she played with a gravy river in her mashed potatoes.

Marie winced at Megan's words. "I'm sure he'll call soon."

"Marie, I have an indelicate question, if you don't mind," Megan said clearing her throat unnecessarily.

Marie immediately started to fiddle with her apron. "I don't have many answers."

"I'm just a little confused. Were you closer to my mother or my father because it seems you've been in contact with both since their divorce?"

"Megan, I grew up with both of your parents. We went to high school together," Marie said defensively as her face turned bright red.

"Yes, but I can't help feeling you're not telling me something. Any detail could be important here."

Marie jumped as Megan's cell phone started vibrating. Megan looked down at the screen as Marie sighed with relief. "Oh it's Nick. I've got to take this." Megan jumped up from the table, grabbed her phone and made her way to the front porch as she got ready to hit the green button. She sat on the steps and realized she was excited about hearing from Nick. Megan knew getting involved with anyone at the moment was a bad idea and especially one of the officers investigating a dead body found on her property. She resolved to forget him as soon as the call ended.

Chapter Nineteen

"Megan?"

"Hi, Nick, yes it's me. Sorry, I was walking out to the front porch."

"Is this a bad time?"

"No, not at all," Megan said as she tried to calm her breathing. "Thanks for calling."

"My pleasure. I wanted to check on you. You looked pretty upset this morning."

"Being told there's a dead body on your property is rather unsettling and then having Grandma Rose put on hospice is a bit over the top. Have you heard anything yet?"

"No, but we should have some information by tomorrow. I wanted to give you a heads up. Davis is planning on stopping by late morning. He's asked me to come with him. He still wants to talk to Rose."

"Why? Does he think she had the strength to bury someone out there?"

"I don't know what he's thinking, but there's no stopping him at this point," Nick said.

"I hope he doesn't labor over the interview. The woman has been through enough," Megan said as she swept sand off the front step with her hand.

"I agree, but we need to get it over with," Nick said, then paused. "Are you feeling any better?"

"Yes, I managed to get some sleep this afternoon and it helped."

"Good. We're starting to worry about you."

"We? Whose we?"

"You know, me, Georgie, Amber. No one wants to call and bother you but everyone wants to make sure you're okay."

Megan smiled. "I appreciate the thought Nick. I'm okay for now, but I want everything to be normal again."

"You and the Misty Point Police Department," Nick said with a chuckle. There was a pause in the conversation before Nick spoke again. "I'd better let you go. Try to get some more rest and I'll see you tomorrow."

"Thanks, Nick. I'll try. See you then." Megan smiled and disconnected the call. Nightfall was close and the air already felt damp. Too wired to go back inside, Megan decided to go for a quick walk. She walked down to the beach and turned left toward the Cape.

As she walked, she watched the lighthouse in the distance. Misty Point lighthouse was one of the last working lighthouses in New Jersey. Constructed in the early nineteen hundreds, it was a round, electrified, brick lighthouse, approximately one hundred twenty five feet high. It was painted red and white and on a good night, the light could be seen fifteen miles away. It marked the inlet on the Cape of Misty Point and many fisherman returned home at night using the light as their guide. Nowadays, party boats enjoyed the same privilege.

Megan could see a light in the keeper's quarters. She used to run up and down the two hundred steps with her friends when she was in grade school, but she had not been near the lighthouse since her graduation from high school. Bill never scolded or chased them out when they were young.

So where was Bill Conklin now? Was he alive? Had anyone checked on him? Megan knew she needed to find him soon. She had a lot of questions and as much as Davis wanted to question Rose, Megan believed Bill may have more of the answers they were looking for.

The breeze blowing her hair, Megan stared at the reflection of the moon on the water as she walked along the water's edge. The sky was ablaze with beautiful stars twinkling in the night. After several minutes, she reached the Cape and crossed from the sand over the wet grass to the concrete walk surrounding the lighthouse. Reaching out, she approached the base and pulled the handle on the old wooden door. It would not budge. She tried again with no success. Megan did not recall the lighthouse being locked at night but it had been years since she visited.

Looking up, Megan called out but was sure her words were lost in the breeze. After several minutes, the light in the keeper's quarters was extinguished. Megan waited to see if anyone would appear at the door, but nothing happened and after waiting another ten minutes she turned around and headed back to Misty Manor. Someone must have been in there.

Megan reached the shore line and walked home as warm ocean water crashed about her ankles. The Grand Victorian looked magical in the distance despite the horror unfolding there. Several windows were lit up and the overall appearance was cozy and inviting. Once again, she envisioned the house as it had been when she was young. Large urns of flowers sat on the beautiful wraparound porch. The windows were decorated and the porch and shutters freshly painted. Grandma Rose was playing croquet with her on the manicured green lawn.

Megan was nostalgic about her childhood at the shore, despite her parent's relationship. The house had withstood storms of many kinds and she would hate to see it all destroyed now, so Megan steeled herself to get to the bottom of this mystery before it was too late. More determined than ever, she decided to return to the lighthouse as soon as Officer Davis and Nick finished their interview in the morning. She would find out who was staying there and what they knew about Misty Manor.

Chapter Twenty

Megan woke to a bright sun shining through her windows. It was a beautiful beach day and held the promise of a great day at the shore, worshipping the sun, playing in the water, enjoying a cold beer and burger off the grill before taking a refreshing shower and then finally reclining to watch a wood fire on the cool sand.

Megan knew none of those things would be available for her today. She quickly rose, got dressed for the day and checked on Grandma Rose. Megan found her in bed, wide awake and wearing a smile. "Grandma, how are you today?"

"I'm well, Megan. How are you, my dear?"

"I'm okay." The side table held a tray with used utensils and a soiled napkin.

Rose noticed Megan looking at the tray and said, "Marie has already been here with a sumptuous meal. She should be back in a minute or two to collect the dishes."

"Oh, I'll take it down to her," Megan said as she began to stack the dishes on the tray. She turned back to Rose. "Did she mention you were having visitors sometime today?"

"Not exactly, but I knew the police would be here eventually. I know what to say to the police. Just follow my lead and we'll be fine," Rose said with a smile.

"Okay, Grandma," Megan said with a shrug. "I wanted to ask you one other thing. I know we've discussed the attic before."

"Yes, and no one is to go in there except for you," Rose stressed.

"I know, but I don't think I can get in there. I don't have a key."

"Megan," Rose began and then stopped when Marie entered the room.

"I'm glad everyone is up," Marie said, looking between the two women. "I hope I'm not interrupting anything. I came to help Rose get dressed for her big day."

"No, not at all, Marie. Thank you for helping out," Megan said as she turned. "I'll take the tray downstairs and watch the door for now."

"While you're down there, you can find your breakfast in the microwave. Make sure you have a good meal this morning since you didn't finish your dinner last night."

Megan laughed and bent to pick up the tray. As she did, Rose caught her at the wrist and said, "Megan, remember, whenever you need to find something, turn to your Bible."

"Okay, Grandma, I will," Megan smiled and promised.

"Megan, the Bible. You know, the one I bought for you when we visited the St. Francis Retreat House in Vermont. Remember?"

Megan looked at Rose and slowly smiled. "I remember, Grandma. I will." Megan turned, lifted the tray and made her way downstairs to prepare herself for the day.

Chapter Twenty One

Megan spent most of the morning organizing papers on her grandmother's desk. The paperwork which officially made her the power of attorney and legal guardian had arrived from the family lawyer. Megan wanted to familiarize herself with her grandmother's affairs so she placed another call to her father's cell phone, but he didn't pick up. Megan surmised the police were calling him as well. As the pillar of support and strength he always was in her childhood, he probably changed his number and pitched his old phone into the closest river.

Megan jumped when Marie poked her head in the office several minutes later. "Are they here?" Megan asked, suddenly realizing how much she was dreading the interview between the police department and Rose as well as the possible consequences if she admitted something unthinkable.

"No, not yet, but there's a phone call for you on the house line. Your grandmother has a phone in the corner, under the stack of papers, if you want to take it in here." Marie pointed to the corner of the desk.

"Oh, thanks." Megan pushed the papers aside to reveal an antique, black, Western Electric desktop rotary phone. "Wow, does this still work?"

"Apparently the ringer doesn't, but try it and see," Marie said as she left the room.

Megan was curious who would be calling her at the house and using the old land line as well. She picked up the heavy metal handle, amazed at the weight difference compared to smart phones. "Hello? This is Megan Stanford."

"Megan, this is Georgie. How are you?"

Megan let out a deep sigh. "Georgie, hi. I'm glad it's you. I couldn't guess who would be calling me on this phone."

"This is the only number I have. I can't believe it hasn't changed since high school. You'll have to give me your cell number so I can text next time." Georgie laughed.

"That would help," Megan said as she rattled off her cell number.

"Thanks, how are you holding up? I hear there's been a lot going on there this week."

"So far, I'm okay, but it's stressful to say the least," Megan replied with a chuckle.

"I don't know exactly what the deal is and I don't want to ask. But, I will tell you a lot of people from high school are talking about Misty Manor, especially our wonderful Jeff."

"Jeff Davenport? Is that jerk flapping his gums?"

"Unfortunately, in a big way," Georgie said. "He never amounted to much, but his father is still the town mayor. Worse yet, I think he has even higher political aspirations."

"Are you serious?"

"Dead serious," Georgie said then cringed at her words. "Sorry, I didn't mean to be insensitive."

"It's okay," Megan said. "I haven't kept up with any of the town activities since I left and I'm sure I missed quite a bit while I was gone. So what has Jeff been doing all this time?"

"Nothing productive," Georgie said. "He's mostly obnoxious, touting his father's power whenever someone challenges him about his behavior or attitude. I think he has a no show job somewhere for his resume, but the tag line really should read, 'Experienced jerk.'"

"Wow, he never grew up?"

"He's actually much worse than when he was in high school. At least he pretended to be classy then." After a few seconds of silence, Georgie said, "Anyway, let's forget about him. What are you doing? It's a gorgeous beach day. Come down to my station for a while. Get out and relax."

"Oh, Georgie, I wish I could," Megan said wistfully. "But I can't leave. The police are supposed to come talk to Rose today and they want me to be here."

"Wow that sounds awful. All right, if you finish early and you want to get to the beach, I'll be at twentieth until 5:00pm."

"Thanks, I don't know if I'll make it but I really appreciate the offer," Megan said.

"Listen, Amber finally called and we're meeting Friday night at the Clamshell."

"The Clamshell?" Megan asked.

"Yeah, it's new. It used to be the Point Tavern."

"Oh wow, that old place?"

"Yeah, they completely redid it. It's beautiful and they have great mojitos, but the reason Amber really wants to go is the band."

"Really? Who's playing?" Megan asked.

"Are you ready for this? Tommy and the Tides," Georgie squealed with laughter.

"Are they new?"

"The band is, but not Tommy. Remember Tommy McDonough?"

"Get out," Megan said. "The Tommy?" She remembered him from high school. During lunch and afternoon breaks, he was always outside playing his guitar and singing. He swore he'd be keeping company with Bruce Springsteen and Jon Bon Jovi one day.

"Yeah, Amber has it bad for him, but for some reason she keeps going out with all those corporate jerks from work."

"She always did like Tommy," Megan said.

"Yeah, but he was another one who lived on the wrong side of the tracks when he was young, so her parents wouldn't let her speak to him," Georgie said.

"Well, I guess that's why things change when you grow up," Megan said, thinking of all the people she avoided as a teenager.

"Anyway, Friday night. Be at the Clamshell at 8:00pm. Whatever's happening, you need a break and we need to catch up on everything. Amber's treat," Georgie said laughing.

"I will if I can," Megan whined.

"No, just be there. See you then," Georgie said and disconnected the call. Megan hung up and turned back toward the desk. Her spirits felt lifted, but dread still lingered as she waited for the police.

Chapter Twenty Two

Two hours later, lunch had been served and dishes removed from the table, when the doorbell rang. Megan went to the foyer, and opened the door to find Officer Davis and Nick standing on the porch. Davis gave a curt nod. "Morning, or afternoon, rather."

"Come in," Megan said as she stepped back to let the two officers in the house.

"As you know, we need to ask Rose a few questions," Davis said as he took his pad from his pocket. "Normally, I wouldn't allow you in the room, but under the circumstances, I'll let you stay."

"Thank you, I think," Megan stammered as she closed the door. She turned to face the officers.

"I have to ask you not to prompt her in any way," Davis said bluntly. "No talking or coaching her words. Will you be able to abide by that?"

"Sure, I mean, yes," Megan said as the knot in her stomach grew. "Can I ask what you're looking for with this interview? You can't possibly think Grandma Rose hurt anyone?"

"Not necessarily, but she may have answers to some questions and not realize it," Davis said.

"Do you have any answers yet about the body?" Megan asked, shaking her head. "Has the medical examiner come to any conclusions? It's been a couple of days."

"Why don't we go speak to Rose and then we can talk again afterward?" Davis suggested as he stared at Megan.

"Okay, if you insist." Megan started to climb the grand staircase. She turned back and looked at the men. "I don't know how she'll react to this, but if she starts getting upset, I'm putting a stop to it. She's sick enough as it is." Megan peeked at Nick who followed Davis up the stairs. He winked and gave her a smile.

The trio reached the bedroom to find Grandma Rose propped up in bed with clean linens and bedclothes. Her white hair was combed back into an elegant silver chignon fastened with a gold comb. The coverlet was pulled up to her waist and she had her hands resting on top with stylish Rosary beads wrapped around her fingers. Grandma Rose was very pale, but smiled as they walked in. The room was quiet. Open windows allowed the fresh salty scent of the ocean to permeate the room as curtains fluttered in the breeze.

Officer Davis approached the bed and cleared his throat. "Ma'am, my name is Officer Davis. I'm with the Misty Point Police Department. How are you today?"

"Why, I'm fine. Thank you for asking, officer. Please have a seat," Rose said as she gestured to a Queen Ann chair, covered in peach damask fabric, arranged at the bedside.

Officer Davis appeared unsettled for a moment, but then sat. "Thank you, ma'am. This is a very comfortable chair." He sat on the edge of the chair and leaned toward Rose.

"Yes, it's one of my favorites," Rose replied with a nod.

"Ma'am, I'd like to ask you a few questions," Officer Davis said as he opened his pad and readied his pen.

"Why, that would be wonderful," Rose said.

"Yes," Davis said and then paused for a moment. "Ah, two days ago, we were called to check the cottages in the back of the house."

"Aren't they lovely?" Rose asked. "The roses are so fragrant this time of the year."

Davis looked up at Megan who simply shrugged. Since Hurricane Sandy, most of the shrubs and perennial flowers had died or washed away. Nothing had been replaced. "Yes, ma'am. Funny thing is when we checked the cottage, we found someone there."

"Really? I do hope you invited them to the house for tea," Rose gushed. "It would be grand to have tea and biscuits on the porch again."

"Well, the problem is this person had passed away," Davis said.

Rose turned to look at him. She remained quiet and several seconds later, a small tear slid down her cheek. "I'm so sorry. Were you friends?"

Davis adjusted himself in the chair and cleared his throat. "Rose, may I call you Rose?"

"Of course, dear. You remind me of my husband."

Davis looked up. "Oh, thank you ma'am. I wanted to speak to you about him."

"George? Why have you seen George recently? I've been waiting for him to come home." Rose leaned closer to Officer Davis and said in a conspiratorial whisper. "He's probably afraid I'll scold him, but I won't."

Megan raised her eyebrows and looked at Nick. With a smile, he looked down at the floor.

"When was the last time you saw George?" Davis asked.

"Oh, I would say it's been almost a year now," Rose said while shaking her head. "He's been very naughty staying away from the house this long."

"You saw him last year?"

"Yes, let's see, that would be about 1955." Rose turned her head. "Isn't that right, Megan?"

Megan approached the bed and placed her hand on Rose's shoulder. "I'm not sure, Grandma."

"Rose," Officer Davis tried again. "Do you know what year this is?"

"Let's see," Rose said, her eyes darting about for hints. "I suspect it could be 1958."

"Who is the president?" Davis asked.

"Why Ike of course," Rose said, "but then, maybe not. What about that cute John Kennedy fellow? Now, what does he do? I don't know." Rose shrugged and looked toward Officer Davis. She then turned toward Megan, eyebrows raised, trying to draw strength from her presence.

Officer Davis smiled. "Rose, I would like to ask you something. Do you ever remember someone missing from Misty Manor?"

Rose stared back at Davis. "My granddaughter Megan was missing for a few years. I think she moved away. I miss her so very much. We used to go to the beach together."

"Ma'am, Megan is home and well," Davis said. "Has anyone else gone missing?"

"She is? Oh, that's lovely. I can't wait to see her." Rose said excitedly as she clapped her hands. "Why, I don't know if anyone else is missing. Everyone is constantly in and out of the house. You'll have to ask George about that."

Davis smiled. "Do you remember when George went missing?"

"George? Now that I think of it, he hasn't been here in a while. I think I called the police, didn't I?"

"Yes, you did call the police," Davis confirmed as he nodded his head.

"That's right, I did. Everyone was so nice, especially his friend, Henry. Yes, Henry Davenport." Rose looked up with a smile. "I'm going to invite them all to a party when George comes home. It should be any day now. I suspect he'll bring presents, too."

Rose grabbed Megan's hand and squeezed. Megan squeezed back and turned to the officer. "Perhaps we should stop here. I'm not sure how much this is helping, but I don't think we should continue."

Davis huffed, put his pad and pen back in his pocket. He leaned toward Rose and said, "Thank you for speaking with me. It was nice to see you again."

"My pleasure. Will you come back for the party?"

Megan felt tears spring to her eyes. She realized Grandma Rose had been weak, but she had never been this confused and Megan did not want her becoming more upset when her husband George did not show up. He had been missing for sixty years.

"Perhaps we can talk again soon," Davis said as stood up with his hat in his hand.

"That would be lovely and please bring your mother along too," Rose said with a smile.

"Yes, ma'am. I'll be sure to ask her."

Megan's head was beginning to spin. Megan's father had not called back and her mother had been missing for at least two years. Her grandfather had been gone a long time and Megan had not located Bill's whereabouts yet. What if the body was a complete stranger? Megan did not want to mention anything to Officer Davis in front of Grandma Rose.

The two officers walked toward the bedroom door while Megan leaned over to tuck the covers around Rose. Megan adjusted the coverlet and as she smoothed back her grandmother's hair, Rose looked up at Megan and winked. Rose then squeezed Megan's wrist and winked again to make sure she noticed.

Chapter Twenty Three

Megan paused for a second before joining the officers in the hall. "Why don't we talk downstairs?" The trio made their way down the elegant stairway and into the parlor. Megan turned to Officer Davis. "Well? Did you learn anything useful?"

"I'm not sure. Sometimes little things can be helpful? Is she always confused?"

"Yes, she is," Megan said as her stomach tensed. Megan had been upset when she realized Rose was not answering correctly. It would be hard for anyone to remember exactly what happened sixty years ago, but Megan never expected Rose to act as if the year was 1958. Was it worse to be confused or purposely misleading the police and most importantly, why? "She has good and bad days."

Megan sat down on the couch and sighed. "Can you tell me where you are in the investigation? Has the medical examiner determined anything useful yet?"

Davis looked at Megan. "We know the bones are old, but we're not sure exactly how old. Bodies decompose at different rates depending on how they're buried. Moisture, depth, embalming all affect how bodies change."

"I don't understand," Megan said. "Was the body in the cottage or buried?"

"The crew noticed the first bone in the debris pile so it could have been either. By that time, the floor, walls, and roof were all mixed together," Davis said. "Your insurance video should be helpful."

Megan looked at Nick. "Of course. Why are the police still out there? What are they doing now?"

Nick shifted his weight as he looked over at Davis. "Megan, they have to do a thorough investigation of the yard. They make a grid and continue to search with metal detectors and other means to make sure they found all they can."

"Have you found the whole skeleton?"

"I'm not sure, but a search has to be made to confirm there's only one skeleton."

Megan blanched at his suggestion. "You're looking for more?"

Davis crossed his arms in front of his chest. "We're doing a thorough investigation. The results will take time, Ms. Stanford. If a body had simply been lying in a cottage, it would be hard to believe someone wouldn't have noticed an odor or increased animal activity. Fresh decomp does not go unnoticed. Beyond that, we don't know if the body was in the wall or under the floor, but we'll find out."

Megan opened her mouth and then promptly closed it again. She had no reason to argue and she had no reason to be defensive about anything they might find. Megan also realized that nothing would happen to Rose even if she had been involved in murder. She was not healthy enough to stand trial or an intense interrogation for that matter. "So, then what is the next step?"

"We'll continue to investigate and you'll hear from us when you need to. We're digging up records from any police activity dealing with Misty Manor. We'll be back with more questions when we do."

Megan reddened at his words. As a teenager, she remembered a few times when the police were called to the house for domestic disputes. Grandma Rose would pull her aside and hide with her in the attic so she did not have to witness the sordid event or speak to the police. Megan blanched at the thought she could have been removed from her home.

"In the meantime?" Megan asked, her face hot.

"Live your life, but please do not touch anything marked as part of the crime scene. It would be best not to discuss anything you've heard outside this house." Davis placed his cap on top of his head. "We'll be going now, but I'm sure we'll be in touch." He gestured to Nick to follow him to the front door. With Davis in the lead, Nick squeezed Megan's arm as he walked by her.

Chapter Twenty Four

Laughter greeted Megan as she walked through the door of the Clamshell Bar. She surveyed the interior and was rewarded with a wave from Georgie across the room. Megan walked over to join her. The place looked great. When she left Misty Point, the building could have qualified for top dive bar of the New Jersey Shore. Completely redone, the interior had a half circle bar which covered the entire left wall. Directly ahead of her were comfortable groupings of tables and chairs. Additional tables were elevated on a platform along the wall directly across from the front door. To Megan's right was a large stage for bands and entertainment. Along the ceiling were suspended surfboards, connected by netting which held an impressive array of decorative starfish, sand dollars, sea shells and colored seaweed. The walls had a mixture of purple and blue up-lighting throughout the bar as well as backlighting a milky glass wall with decorations of clam shells.

Megan joined her friends at a table. Both Georgie and Amber rushed over to greet her with generous hugs all around. Georgie, tall, blond and athletic was dressed in jeans and a brand sweatshirt. Amber wore a fantastic light green sundress with designer wedge espadrille sandals. Her red hair looked luxurious as it hung over her left shoulder.

"You guys look great." Megan stood back to look at her friends as she mentally reviewed her own worn jeans, comfortable t-shirt and sneakers. She was thankful she took a few minutes to apply basic makeup.

"I think Amber may have taken some extra care getting ready for tonight," Georgie said as she burst out laughing. "Just in case she happens to see anyone she knows."

"Shut up," Amber said, feigning hurt feelings, but then started to giggle. "He doesn't even know I exist."

"Whoever it is will notice you tonight, unless he's blind. You look gorgeous in that outfit. Are those designer?" Megan stared at Amber's shoes.

"Yes, I got them at Nordstrom." Amber modeled her shoes for a few minutes.

"Well they're fabulous." Georgie pulled out a chair, sat down and looked at Megan. "We just arrived before you did. I believe Amber is attracted to a certain male who is part of tonight's band."

"Really?" Megan asked, nodding her head as she smiled.

Georgie turned and faced the band to measure their position. "Amber, where do you want to sit? Where will you have the best view?"

Megan looked over at the stage where members of the band were starting to saunter in and set up for the night. "Where will he be able to notice you most easily?"

"Hey, guys, knock it off," Amber said as she blushed. "Let's not be so obvious." After a moment, Amber chose the chair in the middle of table. She faced the center of the stage. With only two small tables in front of them, she would be easy to spot by anyone in the band.

"So, Amber, are you going to tell me who the lucky guy is?" Megan asked with a smile.

Amber looked up and moved closer to Megan. "Yes, as long as you don't make a big deal about it."

"Why would I react that way?" Megan asked curiously. Georgie was behind Amber's shoulder making faces to remind Megan not to let on she already knew.

"Remember Tommy McDonough from high school?" Amber asked nervously.

"Yes, of course I remember Tommy."

"Well, it's him," Amber said with a small grin.

"That's great. Why would I make a big deal about him?"

"Because a lot of people still remember Tommy as being a bit of a delinquent, but he's changed."

Megan laughed. "He was a bit wild back then. I believe he was voted most likely to get arrested before age twenty."

Amber's face clouded over.

"I'm sorry," Megan said. "I believe you, completely. Nick Taylor changed a lot since I last saw him. I didn't recognize him.

"Yes, speaking of which," Georgie cut in. "You have to let us know what's going on over there."

Megan hesitated, thinking back to the warning she received from Officer Davis, not to discuss the case with anyone outside of the investigation.

"Hi ladies, my name is Cassie and I'll be your server tonight. Are you all here or are you expecting anyone else?"

Megan gave thanks inwardly with the realization Cassie had perfect timing.

"We may have a couple of other friends stop over, but we're good to go," Georgie said with a smile.

"All right then. Have you had time to check our specials?"

"Not really, where are they?" Georgie looked around the room for a board.

"Will you ladies be having dinner or appetizers?"

"I'm starving," Megan said with a shrug. When Marie had learned of the Clamshell get together, she refused to cook dinner, knowing Megan would have eaten her dinner at home and then be less agreeable to going out for the evening.

"Okay, take a look at these," Cassie said as she dropped several different menus in front of them. "You can see the specials, but I also want to add the clam chowder is absolutely delicious for anyone who likes soup. Can I get anyone a drink in the meantime?"

"Mojito for me," Georgie said enthusiastically with her hand raised.

"I'd like a strawberry mojito," Amber declared.

"You can get a flavored mojito?" Megan asked, eyes wide.

Amber reached out and touched her arm, concern in her eyes. "Oh honey, you really have been locked up, haven't you?"

"Come to think of it," Georgie said, "I'll have a strawberry mojito as well."

Cassie turned to Megan. "How about you?"

"Sure, I'll try one, but I don't want to drink a lot. I drove here."

"Great, I'll bring a pitcher of strawberry mojitos for the table," Cassie said as she scribbled on her pad. "Take a look at those menus. I'll be back in a few minutes."

Chapter Twenty Five

Tommy McDonough carried his guitar through the front door of the Clamshell. Several of the guys were already there, setting up equipment and lighting. It had been a long day at work, but the gigs were worth the effort. Tommy and the Tides were becoming increasingly popular, playing larger venues all the time. With a little notoriety, he would be able to give up one of his multiple day jobs and concentrate on what he loved doing the most.

"Earth to Tommy, stop daydreaming and hand me that cable."

"Shut up, Eddie. It's been a long day." Tommy pulled the cord around the back of a speaker and handed it over to Eddie so he could plug it into his guitar.

"Yeah, Fridays always are around here. Especially during the summer. Tourists want to go out and see the whales. Bait has to be chopped for the fishing boats, and the boat has to be scrubbed for the booze cruise."

"One day, Eddie, one day soon and bait will be history."

"At least we're not playing on the booze cruise tonight. I just missed getting vomit all over me the last time."

Tommy laughed as he placed his guitar case against the wall. "That was one helluva evening. Those people were crazy, but the pay was great."

"I'm getting older. I don't like to be rocking when I'm rocking. Plus, I don't want to ruin my acoustic guitar with sea spray either."

"Gentlemen, how are we this fine evening?" Gary shifted himself onto the stool behind his favorite drum set.

"Going with the Ludwig tonight?" Tommy asked with a laugh.

"You know it, dude. I love this drum set." Gary picked up his sticks and starting tapping to check the acoustics. "Hey Tommy, see the table in front of us? Look who's there tonight."

"Who?" Both Tommy and Eddie looked up to check out the three women sitting at the large table directly in front of the band.

Eddie punched Tommy on the arm. "My man, that Amber chick is becoming a real groupie. When are you going to talk to her?"

"She's looking pretty hot in that outfit," Gary said admiringly. "You know her from high school, don't you?"

"Yeah and that's the problem. She graduated, went to college, and now works in the corporate world," Tommy said with a sigh. "I clean fish and play in a band for a living. Not exactly compatible."

"You never know," Eddie said as he checked his guitar to see if it was in tune.

"What I do know is she'll remember every crazy thing I did in high school."

"Okay, you were into music. So what?" Gary said, adjusting a cymbal.

Tommy laughed. "So to speak. I was always playing guitar, but I was always the one sitting with my back against the building, in the parking lot or against the wall sitting on the floor in the hall. I was never part of band, or chorus."

"What's the problem?" Eddie shrugged.

"You guys don't get it. Amber was in the drama club, and class valedictorian. She was the soloist for the jazz band. She was really special. I grew up in a different part of town."

"You're ridiculous," Gary said. "You graduated high school years ago."

Tommy grunted and shrugged. "Hey, do you see the other girl? The one with the brown hair?"

Eddie and Gary looked over at the table again. "That's Megan Stanford. She just came back from Detroit. She was in the same circle of friends during high school."

"Are you interested in her?" Eddie asked with a grin. "She's cute, too."

"She lives in Misty Manor."

"Where the body was found?" Gary asked.

"You know it," Tommy laughed. "Speaking of bodies, where the hell is Jason?"

"Who knows? He's on Jason time, as usual." Gary shrugged and nodded his head at Tommy. "Hey dude, you may not want to talk to those women, but at least introduce me. Do it during the first break."

"I don't know," Tommy said.

"C'mon, you owe me," Gary said as he turned away. "Eddie, help me out here."

Eddie grinned and looked over at Tommy. "I'm just curious. Why don't you want to meet her?"

Tommy took a deep breath. "Because I'm always creeping around Misty Manor and so far, she hasn't caught on."

Chapter Twenty Six

"Here we go," Cassie said as she delivered a large, frosty glass pitcher of strawberry mojitos to the table. A waiter standing behind her held a tray with three cold glasses. Cassie reached behind her, grabbed the glasses, placed them on the table and expertly poured the first round. After passing the glasses around the table she stood at the end of the table. "Have we decided on food?"

"I'd like to try the clam chowder," Georgie said as she looked around the table.

"I'm not sure," Megan said. "Everything looks great."

Georgie looked up at Cassie. "Can you bring a sample of clam chowder for my friend here?"

"Of course." Cassie waited a few seconds and then glanced in Amber's direction.

"I don't know. I don't want to eat anything that will make me bloat," Amber said as she shrugged. She made a face at Georgie, silently pleading for help.

Laughing, Georgie turned to Cassie. "How about we start with salad all around? I normally wouldn't order an appetizer, but can you bring a platter of fried clams and nachos for the table as well?"

"Sounds good to me," Cassie said as she prepared to go to back to her station.

"Wait," Georgie said. "One more thing. Please bring another round of whatever the band is drinking to them? Please say it's from us."

"Georgie!" Amber began to blush.

Cassie grinned and turned to leave the table. "Sure, they are cute aren't they?"

"Are you nuts?" Amber blurted out when Cassie had gone.

"No, as a matter of fact, I am not." Georgie looked over at Megan for support.

"It's one of the fastest ways to attract attention," Megan agreed. "If nothing else, it will break the ice." Megan picked up her mojito and took a sip. "Wow, this is really good."

"Enjoy it," Amber said. "You probably need a pitcher just for yourself."

"You got that right," Megan said, finishing half the glass in one large gulp.

Chapter Twenty Seven

The dark water splashed as tall waves hit the jetty. Sea spray covered everything within ten feet of the rocks. Bill Conklin stared at the ocean, spit in the water and turned to watch a night fishing boat slowly pass by. He felt every one of his eighty years as the damp, cold spray penetrated his bones. Trouble was brewing and Bill did not want any part of it. He kept his promise. Rose never noticed him but he stayed in Misty Point, lived in the lighthouse and watched over her for years. Using binoculars, he would occasionally watch her from the lighthouse. The best advantage was from the top. Not like a peeping Tom. He never disrespected Rose and could not see her bedroom from his perch. But when the lights went out, he would go to Misty Manor and do his chores. Repairs were made, the grounds were secured and life was stable. Bill made his promise and swore to keep it. He even brought on a partner, an assistant, in case anything ever happened to him. He was old now, but he'd kept his promise. The years had gone quickly. Too fast and yet, too slow for Bill, but they had passed. So far, they had kept trouble away, but Bill sensed it was brewing as sure as he smelled the brine on a windy night.

After all these years, he hoped trouble would not return, but he knew they were still searching. Still burning, bitter and hungry as they were all those years ago. Mad as hell, too. Yes, trouble would come swarming, now the body was found. Angry, searching and bitter. As he turned and limped back to the lighthouse, Bill reminded himself his promise and devotion stopped the minute Rose died. Once she passed, he was free. One way or another, his journey would end.

Chapter Twenty Eight

"I love this song," Amber said as she faced the band and smiled.

"You love every song," Georgie said. Laughing she held up her empty glass. "If you find the strength to break away for a second, pass me the pitcher of mojitos."

Amber flipped Georgie a rude gesture behind her back.

Megan reached forward and passed the pitcher but not before filling her own glass again. "These are pretty good. I've never had one before." Georgie finished filling her glass and held it up in a mock toast before taking a sip.

The last hour had been filled with salad, fried clams, nachos, oyster crackers and chowder, all washed down with several pitchers of strawberry mojitos. The strange combination of salty sweet food was surprisingly delicious.

"Why did you order all this food?" Amber said as she tasted one small tortilla chip. "There's no possible way we can eat all this."

Georgie laughed and threw a fried clam at Amber. "I'm hoping we'll have help finishing the food."

Amber twisted her head to look at Georgie. "Are you kidding me?"

"Nope. There's always a master plan."

"You're impossible." Amber turned back to face the band as Megan grabbed a tortilla chip and picked up her drink.

Tommy and the Tides rolled through several classics originally recorded by Jon Bon Jovi, Bruce Springsteen and Billy Joel. With the crowd fired up, and a bit inebriated, they began a set of original songs written by Tommy himself.

After the fifth song, the women saw Cassie deliver a generous round of beer to the band while pointing over to their table. Eagerly accepting the refreshing drink, several members of the band turned and saluted the table before guzzling the amber liquid.

"Sending the band a beer round was masterful," Megan said as she wiped her mouth with a paper napkin.

"Thank you, I try," Georgie said as she laughed out loud. Their attention was drawn back to the band when they heard Tommy speaking.

"Thank you for being a great crowd. We're gonna take a little break now. Eat, drink and be cool, but don't go anywhere because we're coming right back."

The women watched as the band put down their instruments and readied themselves for a break.

"Don't look now, Amber, but I think they're looking this way," Georgie said as she began to sip from her drink.

"Really? Oh no, do I look okay? Is my lipstick on?"

"You look fine. You really have to relax and be yourself if you want to attract Tommy. He was a nice guy in high school," Megan said as she giggled over her mojito.

"Oh really?" Amber said, flipping her hair.

"Heads up," Georgie said as she looked upward with a large smile. "Hello, Gentlemen."

"Hey, mind if we sit at your table for a few minutes?" Tommy pulled out the chair between Megan and Amber.

"Please, have a seat," Megan said as she shifted toward the empty chair on her left. Gary and Eddie filled in next to Georgie.

"Thanks for the beer." Gary smiled as he looked around the table. "That was very considerate of you."

"Our pleasure." Georgie beamed back at him. "But we can't take all the credit. It was Amber's idea, so you can thank her."

Megan nodded as she held her glass up toward Amber. The guys followed suit and Amber turned red as Tommy gave the toast. "To Amber, goddess of drink and beauty."

"Awww. That's really sweet," Amber said with adoring eyes as she stared at Tommy. "You sound really good tonight. I love all your songs."

"Thanks, most of the songs are covers, but we had a couple of original songs in that set," Tommy said as he looked at Amber and smiled.

"They were great. I can't wait to download them." Amber smiled back and then looked down at her drink, suddenly shy.

"Thanks, I'll let you know when they're ready."

"Do you mind if I try these fried clams?" Gary said.

"Help yourself," Georgie said as she pointed to the food. "Our eyes are much bigger than our stomachs." Amber glared at her friend.

With a clean fork, Gary reached over to the platter, stabbed several clams and stuffed one in his mouth. "These aren't bad. Eddie, try one of these."

"Come up for air. Stop embarrassing us," Eddie said as he frowned over at Gary.

"Hey, I'm just trying them."

Laughing, Georgie waved over at Eddie. "That's okay, it makes us feel like we're back in high school."

"Yeah, Tommy mentioned he knows you all from there."

"That's right," Georgie said as she extended her hand. "In case you don't know, my name is Georgie, short for Georgiana. Sitting to the right of Tommy is Amber and to his left is Megan."

"It's a pleasure," Eddie said as he raised his beer bottle in her direction. "My name is Eddie and the guy over there eating all your food is Gary."

The women giggled as they shook hands all around. Tommy looked over at Megan and asked, "So how are you doing?"

"As best I can," Megan said, shrugging her shoulders. "Things have been a bit crazy lately."

"So, I heard," Tommy said as he nervously took a draw on his beer. "You just moved back to Misty Manor?"

"Yes. Grandma Rose isn't doing too well so I came back to help her."

"I hear you had a bit of trouble there lately." Tommy picked at the tray of nachos.

"True." Megan took another gulp of her mojito.

"Have the police said anything yet?" Tommy asked casually.

"Yeah, did the police find anything yet?" They all looked up as the chair on the left side of Megan was pulled back and turned around by a man wearing a black t-shirt, faded jeans and a cloud of cologne.

"Jeff Davenport? Who invited you over?" Tommy asked as Jeff straddled the chair and placed his forearms over the top.

"I don't need an invite," Jeff said, picking at the food on a platter near him on the table.

"Sorry, I forgot. As our esteemed mayor's son, you have no rules."

"Piss off, Tommy," Jeff said as he flipped him a finger. He then turned back to Megan. "You know, my father was not too happy when he heard about all the commotion going on at your house. My grandfather almost had another stroke when he heard about it. Don't forget, he was the former mayor. This is a popular beach town and your problems are affecting everyone's business."

"Excuse me?" Megan asked in disbelief. "I didn't plan to have any problems."

"This whole dead body thing is a stain on the community. Media vans have been stopping by town hall for days."

Megan stammered as she recoiled against Jeff's verbal attack.

"What's the matter? Too many mojito's? No wonder you have problems."

"Perhaps you've forgotten Megan's family owns and developed this town," Georgie said sarcastically.

"No, who could forget she always thought she was better than us?" Jeff said angrily.

"What?" Megan was dumbfounded.

"That's enough, Jeff. I think you've worn out your welcome," Tommy said, pushing Megan back as he leaned over her.

"Who died and left you boss? I'll leave when I'm good and ready," Jeff yelled, pushing back his chair. Tommy quickly stood up, his jaws clenched, veins beginning to bulge at his neck. Megan tried to follow the exchange and quickly realized she'd had enough mojito when her head swam from looking up at them. She quickly pushed back from the table and put her head down when her stomach threatened to follow suit.

"You'll leave now," a deep voice said behind Jeff. The group looked over to find Nick Taylor standing behind Jeff Davenport, his arms crossed and muscles taut.

"Oh look, it's the tough cop. My father will have your job," Jeff sneered.

"You know what? He can take it. I'll be worth the pleasure of escorting you out of here and locking your ass in a cell for the night." Nick stood his ground and stared Jeff down. "What's it going to be? You leaving on your own or with me as an escort?"

Caught off guard, Jeff did not have a ready answer.

"Go, call your father. Tell him you were bullying town residents again. Get out of here, now." Nick purposely stood in front of Megan to protect her. He continued to stand with his arms crossed over his well-muscled chest. Jeff turned and with the back of his hand, slapped the platter holding the fried clams across the table. Several clams landed in Amber's hair as the plastic platter caught Eddie on the side of his head. Jeff turned around, knocked his chair to the ground and stalked out of the restaurant.

"What a friggin' idiot." Tommy said as he turned back to the table.

"Megan, are you okay?" Nick asked as he turned to find her cringing behind him.

"What the heck just happened?" Megan asked as she teared up. "I was starting to relax for the first time in a month. I don't understand."

"Oh, honey. Just forget the loser," Georgie said. "He's always been a jerk and he gets worse every year."

Gary was picking clams out of Amber's hair while Eddie rubbed his temple. "What a freakin' ass."

Nick reached out and squeezed Megan's shoulder for reassurance. Megan looked up at him and said, "Thank you. I don't know what would have happened if you didn't show up."

Tommy shook his head and shrugged.

"My pleasure, Megan." Nick said. "Really, it was. I'm tired of him throwing his father and grandfather around." Nick turned to Tommy. "Thanks for standing up to that jerk. I appreciate you standing up for the women."

"No problem, man." Tommy extended his arm for a handshake.

Megan continued to peek up at Nick, noting how desirable he looked in tight fitting jeans and a polo shirt. She had only seen him in uniform before tonight. "Nick, please sit down and join us."

"Excuse me," Cassie said as she arrived at the table with a wet cloth and a tray. She began to clean up the scattered clams and spilt drinks. When she was done she said, "Foster said drinks and food are on the house for the rest of the night, so give me your orders."

Megan turned to Nick. "Who's Foster?"

Nick chuckled which only accentuated a dimple on his cheek. "The bartender, owner and overall boss of the Clamshell."

Cassie handed the tray to a bus boy, turned back toward the table and plopped a hand on her hip. "Foster said to give his thanks, especially to Nick and Tommy. If he had to come over here, he would have kicked Jeff's butt and probably lost his liquor license in the process. So what will it be?"

Megan cleared her throat. "I think I've had enough. To be honest, I should be getting back to the house to check on Rose and Marie."

"Do you have to go?" Amber said, disappointment obvious in her voice.

"Yes, I really think I should," Megan said as her head began to swim.

"And we have to get back to the next set. This was supposed to be a short break." Tommy slid his chair back and turned to Megan. "I'm sorry about all that. I was trying to defend you, not draw you into the middle."

Megan looked over and smiled. "I know. Thanks for your concern, Tommy. Your band is great tonight, but I really have to go." Megan couldn't help but notice Amber making stormy faces behind Tommy before her gaze shifted back to Tommy. "I'm pretty sure Amber and Georgie will be able to stay for a while. Maybe we'll do this again sometime."

"Looking forward to it," Tommy said as he gave Megan a quick hug before he and the other members of the band got up and headed toward the stage. Amber seethed behind him.

"You're right," Cassie said as she put her pad in her hip pocket. "I'll tell Foster, you're all taking a rain check and we'll owe you another night."

Megan grabbed her purse and stood up. "I'm sorry to ruin this evening, but I have to go."

"Megan, how did you get here?" Nick asked as he put a hand on her arm.

"I drove, but after all those mojitos, I think I should walk home."

"How 'bout I drive you home?"

Megan paused for a second. "Okay. Yes, I'd like that."

"You can walk back in the morning and pick up your car."

"Sounds great," Megan said as she felt herself getting nervous to be with Nick alone, which only accentuated her dizziness and nausea. Megan turned toward the table and waved at Georgie and Amber. "This was really fun, at least it was in the beginning. I'll talk to you tomorrow." Nick placed his hand on the small of Megan's back as she turned and walked toward the exit. He then followed her after giving a wave to the women.

As they watched the pair leave the Clamshell, Amber turned to Georgie. "Wow. This evening did not turn out anywhere near what I had hoped for."

"It could have been worse, much worse," Georgie said as she shook her head and picked up her glass. "Hey, Tommy's looking over here, so turn around and smile."

Chapter Twenty Nine

Morning sunlight streamed through the bedroom windows and pierced Megan's closed eyelids. She moaned, covered her head and turned to the side only to have her head swim as nausea threatened to overwhelm her. After several minutes, she slowly opened her eyes to check the time. Eventually, she threw back the covers and rolled out of bed. Swearing softly, Megan grumbled about having to be up early on a Saturday morning, but then felt guilty when she remembered her grandmother.

The hospice nurse and aide were scheduled to arrive this morning to start Rose's care. Megan did not know what to expect and she was nervous. She had heard stories of patients dying as soon as they started hospice. But she also remembered a story she had researched for The Virtual News in Detroit. Her research revealed the average patient stayed on hospice for about a month and many patients improved with the individualized care they received from the team. Of course, every patient had a different experience but most families had positive comments about the time their loved one spent on the program. Megan simply wanted what would provide the most comfort for Rose.

Pulling on the same jeans she wore last night, Megan rooted through her drawer to find a clean t-shirt. Bending over to retrieve last night's shirt and bra from the floor caused her head to start pounding. Her mouth was dry but the thought of brushing her teeth made her want to heave. Thinking back to last evening, her face began to flame as well. Megan's memory was a bit fuzzy but she was fairly certain she remembered most of the evening.

Both Rose and Marie had insisted she go to the Clamshell and meet her friends. She had been working feverishly to take care of Rose as well as clean up the house and grounds. The property had not had much attention since Hurricane Sandy and there were many areas of general disrepair. Megan now realized how hard her grandmother worked to beautify the house and Megan wanted to regain some of the splendor Misty Manor had enjoyed when she was young. She was hoping to replace the large planters on the front porch and replant the beautiful gardens and flowers which had been destroyed in the hurricane.

Since returning to New Jersey, Megan had spent all her time concentrating on helping her grandmother and the agonizing repair process to make Misty Manor presentable again. Last night was the first time she agreed to let her guard down and relax. What good came of that? And what the hell was Jeff Davenport's problem?

As Megan walked downstairs, she realized she was trying not to think about the drive home with Nick. Courteous and polite, he held the door open while she climbed into the Camaro.

"Nick, your car is gorgeous."

"Thanks. I like it." Nick tried, but could not hide his smile.

"I'll bet you love it," Megan said. "You always did love cars."

"You remember that?" Nick asked in disbelief. "But you don't remember the prom?"

"I don't know where the memory came from," Megan said with a laugh. "About the prom, I want to forget it ever happened. I can't believe I went with Jeff the jerk, but that's old history." Megan shook her head. "What an ass. Some things never change."

"Try to forget it," Nick said as he drove toward the beach. "Are you in a hurry to get home or do you want to take a little drive?"

Megan had her window open. "The breeze feels good," she said as her head began clearing.

Nick drove down Ocean Ave along the boardwalk. The night was quiet on this side of town, but got louder as they followed the boardwalk.

"We can take a ride down to the amusements one night, if you'd like," Nick said softly.

"Sounds like fun," Megan said as she watched the colorful neon lights sail by.

They drove around for fifteen minutes and talked about Jeff Davenport's rude behavior. Jeff had been using his father's influence for years which was wearing thin on the whole town.

Realizing she was still a bit tipsy, Megan purposely did not ask Nick how the case was progressing. She wanted to wait until she had some sleep and better focus.

Unfortunately, the morning greeted her with a major hangover. Her focus and energy were worse than before.

Reaching the kitchen, Megan picked up the coffee grounds and starting spooning a heavy amount into the coffee pot. She did not understand why she felt her stomach knot when she thought about Nick. Nothing had happened last night. At least, not until the hug.

They had reached Misty Manor and Nick jumped out of the Camaro. He ran to Megan's side and opened the door for her. He offered his hand to help her out of the car. "How are you feeling?"

"Fine. I'm sorry I caused such a spectacle tonight. I'm embarrassed, really."

"Don't even think about it. I'm glad you had a few mojitos. You relaxed a bit and I got to spend some private time with you."

Megan felt herself blushing as they walked up the stairs to the wrap-around porch and reached the front door. The surf hit the shore in the distance. The sky was clear and full of stars playing hide and seek behind the clouds. A gentle breeze wrapped around them. Megan unlocked the door and turned to face Nick.

"Thanks so much for driving," Megan said as she looked up at him. She marveled at how handsome he was.

"My pleasure." Nick leaned with one arm against the door frame. "I can run over and get your car if you give me the keys."

"No, I'll get it tomorrow. You've already done so much," Megan protested. "Is it all right if I leave it at the Clamshell tonight?"

Nick looked down at her and smiled. "I'm sure it will be fine. Can I call you tomorrow?"

"I'd love that," Megan whispered.

"Great, I'll talk to you then," Nick smiled. "Get a good night's sleep."

"I'll try. You too," Megan said, fumbling for words.

Nick straightened up, placed his muscular arms around Megan and pressed her into a close hug. "You smell great," he whispered to the top of her head. Leaning down, he kissed her cheek, turned around and walked off the porch.

Chapter Thirty

The doorbell rang twice before Megan shook herself out of her reverie and answered the door. She wished she had been able to drink a strong cup of coffee before this moment but she was still in a fog from last night.

Megan opened her door to find two women standing on her porch.

"Good morning," Jessica said as she held a small briefcase in her hand. "We met the other day."

"Yes, I remember you." Megan stepped back and let the two women into the house.

"This is Nicole," Jessica said as she introduced her companion. "She is the nurse case manager who will be in charge of your grandmother's care."

"Hello," Megan said as she looked at the thirtyish, brown haired woman.

"Nice to meet you," Nicole said with a kind smile.

Megan shook her hand. "Thank you for coming. I'm sure Rose will feel better when you start taking care of her."

"Well, I can't wait to meet her," Nicole said.

"Great, so what's our next step?" Megan felt a sudden sense of panic. She had not had time to check in on Rose this morning. Marie had been at the house when Megan arrived home last night and assured her Rose was sleeping comfortably. According to Marie, she had eaten a good portion of her soup and seemed in good spirits for the remainder of the evening. Megan was so shaken by her experience at the Clamshell and Nick's hug, she did not want to disturb her grandmother if she was sleeping so she only peeked in the door.

"I need to spend some time with you and Rose this morning," Nicole said. "I have some admission paperwork to go over and I'd like to do a physical exam. After that, we'll go over medications I can order and talk about any equipment Rose needs to make her more comfortable."

"What kind of equipment?" Megan asked.

"We'll decide after we talk to Rose, but sometimes a patient may be more comfortable in a hospital bed or need a wheelchair. We usually send oxygen to have on hand as well."

"Oh, I'm not sure if we need any of that," Megan said.

Nicole smiled and said, "Once we spend some time with you and Rose, we'll try to make things as comfortable as possible for her, but first we need to see what her needs are."

"I see," Megan said. "Can you give me a minute to go talk to Rose? I'm not sure she remembered you were coming today and I don't want her to be surprised."

"Of course," Nicole said while Jessica nodded.

"Why don't you have a seat in the drawing room?" Megan suggested as she pointed toward the left.

"Your home is gorgeous," Jessica said as she looked around.

"Thanks, this house was built by my great grandfather in the early 1900's."

"It's beautiful," Jessica said as she admired the foyer and the grand staircase.

"I'm told it was quite impressive when it was built," Megan said. "The layout is considered a bit old fashioned now. My family has made improvements over the years but they kept the best rooms as close to original as possible, such as the library."

"Feel free to look around. I'm going to run upstairs to check on Rose and will be back in just a minute."

"Great, we'll be here," Nicole said as they started toward the drawing room.

Chapter Thirty One

Megan reached her grandmother's room and opened the door. She quickly went to the window and drew back the drapes.

"Megan? Is that you?" Rose whispered as she looked toward the window.

"Yes, Grandma. How are you today?" Megan walked over to the bed and straightened Rose's blankets. The room was immaculate as Marie promised when she pushed Megan to go out.

"I'm okay. Did you have a fun time last night?"

Megan smiled in spite of herself.

Rose smiled as well. "A night with some friends and a little booze never hurt anyone."

"Grandma Rose," Megan said as her face reddened.

"Don't Grandma Rose me. I was your age once. I managed to have quite a lot of fun with your grandfather." Rose paused for a moment as her face clouded over.

"Grandma, don't get upset," Megan said as she hugged her shoulders.

Rose reached up and squeezed Megan's arm. "I'm okay. Our anniversary is coming up soon. He's been gone for sixty years but I miss him as much now as I ever did."

"I'm sure you do," Megan said as she picked up a comb and straightened her grandmother's hair.

"Well, enough of that," Rose said. "I'll be with your grandfather soon enough. Let's move on with our day."

Megan put the comb down and turned toward the bed. "The nurse and the social worker are here. They want to talk to us and do a physical exam on you. Are you ready?"

"Sure, let's get started," Rose said with a smile. "The sooner they start, the sooner they'll leave."

"Grandma, they're here to help you. Plus, you'll have some company."

"I know, but peace and quiet are nice as well."

Megan laughed. "I promise you'll have some peace and quiet today, as soon as we finish with all their questions."

"Okay, I trust you."

"Good," Megan said as she turned and headed for the door. "They're downstairs. I'll go get them and be right back."

Chapter Thirty Two

Megan escorted the two woman into Rose's room and pulled a couple of chairs up to the bedside. Nicole introduced herself from Cape Shore Hospice while Megan held her breath. She was not sure what understanding Rose had of hospice and she was afraid Rose would think it involved the grim reaper in a black hooded cape.

Within minutes, Nicole had lightened the mood as she introduced Jessica and then took the time to explain the supportive services which were commonly provided from a hospice company. Rose could stay at home and would be provided with medical equipment, medications related to her disease, an aide for a couple hours a day as well as visits by nurses and other team members.

Rose smiled as she warmed up to the women and Nicole began to ask questions about Rose's medical history. Rose answered a few questions without difficulty but soon began to tire. Noticing a few inconsistencies, Nicole repeated a few questions and again received different answers. Acknowledging Rose was tired, Nicole put down her clipboard and asked if she could do a physical exam.

Megan moved aside to make room for the nurse and jumped when her phone started vibrating in her pocket. She ignored the signal until it stopped, but after a moment it started again. Afraid it may be important, Megan excused herself and walked out of the room. Digging her phone out of her pocket, she checked the caller ID and answered.

"Hello?"

"Hi, may I please speak to Megan Stanford?" A pleasant woman's voice sounded.

"Megan speaking, who is this?"

"Hi, this is Maureen Forsythe. I'm calling back from the Misty Island Taxi Service, you called us a couple of days ago."

Megan's stomach jumped as she came to full attention. "Yes, I did call. I wanted to know if you were able to find any records of picking up my mom, Donna Stanford. I know it was a couple of years ago, but it's really important and I was hoping you kept records for a while."

"I understand darlin'. Normally we don't give out information, but I know the police want the same information. Besides, I've known your family for a long time. So here it is, we did pick up your mom from Misty Manor approximately two years ago."

"I knew it," Megan said. "Thank you so much for letting me know."

"Okay, do you want the rest of it?"

"There's more?" Megan asked, surprised.

"Yes, according to the records, we picked her up again, from Misty Manor, about four months ago."

"Four months?" Megan was astonished. "Are you sure?"

"That's what the records say," the woman said. "It was Valentine's Day as a matter of fact. Of course, I wasn't the driver so I couldn't swear it was the same woman."

Megan's head was reeling. Her mother was at Misty Manor four months ago? That would be about three months before Megan was fired and returned home from Detroit. If that was true, how could she possibly leave Grandma Rose in this condition? Megan had not seen or talked to her mother in a long time, but Megan did not believe she would abandon Rose in her time of need.

"Do you know where she went?"

"We dropped her off at the train station. That's all we have sweetie."

"Wow, that's very helpful," Megan said. "Thank you, thank you very much."

"You're most welcome and please say hi to Rose for me."

"Will do. Thanks again." Megan hit disconnect on the phone. Nick had said the bones were old. She didn't know how old, but she was fairly sure the bones were older than three months.

Walking back into the bedroom, Megan observed Nicole bringing the blankets back up to her grandmother's chin. "So how is she?"

"She's great, right Rose?" Nicole turned to Megan. "Why don't we go downstairs to talk and let Rose get some rest?

"Sure," Megan said, slightly confused. "Is it okay with you, Grandma?"

"Yes, dear. Go talk about me. I'm gonna take a little nap now anyway."

Megan looked at Nicole, her expression showing concern.

"She's fine, just a bit tuckered out by the activity. Why don't we let her sleep and go downstairs?"

"Yes," Megan said as she gave her grandmother a kiss on the cheek. The three women left the room and headed downstairs toward the drawing room.

Megan turned to Nicole when they settled. "Did you give her any medicine?"

"No, absolutely not," Nicole said. "We don't carry any medications. When someone is admitted, we have to review the chart with our medical director. He'll decide which medications are related and offer any suggestions for meds she may need."

"Oh, I'm sorry. I was surprised to see she was so sleepy when I came into the room."

"Lethargy is a common symptom with her disease but it's also a common reaction to the first hospice visit. The anxiety can be exhausting. We try to explain everything as thoroughly as we can, but it's a scary moment. Families never know what to expect."

Jessica broke into the conversation. "Speaking of expectations, we'd like to take a moment to discuss our next steps with you."

Megan fell silent and then nodded. "Okay, so what happens next?"

"We have to go back to the office and write up her chart," Nicole said as she leaned toward Megan for a conspiratorial whisper. "We're supposed to do bedside charting but the signal near the ocean is so weak, it would take us forever."

"Oh, you're right," Megan said, nodding. "Sometimes, the wifi isn't great, especially if a storm is moving in."

Jessica cleared her throat as she shot Nicole a reprimand with her eyes. "Anyway, someone will be arriving later today to deliver medical equipment for Rose."

"What type of equipment do you think she needs?"

"Usually, we send a hospital bed, a commode, otherwise known as a potty chair. We'll send a wheelchair if Rose wants to get out of bed. You'll receive a delivery of oxygen and an emergency box of medications as well."

"Wait a minute," Megan said. "I don't think Rose would want a hospital bed. I have to ask her."

"Of course, please speak to Rose and let us know," Jessica said.

"I will, but for now, I think she'd feel more comfortable in her own bed."

"It doesn't have to be now. We can send a bed any time," Nicole said. "It may be easier for everyone to care for Rose in a hospital bed when she declines, but we can cross that bridge when we come to it."

"Thank you," Megan said with a small smile.

"As we mentioned earlier, we'll also send some oxygen for Rose. We like to have it here in case she needs it for comfort. Does anyone in the house smoke?"

"No, of course not," Megan said. "Why?"

"Because any open flame near oxygen could cause an explosion."

"Oh, that's dangerous," Megan said, eyes wide.

"Yes, it can be," Nicole said. "We take extra precaution with patients who smoke or cook over an open flame. They shouldn't do that while wearing oxygen."

"I can see why," Megan said. "Rose has a fireplace in her room. Is that a problem?"

"No, it shouldn't be. As long as you keep the oxygen tank and tubing away from the fire," Nicole explained. "She shouldn't wear any lip balm or petroleum rub on her face or near the oxygen. That can cause a problem."

"Wow, it's that dangerous?"

"You should be fine as long as you don't use petroleum or go near a flame of any sort. We also like to send a small box of emergency medication, just to keep on hand if Rose develops sudden symptoms."

"Like what?"

"Pain or shortness of breath. The box may contain a narcotic, so, once again, we want to make sure no one will open or touch the box without consulting the nurse first," Nicole explained.

Megan took a deep breath. "Okay. Things are starting to sound a bit complicated."

"It sounds more difficult than it is, but we do have to warn you," Jessica said.

"I understand," Megan nodded. "What else should I know?"

"Someone will be stopping by tomorrow to check on Rose. Also, you may hear from other members of the team on Monday. Hopefully, we'll have an aide start on a regular basis."

"That's fine," Megan said. "When I'm not here, she has a wonderful friend, Marie, who helps to take care of her."

Jessica was busy scribbling in her pad. "Marie is a family friend?"

"Yes, she's known the family for years."

"Okay. Can I ask how many children Rose has?"

"She has one child, a son named Dean, who is my father."

"Does he live nearby?" Jessica asked. Nicole sat on a nearby couch typing on a tablet balanced on her lap.

"Well, if he were in the country, he'd be living here. But he's in Europe with his girlfriend."

"Oh, I see," Jessica said. "Can I ask about your mom?"

"I haven't seen my mom in many years. She and my dad split a while back."

"I'm sorry to hear that," Jessica said warmly. "Do you have any other support? Siblings or other relatives?"

"No, at the moment, it's just me," Megan said. "I was living in Detroit and returned several weeks ago to take care of my grandmother." Megan's face flushed. "I would have been here earlier if I knew she needed me."

Jessica looked up at Megan. "Then how did you find out she needed help?"

"My father called me from Europe. He asked me to come back to New Jersey to handle some property issues caused by Hurricane Sandy. When I got here, I was appalled to see how much help Rose needed. Her doctor had made a house call and he was the one who suggested hospice."

"I see," Jessica said as she nodded. "I hope you don't mind my asking but does that have anything to do with the police being here the other day?"

Megan opened her mouth and then closed it again. Finally, she answered. "I guess I could tell you. It's all over town anyway. There were some cottages in the back which had been pretty heavily damaged by the Hurricane Sandy. They needed to be demolished and because nothing had been done, the town was beginning legal proceedings."

Jessica looked at Megan. Nicole had stopped typing and was paying attention as well. Megan shrugged and continued. "Anyway, they found a dead body in one of the cottages."

"Oh my," Jessica said as she inhaled sharply. "What happened?"

"That's the problem. We don't know who it was or how long the body's been there,"

"Do you know how the person died?" Nicole asked. "Was it a trespasser?"

"The police are trying to find out. It's possible it could have been someone using drugs in the cottage or caught in the storm. Rose has been the only one here for a long time. I think she's been ill for a while so it's possible she may not have noticed. I doubt she was able to keep a close eye on the property."

Jessica and Nicole were speechless for a few moments. Jessica was the first to break the silence. "One of the things we have to do is ensure the safety of our staff. Megan, did the police indicate there was any danger or threat being here?"

"Not that I know of. They didn't warn me to do anything different," Megan said shifting uncomfortably.

Jessica nodded. "Okay. I have to ask. Do you have any guns in the house?"

"Not that I'm aware of," Megan said with a grimace, her annoyance starting to grow. "I've never seen any. I didn't bring any with me and I don't see Rose as a gunslinger either."

"Okay, I'm sorry, but I have to ask," Jessica said.

"Are there any pets here? If so, they have to be locked up when we're here."

"No pets." Megan nodded as her headache returned. "Are we just about done?"

Jessica looked over at Nicole. "Yes, that's about it for today."

"Good, because I.." Megan's thought was cut off as her phone began to ring. She looked down at the caller ID to find Nick's name. "Oh, excuse me one minute, I have to take this."

"Yes, of course." Jessica said as she looked over at Nicole when Megan walked out of the room. "This ought to be an interesting discussion at team."

"You know it," Nicole said. Her thought was cut off as they heard Megan's raised voice in the hall. Nicole picked up her belongings. "C'mon, we'd better get out of here."

Chapter Thirty Three

"What? Are you serious?" Megan shouted into the cell phone.

"Megan, calm down," Nick said as he started to explain. "Foster simply called me and said we better get down there and check your car. Apparently, there's been some damage."

"Nick, I can't…I mean I'm doing something for Rose." Megan looked up to see the two women from Cape Shore Hospice leave the drawing room and edge toward the front door. "Nick, please hold on."

"Are you leaving?" Megan asked as she placed the phone by her side.

"Yes, we have all we need for today and you seem a bit busy at the moment," Nicole said. "Someone will be back tomorrow and if you need us, please call the big number on the front of the admission packet any time day or night. Okay?"

Megan looked at them. "Sure, I'm sorry. I have another problem I have to attend to."

Nicole waved her on as Jessica began to open the door. "Of course, do what you have to do. We'll talk again soon." The two women waved as they scooted out the front door.

Megan walked toward the door to make sure it was closed and secure the lock. She placed the phone near her ear. "Nick? I'm sorry, the hospice people were here to see Rose. They just left."

"Okay, good. Go check on Rose. I'm on my way to pick you up. Can you get Marie to come over and stay there for a while?"

"I'll try. I'll call her as soon as we hang up. What aren't you telling me?"

"Nothing. Call Marie and I'll be there in ten minutes," Nick said as he disconnected the phone.

Shaken, Megan checked her contacts and dialed Marie as she ran up the stairs to check on Rose. Luckily, Marie was home and agreed to come right over.

Megan did not know what to expect and the last thing she needed to deal with at the moment was paperwork for an insurance claim. What was she thinking? She should have accepted Nick's offer to walk back to the Clamshell and drive her car home. There were probably a few drunk people who drove away from the bar last night. She should have realized the chances of her car being hit would be high.

Megan peeked at Rose from the bedroom door. She was asleep and appeared to be dreaming. Megan watched as Rose began to smile and coo. At least the dream was pleasant and Megan was grateful for that.

"Hello? I'm here." Marie called out from downstairs as she closed the front door. Megan softly closed the door and went downstairs to talk with Marie about the hospice visit. She warned her someone may come with medical equipment and supplies later in the day.

"Marie, I don't know what I'd do without you. Things have been so crazy, I can't seem to catch up with myself."

Marie offered a light hug. "No problem, honey. I was cleaning my house so I'm more than happy to take a break and come over."

"I just checked on Rose and she's resting. I think all the activity wore her out."

"I don't doubt it," Marie said, shaking her head. "The poor dear."

"I know. She breaks my heart."

"You were always her favorite, but don't worry. We'll be fine. Go do what you have to do. Then go to lunch. It's a beautiful day."

"Thanks Marie. I don't know how long I'll be. Nick called and said there was some damage to my car. Once we look it over, I'll probably have to file a report."

A car horn sounded outside several times.

"Just go. If she's sleeping, I'll start putting up a dinner."

"Okay, I'll see you later." Picking up her bag, Megan turned back. "Thank you, seriously from the heart." She then turned and ran out the front door and across the lawn to Nick's waiting car.

Chapter Thirty Four

"So what happened?" Megan asked as she fastened her seat belt and turned to look at Nick.

"Foster called and said we should come check out your car as soon as possible," Nick said as he turned and placed his hand on her shoulder.

"How did Foster know it was my car?" Megan wondered aloud.

"I called him last night and asked him to keep an eye out since we didn't go back." Nick put the Camaro in reverse and backed out of the driveway before heading toward the Clamshell.

"I was so tired last night," Megan whined. "Leaving your car in a parking lot never used to be a problem in Misty Point. Someone probably backed into it, right?"

"Um, I'm not positive, but I asked one of the patrolman to go and start a report." Nick sailed down Main Avenue toward the bar. He slowed when they reached the lot and turned in to park. Officer Peters was already there and slowly circling Megan's car while taking photos with his phone.

"The rear bumper looks okay," Megan said as they approached the car. "Maybe Foster was jumping the gun."

"Don't think so," Nick said as he looked over at Peters, who was shaking his head.

The two approached the car from the passenger side. "How did this happen?" Megan shouted when she saw the damage. The windshield was shattered in several places.

"Looks like a baseball bat to me," Nick said as he stared at the breakage pattern.

"Better come over here and look at this, Nick," Peters said from the driver's side. The two came around the passenger side to find the driver's side window also smashed. The door, covered in spray paint, had the word, "DIE", circled several times in red. The two tires on the driver's side had been punctured with something and were flat.

Megan was speechless as the impact of the damage settled in. Her eyes welled up as she turned to Nick. "It's okay, you're safe," Nick said as he slung an arm around her shoulders.

"Damage was definitely targeted," Peters said as he took several more photos. He then stood and turned toward them. "Foster called the station as soon as he got to work this morning. He said the car was fine when he left last night. After you called, he made it a point to check." He then asked Megan, "I'm sorry about your car. Do you know anyone who would do this?"

Megan shook her head. "No, I don't know what's going on anymore."

They looked up as Foster came out of the bar and walked toward them. He was drying his hands and then threw the dishtowel over his shoulder.

"Hey, Nick. I'm sorry about what happened here. I called right away. I'm always the last to leave because I want to make sure the staff and customers are out safely. I call a taxi and pull keys for anyone who's not able to drive so I always make note of what cars are still in the lot. There were three when I left, two when I got in this morning. The other car is fine, but this car had the damage, so I called right away."

"Thanks Foster, I appreciate it," Nick said with a nod.

Foster turned to Megan, "I'm sorry Miss. I feel really bad about this, especially after last night."

"What happened last night?" Peters asked looking over at them.

"Jeff Davenport," Nick said as he recounted what had happened in the Clamshell.

"Jeff's an ass," Peters said. "It's no secret he hides behind his daddy's position, but I've never known him to be this obvious."

"I agree and that's what has me worried,"

Officer Peters looked at Nick. "How do you want to handle this? Have there been any other threats you know of?"

"Do you think this has anything to do with the dead body?" Megan asked, her voice rising in concern.

"We don't know anything at this point," Nick said. "We're going to have to do some digging." He turned to Peters. "Let's tow it down to the municipal garage and see if we can get anything off it. Have you looked inside yet?"

"Nothing other than a visual. I didn't see anything obvious in the car or the hatch, but we'll check it out down there. Maybe we can find something to trace."

"Sounds like a plan," Nick said. "Let me know when the report is done. In the meantime, I'll go over things with Megan and see if we can find a thread."

"Okay, I'll call for the tow," Peters said as he pulled out his phone and walked away.

"Foster, thanks for calling," Nick said as he shook his hand. "Do you keep a camera on the parking lot?"

"I do, but it's not the best system. I keep it running mostly for insurance purposes. If the damn thing isn't cloudy, the high winds knock the view off."

"Is there any way we can look at the footage from last night?"

"Sure, but it's not here. It's handled by a virtual alarm service so we have to call them to send it over. I'm not sure they'll do that on a weekend."

"Okay, please give them a call and then let Officer Peters know what they say so he can follow up."

"You bet, Nick."

Chapter Thirty Five

Nick pulled Megan toward his car. "C'mon, I'm buying you a cup of coffee."

"Seriously, I don't know what's going on," Megan said as she got into Nick's car. "I'm starting to get scared."

"I don't think you have to worry," Nick said, thinking aloud as he pulled out of the parking lot. "Someone obviously wanted to send you a message. If they wanted to hurt you, they would have come to the house."

"Thanks, I'm nice and calm now. That's some message," Megan said sarcastically. "Now, every creak in the house is going to scare me. I'll think someone is breaking in to kill me and what about Rose?"

"Who would want to kill Rose?" Nick asked as he pulled up to the sidewalk next to Stanley's Bagels.

"No one," Megan said. "Wait. You're saying they're going after me?"

"If someone wanted to kill you, the damage would have been at the house. Someone appears to be sending a message, but why?" Nick popped out of the car and walked around to open Megan's door. He extended his hand to help Megan step out. The two walked in silence into the bagel shop. Nick looked at the college student working behind the counter.

"Seat yourself, wherever you like," he said, wiping his hands on a white apron as he collected orders from the line of people in front of the counter.

Megan and Nick walked toward a small table in the back of the small room. Most of the families had already had breakfast which left the room empty. The college students who worked and lived at the shore during the summer were late risers after hanging on the beach or a nightclub until the wee hours of the morning.

"Did you eat today?" Nick asked while picking up the small paper menu stuffed next to the black napkin holder.

"Not really, I barely had time for coffee before the hospice agency arrived this morning," Megan said.

"Wow, how's that going for Rose?"

"Okay, she's very quiet. I'm not sure if she realizes who they are but I'm sure they'll help her."

Nick reached over and placed his hand on top of Megan's. "Not to sound blunt, but is Rose…ah, you know, close to dying?"

Nick's hand felt very warm against Megan's cold fingers. She looked up at him with tears in her eyes. "I don't think so but I don't know. I don't know what to look for. One minute she's telling me about the history of Misty Manor. The next she's talking about crazy things. I haven't been able to make sense of it."

"What can I get you?"

Megan jumped at the sound of a voice beside her. Nick smiled and squeezed her hand before letting it go. Turning to the student she said, "I'd like a vanilla latte, please."

"Order some food too," Nick said as he looked at her.

"Okay, how about Taylor ham, egg and cheese on an everything bagel?"

Turning to Nick he said, "Okay, how about you?"

"Egg white and sausage on a sesame bagel, raspberry iced tea with a lemon wedge."

"Sounds great to me, dude." The college student headed back to the counter.

Nick turned back to Megan. "I don't believe in coincidences. When you look at everything going on in your life, there has to be a connection."

"Like what?" Megan asked as she played with the sugar packets.

"A dead body, Fran stealing from Rose, Jeff's anger, a smashed car, and that doesn't take into consideration Hurricane Sandy and Rose's health. Your parents not being around doesn't help either."

"When you say it like that, the situation sounds awful," Megan said. "I thought you were supposed to be calming me down?"

Nick looked up and started to smile. "I'm sorry. I guess I'm thinking more like a cop and not as a friend. We're missing a big piece here and hopefully we'll figure out what it is."

"Speaking of my mother, I got a call from Maureen Forsythe. You know, she drives for the Misty Island Taxi Service."

"Why would she call about your mom?"

"After you talked to me in the kitchen the other day, Marie told me my mother had been in Misty Point two years ago. Since my mother doesn't drive, I called all the taxi's to see if anyone kept a record of picking her up.'

"And they told you that?"

"Well, it was Maureen and I was looking for my mom. Anyway, she confirmed my mother was here two years ago. They picked her up at the house and took her to the train station."

"Two years? I'm waiting to hear how old those bones are."

"Wait, I'm not done yet. According to Maureen, my mother was also in Misty Point four months ago."

"Four months? Are you sure?"

"Yes, that's what Maureen told me. We've all lived in town for a long time. I'm sure she knows my mother. I can't imagine why she was here and if so, why would she leave Rose in that condition?"

"That would have been back in February," Nick mused to himself.

"That's right. As a matter of fact, she said it was on Valentine's Day," Megan said. "Why the heck would my mother be at Misty Manor, of all places, on Valentine's Day?"

"Damned if I know, but I'll check it out."

"Watch out, the coffee is hot." Megan and Nick looked on as the waiter placed the coffee, tea and bagel sandwiches on the table along with a small dish of creamers. He then pulled a bottle of ketchup out of a back pocket and plopped it down on the table. "Anything else I can get you for now?"

Looking over the items on the table, they both shook their head. "No, looks good," Nick said.

"You got it, dude. I'll be back to check your drinks."

Megan couldn't help but smile despite her mood. "He's funny. I remember when life was so simple. Beach during the day, party at night and summer job on the side."

Nick laughed. "No mortgage, car payments or insurance to worry about."

Megan groaned. "Oh jeez, I'm gonna have to call my car insurance soon."

"We can worry about that later. Hey, maybe you want to drive the Studebaker in the meantime." Nick squirted ketchup on his sandwich and then on Megan's as she slid her plate forward.

"Not likely, Nick. I'd look like I'm driving around town in a lime," Megan said. "Besides, I was never allowed to go near the Studebaker when I was a kid, but I have no idea why." She pulled her plate back and repositioned the top of the bagel. "I always had the impression Rose wanted everything to be exactly the same when Grandpa George showed up."

Nick laughed and picked up his bagel. "Wow, that car would be a classic now. I wonder how much it's worth."

"Who knows?"

Nick bit into his sandwich and chewed slowly. After swallowing, he wiped a bit of ketchup off his chin with a brown paper napkin. "I'm thinking back to February. I don't know what was going on with your mother but I know Rose was not as bad as she is now."

"How do you know that?" Megan asked slowly chewing a piece of her bagel.

"Back then, Davis and I were trying to talk to Rose about getting the property cleaned up. The Chief wanted to get all the township business wrapped up before the summer crowd started coming in. Although Rose was very polite, I don't think she understood everything we were asking her to do, which is why the town decided to serve papers and make it official. To be honest, they were going after your father. Rose seems to have had a significant decline in the last three months."

"Isn't that why the doctor suggested hospice in the first place?" Megan placed her sandwich on her plate and looked over at Nick.

"I would assume so. There seems to be a lot of different things happening at once over there."

"I'm not defending my father, but the reason he called me was to come out here to take care of Rose and get the town off his back."

"I'd like to know why he isn't here."

"I don't know, but I put my life on hold and beat it out here as soon as I heard Grandma Rose was ill. I would have come sooner but I didn't realize how bad she was."

"It's a good thing you're out here now," Nick said, finishing his iced tea.

Megan stared out the window for a seconds, then quietly said, "The problem is I'm going to have to make a decision about my apartment soon. I still have things in Detroit."

Nick picked up Megan's hand again. "I don't know if I'm entitled to a vote, and I have no clue what's going on yet, but I hope you decide to stay for a long time."

Chapter Thirty Six

When they arrived back at Misty Manor, Nick walked Megan to the front door. "Are you going to be okay?"

"Yeah, I'm just really tired. I guess everything is catching up to me," Megan said as she offered a small smile.

"I'm sure you'll feel ten times better with a nap. Go rest and I'll call you later."

"Sounds grand." Megan nodded. "Thank you for breakfast and everything," she said with a shrug.

Nick gave a lopsided smile, pulled her into a quick hug and placed a kiss on her cheek. "No problem. Go ahead inside." He waited until she opened the front door, slipped inside and locked the door behind her. Megan turned and watched from the window as Nick left the porch. She then slipped off her windbreaker and found Marie in the kitchen. "How is she?"

"The poor dear, she's still sleeping," Marie said as she turned from the kitchen sink. "She's trying so hard to be strong and not complain. Quite frankly, you don't look too well yourself."

Megan pulled out one of the kitchen chairs and plopped down in the seat. "I can't believe what's going on. Nick picked me up. We had to go to the Clamshell because someone took a baseball bat to my windshield and punctured two of my tires. To make matters worse, there was a threat spray-painted on the side of the car."

Marie's face blanched at the news. She sat across from Megan. "Do they know who did it?"

"No, but Foster is trying to get the footage from a camera in the parking lot. Something very strange is going on around here."

"Like what?"

"I have no idea but I intend to find out," Megan said. "I can't sit around waiting for something to happen."

"Is that safe? Shouldn't you talk to the police?"

"Nick knows and I'm sure he's going to look into it. He was trying to act nonchalant while we were out, but I don't think he'll let it slide."

"I hope not." Marie said, her voice wavering.

"I have to ask you something else," Megan said, looking straight at Marie.

"What? You're making me nervous."

"I talked to Maureen Forsythe today. She confirmed my mother was in town two years ago and the taxi service picked her up and delivered her to the train station."

"I knew it," Marie said, shaking her head.

"Well, did you also know she was in town four months ago?"

Marie looked surprised. "She was?"

"You didn't know?"

"No, I did not know that. She certainly didn't stop and see me. Do you know why she was in town? Did she come here?"

"She was picked up from Misty Manor so I know she was at the house. I don't know what she was doing here and I can't imagine why she would have left without making arrangements for Rose."

"I don't think Rose was as weak then," Marie said. "She is and always has been such a stoic woman."

"Marie," Megan paused. "Nick said the same thing. You don't think she would have done anything to cause Rose to get worse, do you?"

"Donna? No way, Megan. Your mother had a good relationship with Rose. There was a time when I was very close to your mom. We talked a bit and with certain arguments, Rose supported Donna over her own son, your father."

"You and my mom were pretty close then?"

"Yes, we shared a common bond."

"And that would be?"

Marie shifted uncomfortably in her chair. Looking down at the table she said, "Do we really have to do this?"

"I think it's time," Megan said as her gaze narrowed. "You're hiding something from me and it's time I know. This isn't funny."

"Oh Megan, you weren't even born yet."

Megan raised her hands. "I don't care. Tell me already."

"Okay, give me a minute." Marie's hand shook as she held it up and then cleared her throat. "Years ago, your mother, father, and I were in high school together. After we graduated, your father and I dated and he asked me to go steady."

"Really?" Megan asked, surprised.

"Yes, don't look so giddy," Marie said with a frown. "Anyway, I thought things were going well and one day, I got out of work early. I had received a small raise and I wanted to celebrate so instead of going home, I decided to go to Misty Manor and order a pizza with your father."

"And?" Megan asked mesmerized by the story.

"I found your father involved with someone else, your mother."

"That's creepy to hear about them that way. What were they doing? Talking?" Megan asked.

"No, back then we called it necking."

Megan laughed in spite of herself. "I'm sorry, but also surprised."

"So was I since we were going steady."

"Marie, I had no idea you dated my father. So what happened?"

"Well, I was upset to say the least. I started yelling at them. Your mother was so embarrassed she started to cry and left. Your father and I had quite an argument after that and we officially broke up."

"Wow."

"Your mother tried to apologize but I wasn't having it. I kept warning her she should watch out."

"Did you threaten her?" Megan asked, beginning to bristle.

"No, of course not," Marie said, her face turning bright red. "I was trying to warn her about your father's wandering eye."

"You knew back then?"

"Megan, I feel embarrassed discussing this with you."

"Please finish. I am well aware of my father's reputation."

Marie sighed and fiddled with a dish towel. "Your father always had roving hands if you know what I mean. I knew it, but I didn't want to break up with him until I found him with your mother." Marie looked up. "Megan, I was honestly trying to warn her and I admit I was angry as well. I'd had enough at that point. She didn't believe me and thought I was bitter he had chosen her over me."

"So what happened?"

"They got married and at first things were fine. I was still angry at times, even then. What's the saying? A leopard doesn't change its spots? You can pretend all you want, bad traits tend not to change. Anyway, it was simply a matter of time. After a few years, your father was less attentive to your mother. Then she became pregnant and your mother was thrilled. She couldn't wait until you were born. She was hoping your birth would bring them closer together, but it didn't. As a matter of fact, that's when he officially had his first affair with some floozy in town." Marie looked over at Megan. "I hope I'm not upsetting you with this."

"I'll admit, it's not what I expected, but I asked for it." Megan shrugged.

"Anyway, by the third affair, your mother called me one day and apologized. He cheated on me which is really nothing compared to what she was going through, but I probably understood her the most. We were both hurt and dumped by the same guy, so to speak. That was our bond and through that, we actually became close friends." Marie reached out and took Megan's hand. "I know it's very confusing but she does love you very much. She never divorced because of you, but you'll have to hear the rest of the story from her one day. I'm not at liberty to go any further and it doesn't involve me other than I was her friend, especially when she needed a shoulder to cry on." Marie squeezed her hand and Megan squeezed back.

Megan remained quiet for a minute or so. "Thank you, Marie. I'm sure it wasn't easy and I appreciate you telling me."

"You asked me, sweetie. It was one of the skeletons in the closet, but I honestly don't think it has anything to do with the weird things going on now."

"As I said, I don't know what's going on but I'm going to keep digging until I find out," Megan said, stifling a yawn.

"Maybe, you should start with a nap," Marie laughed. She slid back her chair. "Go ahead, I'm going to start making something for dinner. You go rest. I'll keep an eye on Rose and watch the door for those supplies."

"Thank you, Marie. You've been a good friend," Megan said as she stood up and hugged her.

"I feel bad saying things against one of your parents, but it's the truth."

"I'm old enough and have seen enough to know you're right about my Dad." Megan started to laugh. "Can you believe he's still in Europe with GiGi? It's insane."

Marie paused and looked at Megan with a frown.

"What?" Megan asked.

"Are you sure he's in Europe? How do you know?"

"Because he told me," Megan said. "The caller ID had his name."

"You couldn't tell where he was by that," Marie pointed out. "Sorry to say, but he's been known to lie on occasion so how do you really know?"

Megan thought for a while. "You're right. I don't really know. I'll ask Nick though. Maybe the police can check his passport or something."

"I'm sure you'll do whatever you think is best," Marie said with a smile. "Go take your nap. Dinner will be ready when you get up. Go," Marie said as she shooed Megan away from the kitchen.

Chapter Thirty Seven

Megan rolled over and felt the warm breeze caress her face. After talking with Marie, she went upstairs and peeked in on Rose who was snoring softly. Megan gently closed the door and went to her room. She had not had a hangover in a long time and needed to close her eyes for a little while. Once asleep, she did not wake for an hour.

Megan remained on her side, facing the open windows. She felt relaxed and needed quiet time to think. So much was happening all at once. Megan took a moment to review one of the dreams she had. It was more of a memory, which saddened Megan realizing so much had changed in her life.

The water was warm as she laughed and kicked at the foam causing large splashes into the ocean. It was a beautiful day at the beach and one of the most fun she could remember. Grandma Rose had free time and suggested the two of them spend the whole day there to celebrate Megan's sixth birthday. They had a big blanket, chairs, toys and a basket of food. And there was suntan lotion. Lots of lotion as Grandma insisted on reapplying every two hours. Together they swam, built a sand castle, collected shells and rested in the sun.

"Don't go in too far, Megan," Rose had cried out when Megan ran into the waves.

"It's beautiful," Megan laughed as she splashed and played.

"Things aren't what they always seem," Rose said as she walked up to Megan and took her hand. "There can be many things hidden under the surface and the undertow is strong. It can pull you under before you blink."

Megan laughed and as if Mother Nature wanted to prove her point, a big wave suddenly hit Megan in the face. If she hadn't been holding Rose's hand, she would have been knocked over and thrown along the sand. Coughing, she let Rose hug her as wiped sand out of her eyes.

"Quick, go chase the birds away from our blanket. They're trying to find our snacks," Rose said as she pointed her away from the water.

Megan rolled over. She didn't realize how true Grandma Rose's words were. Rose had been trying to give her clues and Megan awoke with the realization there was something to be found in the attic. She needed to find the key as soon as possible. Megan had some other things to check out. She wanted to go back and review the video of the cottages, then go outside and look around the property. The yellow police tape was still there, but a part of it was fluttering in the breeze. She could say she thought it was okay if the police caught her but purposefully would not tell Nick so he couldn't be blamed. She needed to find Bill and speak to him as well. Something was going on and Megan was determined to get to the bottom of it.

Rose said she would find all the answers in her Bible. Did she mean metaphorically? But then Rose had specified the Bible she had bought when they vacationed in Vermont and visited the St. Francis Retreat Center. Megan had been so enamored by the gorgeous church and grounds in the high mountains of Vermont, she asked for a souvenir. The rectory had a small table with mementos for a donation. Rose had purchased a beautiful pair of rosary beads as well as a ceramic Bible. The lid could be removed in order to store the beads or other special cards or trinkets.

Megan loved the Bible and used it to hide little secrets from the world, especially on the days she fled to her room when her parents started fighting again. After graduation, Megan accepted her first job offer and fled to Detroit. She had purposefully left the Bible and beads behind, feeling they did not hold any special blessing in her family. Perhaps Rose found them and hid a clue in the ceramic Bible?

Megan was excited she was on to something but first she had a major concern for the Bible. Exactly where the heck was it?

Chapter Thirty Eight

Nick parked his patrol car in front of the Colonial house, called in his location and got out. He walked up the driveway contemplating his fate, but he was tired of the bullying and lack of responsibility. Stepping onto the porch, he rang the bell and waited until a small, thin woman opened the front door.

"Can I help you?"

"Yes, Office Taylor to see Jeff Davenport. Is he home?"

"Please give me a minute," she said and closed the door. Nick looked around as he waited for the door to reopen. The property was immaculate as expected for the Mayor's house. After a moment, the tiny woman beckoned Nick inside. "He's in the study with his family. Please follow me."

They walked down a hall and into a family room, bright with green pastel walls, white couches, glass tables and a plush gray rug. Large windows opened toward a relaxing view of the bay. The room was warm and inviting except for the three men seated on the furniture.

The small woman gestured for Nick to enter the room and she quietly backed away to pursue other duties.

"Nick, how can we help you?" Andrew Taylor asked. "I understand you're here to see my son?"

"Yes sir, I need to ask Jeff a few questions," Nick said as he shook hands with the Mayor of Misty Point. Nick chose his words carefully. Seated in the room was Jeff, Andrew and Henry Davenport. Jeff's father, Andrew, was the current mayor. His father, Henry, had been the mayor before that. The Davenport men had controlled the town for many years but Nick was convinced the tradition would end with Jeff who did not have the brains to run a juicer much less a town.

"What do you want, Taylor? Come to beg for your job? I didn't even get a chance to tell them about you," Jeff said as he jumped up from a chair.

"On the contrary," Nick said as he faced Jeff. "Will you please step outside?"

"I'm not going anywhere," Jeff said, crossing his arms over his chest. "Whatever you want to say, you can say in front of my father and grandfather. That'll make it easier to fire you."

"Have it your way," Nick said quietly as he grabbed a pen and his pad from his pocket. "I'm here to investigate damage to Megan Stanford's car."

"What the hell are you talking about?" Jeff spit.

"Where were you last night after you left the Clamshell?"

"None of your business."

"Officer Taylor, why don't you tell me what's going on?" Andrew Davenport said as he gestured for his son to remain quiet.

Nick turned to the mayor. "The police were called by Foster Marshall, the owner of the Clamshell to report damage to a car in the parking lot. The car belongs to Megan Stanford."

"Why would my son scratch her car?"

"Actually, sir, the windshield was shattered, tires were punctured and threats were spray-painted across the side."

"That sounds very serious, but once again, why my son?"

"Earlier that evening he harassed Miss Stanford inside the bar. He then toppled furniture and threw a platter of food across the table. There are many witnesses. He's lucky he wasn't charged with disorderly conduct or assault and battery. He targeted Miss Stanford and stated her personal affairs were a nuisance to the town her family established."

Andrew turned to his right. "Is this true, son?"

"Oh please, he's just protecting her to look like a tough guy," Jeff said as he flipped a rude gesture toward Nick.

"Did you do those things?" Henry Davenport asked, ensconced in an armchair in the corner. "And to Megan Stanford?"

"I'm sick of hearing people talk about her so I gave her a piece of my mind to knock her down a peg or two, but I sure as hell didn't touch her car."

"Jeff, leave Megan Stanford alone," Andrew said to his son. "That's not the behavior I expect from my son."

"You should keep a closer eye on your son, sir," Nick said putting his pad and pen away.

"Go to hell, Taylor," Jeff said, throwing a remote toward his head.

"JEFF!" The men all jumped when Henry threw off his small afghan and shakily stood up from his easy chair. His face was red with anger and his finger shook as he pointed it. "You will leave Megan Stanford and Misty Manor alone. Do you understand?" They watched as Henry's whole body began to shake with rage.

"I'm sorry, Grandpa. Calm down," Jeff said, frightened by his grandfather's visage.

"Just leave them alone," Henry said as he turned pale and started to wheeze. He reached behind him for the arms of the easy chair and lowered himself into the cushion.

Andrew turned to Nick. "Officer Taylor, if you don't have proof or plan any further action, I'd appreciate it if you go now. We were having a conversation about moving Dad into a nursing facility and all of this emotion is very upsetting for him."

Henry's breathing began to ease as the men watched him for a moment.

"Will he be okay?" Nick asked Andrew. "Would you like me to call for help?"

Andrew spent a minute or two looking at his dad. "I don't think we'll need an ambulance. He looks like he's feeling better, but you should go."

"This is crap," Jeff yelled. "You got nothing, Taylor. This is harassment."

"Foster is pulling the parking lot video. If you're on the video, we'll be back," Nick said as he started to back out of the room. He turned to Andrew and Henry. "I'm sorry my visit has been upsetting, Mayor, but we have to investigate."

Andrew nodded as Nick left the room and showed himself the front door.

"What an ass," Jeff said. "Dad, are you going to let him push us around like that?"

"Jeff, for once, shut up," Henry said from his chair. "I am warning you, leave Megan Stanford and Misty Manor alone." Henry looked at his son, Andrew. "You make sure he does so and that's all I have to say about it."

"Of course, Dad. Just relax, you're making me nervous," Andrew said.

"Are you kidding me?" Jeff raised his voice and arms with the question.

Andrew wheeled on his son. "Unless you want to be responsible for killing your grandfather here and now, get the hell out. I don't know what you've been up to, but I'll deal with it later." Andrew pointed to the door. "Jeff, get out."

Jeff grabbed his phone and his keys. "Screw all of you." He walked out of the room and slammed three doors as he ran out of the house.

Chapter Thirty Nine

Megan searched through cubbies and drawers looking for the ceramic Bible. She did not take it with her when she moved to Detroit seven years ago and had little memory of where things were when she left. Feelings of guilt crept in as she searched through her personal things and the dream only added to her guilt of not being close to Grandma Rose over the last seven years. Her grandmother had always cared for her, protected her through all the family disputes and fights. Rose had worked very hard to make Megan understand her parent's behavior had nothing to do with her. She was neither the cause nor cure for her parent's dysfunctional relationships. Why hadn't she kept in touch?

Megan dropped to the floor and slid the large drawer out from underneath her bed. She found some of her favorite socks, books, papers, photos, small handbags, scarves and a collection of her favorite sea shells. No ceramic Bible or rosary beads.

Frustrated, Megan left her bedroom and ran to the steps leading to the attic. She rattled the knob on the attic door with no results. The lock was different from the one she remembered and she needed to find the key. When and why had Rose decided to change the locks?

Climbing downstairs, to the second floor, Megan turned toward her grandmother's room. She had not had a chance to talk to her since the hospice staff had left and she wanted to make sure she was feeling all right. Walking down the hall, Megan heard loud voices. Hurrying to see what was happening, she opened her grandmother's door and found several men as well as Marie in the room.

"What's going on?"

Marie walked over to Megan. "It's all okay. These men are from the medical equipment company and they're delivering things for Rose."

Megan looked up to see a commode near the bedside as well as a walker. In the corner of the room, a wheelchair rested against the wall. One of the men was arranging a small oxygen tank near the head of the bed. He was connecting clear tubing which he then left on her pillow. He looked at the two women.

"I can't start the oxygen. You'll have to call the nurse to see what orders her doc wrote. It looks like they wanted a nasal cannula but I have no idea how many liters per minute she's supposed to have on her flow."

"Yes, of course," Megan said as the man handed her a clipboard with a pen.

"As you can see, we delivered a commode, a walker without wheels, a wheelchair, and oxygen with tubing. Would you please sign this delivery confirmation?"

"Oh, sure, I guess so," Megan said as she scribbled her name on the paper and handed the clipboard back to the man.

"Thank you, ma'am," he said as he took the pen and paperwork, ripped off a copy and handed it back to Megan. "If there's any problem, you can call the phone number listed on there for help. Of course, you should always call your nurse first."

"Oh, okay," Megan said as she glanced at the paper.

The men made their way toward the door and Megan walked over with them. "Let me walk you to the front door." She looked back at Marie who nodded.

Megan escorted the men down the spiral staircase, to the front door. She reached into her pocket to find a couple of bucks to give them, but she was stopped. "No, thank you. We're not allowed to accept tips." The men waved as they crossed the deck and headed toward the driveway.

Chapter Forty

Andrew Davenport poured a healthy amount of Jameson Whiskey into two crystal glasses, and handed one to his father. Henry's hand shook as he took the glass and sipped the amber liquid. "What the hell has gotten into him?" Andrew said as he swallowed a decent amount of liquor. "That kid becomes more of a problem, every day."

"Drew, you have to reel him in," Henry said as he took a deep breath and let it out slowly. "He's enjoyed a certain amount of latitude in this town, but his favors are wearing thin. He's become an aggressive bully and we're going to burn for it."

Andrew turned to his dad. "We?"

"Yes, we," Henry said, taking another healthy slug of whiskey. "I was mayor in this town for a long time before you. A lot of my cronies have passed on, but we still enjoy a certain level of respect and favoritism from their families. As a matter of fact, half of your supporters came from those relationships."

"I had a little to do with my own success, Dad."

"Yes, I understand that, son. But, Jeff is pushing the envelope too far. You can't cross the line and get away with it anymore. You need to talk to that boy. He's out of control."

"All right, don't get yourself worked up. Why is this so important to you anyway?" Andrew asked, finishing his drink and placing the glass on the table.

"There's a lot of media in town due to the Stanford situation. News vans, reporters, and plenty of social media to pick up and share a story. Jeff doesn't need to be part of the story and a criminal one at that. The kid thinks he's invincible and he's acting stupid."

"I know, Dad, I know. I tried to fix him up with a job at town hall and he laughed at me."

"Being a politician means keeping your head down, mouth shut, and keeping a lot of secrets."

"Don't I know it?" Andrew said shaking his head.

"Now go get that kid."

Chapter Forty One

Megan ran back upstairs to her grandmother's room. When she opened the door, Marie was tending to Rose and came over to the door. "Megan, your grandmother needs to be cleaned up. I'll take care of this. Why don't you take a little time for yourself? This shouldn't take us too long." Marie shooed her out of the room and closed the door.

Standing in the hall, Megan was lost in thought for a moment. She decided to take the opportunity to return to her room. Sitting at her writing desk, she plugged in her iPad and pulled up the video file she had taken for the insurance company before renovations started. The back property had originally held five small cottages scattered throughout the yard. Megan held fond memories of the cottages when she was young and use to play house in them when they were empty of summer guests.

Misty Manor was built a century ago but it had constantly been improved and fortified. Megan was not sure how old the cottages were, but knew they were built long ago. Simple wood framed structures, their heyday had come and gone. The damage from Hurricane Sandy helped make the decision about their fate.

One video after another, Megan watched the footage of the buildings. They were simple square buildings and each measured one hundred fifty square feet. Each cottage had a window on three sides, a small bathroom with a shower in the corner and then open space which held a bed and small table. A wall counter and cabinets contained simple kitchen amenities such as dishes, utensils, coffee pot, microwave, toaster, and small refrigerator as well as a large sink for dishes. Simple and cozy, but more than enough for the purpose of having a place to stay while visiting the Jersey Shore for vacation. A short walk would bring one to the lighthouse, beach or boardwalk depending on the direction they chose.

Megan reviewed footage of the complete exterior and interior of each cottage. Although intact, they had fallen into disuse over the last decade. Some had amenities missing. The paint was peeling and some windows were broken. They probably should have been demolished long before the hurricane.

Megan watched closely but there was no sign of a body or anything else unusual. She certainly did not remember an odor or sensing unnatural activity. The exterior footage of the buildings caught the surroundings and Megan was admiring the growth on the trees for early June when she noticed a dark shape in the background of the last cottage. She had been so intent on the buildings for the insurance company, she did not realize someone had been on the property when she took the video.

Starting over, Megan hit pause and saved a still of the person who was in the background. She continued to watch and saw the person running from tree to tree in order to hide from the camera. After a few seconds, the shape was gone.

Closing the video, Megan pulled up the photo she had saved. She zoomed in on the shape and was shocked when she was finally able to make out the face. The person sneaking from tree to tree was Tommy McDonough.

Chapter Forty Two

The kitchen smelled great when Megan ventured downstairs a short time later. Marie was loading a ceramic bowl filled with soup onto a tray which already held a small plate of meatloaf and mashed potatoes covered in gravy.

"Is that for Rose?"

"Yes, I'm hoping she'll be able to eat most of it. She's had some trouble swallowing so I thought softer foods might be better."

"The hospice nurse said she was going to have a dietician speak to us about pureed food," Megan said with a grimace. "Doesn't sound appetizing. I know they don't want her to aspirate any food and are worried she can't chew it thoroughly." Looking at the tray, Megan said, "They said thin foods would be hard too, so I'm not sure about the soup."

Marie heaved a big sigh. "I feel so bad for her. She's a special lady."

"I know she is," Megan said. "I feel guilty I wasn't more in touch with her while I was living in Detroit."

"Megan, you had to go live your life. Your grandmother knew that and she knows you love her very much. She's thrilled you're back."

Feeling choked up, Megan hugged Marie. "Thank you for all your help. I don't know how I would have handled any of this if you weren't helping me."

"Oh, you would have figured something out," Marie said, as she turned and wiped her hands on a towel.

"You've been here all day, Marie. I'm going to take the tray upstairs and feed Rose. I'll take care of her the rest of tonight. Why don't you go home and relax?"

Marie looked up. "If you think you'll be okay. There are a couple of things I need to do."

"Honestly, we'll be fine. If there's any problem, I'll call the hospice. They said they have a nurse on call twenty four hours a day."

"Well, if you're sure you'll be okay."

"I'm sure." Megan took the towel and smiled. "Now go. I'm sure I'll be seeing you tomorrow." Megan saw Marie to the door. Despite their small financial arrangement, Megan was grateful for all the help Marie offered and did not want to abuse her efforts. Besides, Megan would feel better being alone with Rose. Beyond that, she needed some quiet time to decide what to do about Tommy.

Chapter Forty Three

Megan balanced the tray in her right hand and a glass of wine in her left as she climbed the steps up to her grandmother's room. Rose used to love a glass of White Zinfandel with her dinner each night. Megan had placed a small shot glass on the tray in case Rose wanted to try a few sips. Hopefully, she would not have any trouble swallowing. If so, Megan would enjoy it as she fed Rose.

Reaching the room, Megan softly pushed open the door to find Rose lying against a bank of clean pillows. Marie had cleaned up before she left and Megan would never be able to thank her enough for helping to maintain dignity for Rose at this time in her life.

The large glass windows looked out on the sea and beach. Partially open, Megan smelled the fresh ocean scent gently blowing into the room. In the west, the June sun was only beginning to set so Rose was able to enjoy some light with traces of a beautiful pink sky.

Rose turned toward the door and smiled as she saw Megan enter the room.

"Hi Grandma, how are you feeling tonight?" Megan asked as she placed the tray on the side table.

"I'm well Megan. How are you?"

"I'm okay, but it's been a busy day." Megan pulled up a chair to the bedside and started arranging the dishes on the tray.

"Yes, the nurses were very nice," Rose said with a sigh. "I know they mean well, but it's all a little much."

"I trust they'll do their best to take care of you," Megan said. "Marie has been fantastic."

"Yes, she's very kind." Rose took Megan's hand. "She has a hard life. Please make sure you remember her once I'm gone."

"Grandma, let's not talk about that right now," Megan said as she stirred a bowl of thickened soup. She shook out a large linen napkin and tucked it under Rose's chin. "Marie also left us a delicious dinner. I'd love to see you finish it."

Rose reached over and took hold of her granddaughter's hand. "Megan, I'll try but you know I haven't had an appetite in a while. I worry about you. I'll try to eat if you tell me what's going on. What are the police saying? You look tired, honey."

"The police haven't told me anything and I plan to get a good night's sleep tonight," Megan said. "Okay, let's try some soup. Marie made it nice and thick for us." As she turned toward the bowl, her cell phone began to vibrate in the back pocket of her jeans. Surprised, Megan jumped a bit and pulled the phone out. The screen indicated Nick was calling, but Megan clicked off the call and placed the phone on the table.

"Do you need to take that, dear? It's all right."

"No, Grandma. It's Nick. I can call him back later." Megan lifted the soup and began to ladle a bit with the spoon. Rose was able to swallow with ease with the thickened consistency and Megan was thrilled.

"He seems to really like you Megan. I remember how disappointed he was about the prom."

"That's a time in my life I never want to revisit," Megan said as she continued to feed Rose. "Nick asked me to go, but he was so different then, very smart but kind of nerdy. He's grown up and matured."

"You have a certain smile when you talk about him."

"What smile, Grandma?"

"The kind which tells me you go weak in the knees when you see him."

Megan blushed and turned toward the table. "I don't know. It's all been so confusing."

"So tell me about it, like you used to when you were a little girl," Rose said. "I haven't lost all my marbles yet and I do feel much better since you've come home and Marie started helping me. I have a little strength back."

Megan angered when she thought back to how weak she had found Rose when she returned to Misty Point. Neglected, hungry and disheveled. Since she had been getting proper care, Rose did look much better. The doctor felt she was still appropriate for hospice and palliative care, but at least she would always be well cared for from this moment on.

Megan put the dish down and looked at her grandmother, so frail and small against the pillows. Megan pushed a wisp of Rose's gray hair to the side and teared up as she held her hand.

"What's wrong, Megan? Why are you so upset?"

Megan swallowed hard a few times while she took a moment to collect her thoughts. In a husky whisper, she said, "First, I am so sorry I went to Detroit and didn't stay in touch. I should have called or come to visit you more often and I feel so bad after all you did for me as a kid."

"Nonsense, honey," Rose said as she wiped a tear from Megan's cheek. "I did whatever I could to try to make your childhood normal. I know your parents were not focused on you and for that, I am sorry."

Megan smiled. "It wasn't your fault."

"No, but it wasn't fair to you."

Megan looked down and swallowed hard. After a moment, she said, "Someone told me my mother was in town several months ago. Do you know anything about that?"

Rose paused and looked down at her hands. When she looked up again, she had a small smile. "Yes, she came to see me."

"I don't understand," Megan said. "She hasn't talked to me in years and how could she come to Misty Manor and leave you in this condition?"

"It's not that simple, Megan. I hate to say this, but your father, my son, is a very controlling, cold man. Your mother is beautiful, Megan, and so are you. But, your mother had a few issues as well and your father did not make life easy for her. As time went on, she wanted to leave and try counseling and therapy. Your father did not cherish or acknowledge her, but he wouldn't let her go." A shadow of sadness passed over Rose as she continued to speak. "I don't know why he is like that. Your grandfather was a wonderful man and I miss him so much."

"Grandma, let's not talk about this. I don't want you to get upset."

"No, this has to be said. Your mother was miserable. She started having panic attacks. She was depressed and anxious. Your father took no responsibility and used her illness against her to garner even more control. Finally, I told her she should simply leave. At first, she refused to go. She was worried about you, but I promised her I would look after you."

"You helped me with college and everything. Dad did nothing but complain she was worthless and a bad mother. He said she left because she hated me."

"Oh Megan, I could throttle him. He was furious when she left. Not because he missed her, but her walking out reflected poorly on him. So he spun a story to shift all the blame onto her. He also went to a lawyer and did all he could to make matters most difficult for her. He made sure she had no legal right to see or contact you, with penalties if she tried. Your mother loved you very much. She was so upset, she almost committed suicide."

"But I'm grown up now. None of that applies anymore, right?"

"That was part of the reason she was here. She finally landed a decent job with benefits and went to therapy. She made a few close friends but it's hard to trust other people after experiencing something like that. After many years, she hired a good lawyer. She wanted to tell me she filed for divorce. She no longer cared about his threats and didn't want any part of his life except her freedom. Her next step was to try to win you back. She wanted to make sure you realized how much she loved you but was unable to be a good mother." Rose took a breath. "It's hard to simply walk up to someone after years of silence and tell them you want to be a part of their life."

"But if she was here, how could she leave you like this?" Megan's face flushed with anger.

"I wasn't this weak then, Megan. It would have been very awkward as well. It was my fault. I reached a point where I was upset about your father. I missed you and my husband so much, I just gave up. I stopped eating and didn't take care of myself so I got much worse. I'm not afraid to die. Don't blame your mother."

"She could have called me. Someone could have called me," Megan protested.

"Your father finally did," Rose said. "Deep down, I know it's only because the house and my neglected condition were a black eye for him. Neighbors and town officials started to get involved."

"But I would have come sooner."

"You had your childhood ruined. I wouldn't dream of imposing on your adult life."

The two were silent for a moment. Rose placed her hand on Megan's knee. "If I promise not to die tonight, can I have some of that wine?"

Megan burst out laughing. The tension relieved, Megan handed Rose the glass of wine. "Drink it slowly, Grandma."

After a few greedy sips, Rose sighed contentedly and passed the glass back to Megan. "Oh my, that was good."

"I'm glad you enjoyed it," Megan said. "Now let's work on some protein."

Megan mixed some of the potatoes and meat together and began to feed Rose. After swallowing, Rose asked, "Did you look to your Bible, Megan? It's important."

Megan put the fork down. "I looked for my ceramic Bible, but I don't remember where I left it."

Rose chuckled. "The last I saw, it was in your very special hiding place. The one you thought I never knew about."

Megan smiled. "Which one is that?"

"Weren't you ever suspicious I never had the loose air vent cover fixed under your window seat?"

Memories hit Megan in the head in a flash. "You knew about that?"

"I did," Rose laughed. "That's where you put the really secret things, but I didn't go through them, Megan. They were yours to keep and I never invaded your privacy. Before Hurricane Sandy, I was worried what would happen after the storm. I didn't know if strangers would have access to the house so I had new, strong locks placed on the attic and cupola doors and I hid a key for you in your Bible. I knew you'd remember to look there at some point. But that's the only thing I looked at. I swear."

Megan laughed as she watched her grandmother cross her heart.

Chapter Forty Four

Megan added dish detergent to the hot steamy water and watched suds fill the kitchen sink. Although she enjoyed the lengthy visit with her grandmother, Megan realized it had worn Rose out. Megan was not as upset as she had been. They had needed to have a heart to heart for a while and time was running out.

Rose was better now than when Megan first arrived due to personal care. She was being fed, cleaned and dressed by people who loved her. The hospice aide would only make things better.

Megan rinsed a plate and the wineglass when she heard her cell phone ringing. Wiping her hands on a towel, she walked over to the kitchen table and hit the green accept button on her phone.

"Hello?"

"Hey, Megan. How are you?" A bubbly voice boomed over the phone.

"Hi, Georgie. I'm okay, just a little tired. How 'bout you?"

"I'm good. What are you doing tonight? Any chance you can come out and play? We were thinking of making a bonfire at the cove."

"Oh, I can't tonight," Megan said as she pulled out a chair and sat down. "It's been a hell of a day for me, Georgie."

"Why is that honey? Is everything all right with Rose?"

"Yeah she's okay."

"Then what? How did things go with Nick last night?" Georgie giggled as she asked the question.

"They were fine," Megan said as she protested the question.

"Well, after you left, Amber was fit to be tied," Georgie laughed.

"Why? Did something else happen?"

"Let's say the night didn't turn out the way she hoped."

"Well, it wouldn't have been a problem if Jeff hadn't come along. I can't believe how rude and arrogant he was."

"True, but it wasn't Jeff who really annoyed her."

"Who then?" Megan wiggled in her seat as she rearranged papers which were resting on the table.

"She wasn't very happy with the way Tommy jumped to defend you when Jeff started acting out."

Megan blanched. "What? I imagine he did what any self-respecting guy would do."

"I don't know, Megan. Amber was turning a bit green last night, if you follow my drift."

"Oh, that's ridiculous," Megan said. "Believe me, she wouldn't want any part of my life right now."

"Oh honey, I'm sorry about Rose," Georgie said.

"It's not just her. The hospice started this morning and while I was talking to the nurse, Nick called to pick me up. I had left my car in the parking lot of the Clamshell last night. Apparently, someone decided to take a bat to the windshield and body of the car. They left a nasty message in paint as well."

"Wow. That's scary," Georgie said with concern.

"Did everything look okay when you all left?"

"There was nothing obvious in the parking lot, if that's what you mean. To be honest, we weren't feeling much pain at that point, so I couldn't be totally positive."

"Did you and the band ever reconnect?"

"No, we didn't. When the band finished the next set, they immediately started packing up their equipment to leave. They waved a time or two, but I dragged Amber out of there before something else happened."

"Good for you. We did have fun the first part of the night."

"Yes and we'll have to go out again," Georgie said. "Soon. You've been working so hard since you've come back to Misty Point. You have to get out a little more to keep your sanity."

"Georgie, can I ask you a question? I mean, if I do, can you keep it to yourself?"

"Of course, sweetie. What is it?" Georgie waited until Megan made up her mind.

"I'm not supposed to talk about it, but waiting for the police is driving me crazy," Megan said in a rush. "I wanted to start looking into things myself."

"Are you sure you want to do that?" Georgie asked, alarmed.

"Little things. I took a video of the cottages for the insurance company before they started knocking them down and I watched it today."

"And?" Georgie asked, hanging on to every word.

"I didn't see anything in the cottage, but the camera caught someone watching from the woods."

"Seriously? What creeper would be doing that?"

Megan paused. "That's the awkward part. It was Tommy."

"What?" Georgie spurted out.

"I'm telling you, Tommy McDonough was watching me from the woods while I was filming the cottages."

"That is so creepy," Georgie said.

"I need to find out why, but I don't want to ask him alone," Megan said. "Will you go with me?"

"Me?" Georgie asked. "Why me? What's wrong with Nick? He's the police officer."

"He'll get mad if he thinks I'm meddling."

"You are meddling and he should be. Let him check it out."

"Why would he be watching me?"

"I don't know, but you better let Nick check it out. Tommy seemed to be very concerned about you last night, so it doesn't make sense. On the other hand, if he is a creeper, we need to do something about Amber right away. We can't let her throw herself at a weirdo."

"Okay, let me think about it tonight," Megan said, stifling a yawn.

"Am I boring you?" Georgie laughed.

"No, I'm not used to staying out or drinking," Megan said as she pushed back her chair and walked out of the kitchen.

"Jeez, all right go to bed already. I'll call you tomorrow to see what you're going to do about Tommy, Nick and Amber. This sounds like it could be a delicate situation."

"Fine, but let me sleep in." Megan said as she turned off the lights on the lower level and checked the locks on the doors and windows.

"Will do. Sweet dreams," Georgie said as she hung up the phone.

Chapter Forty Five

"George, you came to see me," Rose said as she smiled at her husband. "I've missed you."

"*I've missed you too, Rose. It won't be long now,*" George said as he *beamed at his wife. "We'll finally be together again.*"

"Why can't it be now?" Rose reached out to try to touch him.

"*Because you have work to do,*" George smiled. "*Megan still needs you. But, I have a treat for you tonight. Listen.*"

Rose was silent for a full minute, then smiled as recognition dawned across her face. "Is that our wedding song?"

"*You remember after all these years?*"

"I could never forget. It seems like yesterday, but it's been so long."

"*Just a little longer, my love,*" George said. "*Then we can dance all night in the light of the moon.*"

"I love you, George. You know that don't you? I've always loved only you."

"*I know, Rose, and I, you. Megan will need you a bit longer. Help me protect her, Rose. Very soon, all will come to pass.*"

"Yes, George. For Megan. Promise you'll stay with me?"

"*Always, Rose. Forever and eternity.*"

Chapter Forty Six

The gulls were loud. Megan opened one eye and squinted toward her bedroom window. Seagulls flew back and forth across her view, against the morning sun, but they seemed much closer than normal. Everything seemed different these last several weeks. People, animals, and the weather, the world was changing.

Closing her eyes for a moment, Megan yawned. She then grew rigid, snapped her eyes open and stared at her window seat. Without leaving the bed, her eyes traveled down the wall and spied the loose grate cover. A small chuckle escaped her as she took a moment to remember all the secrets she stored away in the vent. She was not surprised Rose knew about the hiding place.

She hopped out of bed to remove the grate cover. She had stored all her major possessions in this hiding place. Her diary, which detailed her first kiss. Notes she had passed with Georgie at school, discussing which guys were the hottest. A favorite piece of sea glass.

Megan pried for a few seconds before the cover popped off. She reached inside and began to remove special treasures. Favorite toys, dolls, and cards were lovingly tucked away in the vent. She smiled and shed a few tears of nostalgia as she studied her possessions.

Megan stopped and flushed as she found a photograph of herself, her parents and Rose at the beach. She was around six years old. The day was sealed in her mind. It had started out well, full of anticipation of swimming, sleeping, and playing in the sand. At first, everyone had fun and they had taken an instant photo to commemorate the day. Then something went wrong. Her mother and father started screaming, then started throwing wet sand at each other. Birds started swirling around with hope the globs of sand were pieces of food. Other beachgoers stopped and stared, convinced someone was drowning. Finally, a life guard or two showed up with summer police in tow. The crowd was dispatched and her parents were separated immediately. Grandma Rose was so upset, she packed everything and walked Megan back to the house. Megan spent the next couple of hours crying in her room from disappointment and then took the photo and with a pen, scribbled over her parents face and then hid the photo away.

Placing the photo aside, Megan continued to search the vent and found the ceramic Bible. She withdrew the piece and gently lifted the lid. Inside, she found a piece of tissue paper and when she opened it, she found a key. A shiny, heavy gold key. Megan let out a whoop, closed the Bible, placed everything back inside the vent and hung the loose cover in place.

Chapter Forty Seven

Fully dressed, Megan slipped the key into her pocket and focused on making a pot of coffee. She felt much better than she had the day before and was determined to search the attic before the day was out.

Megan walked down the hall and paused near her grandmother's bedroom. Peering into the dark room, she noticed Rose was resting peacefully so Megan gently backed into the hall and headed downstairs. The seagull's cry was loud near the window and Megan hoped it didn't wake her.

Filling the coffee pot with water and her favorite grounds, Megan flipped on the switch and waited while the aroma from her favorite brew filled the room. With sleep and a good cup of coffee she was eager to continue her search for clues. She wanted the mystery cleared up as soon as possible, but each day presented new problems.

Popping bread in the toaster, Megan jumped when she felt her phone buzzing in her pocket. She pulled out the phone and popped it on the counter without answering, but within several minutes the phone started vibrating again. Megan reached out and grabbed the phone before it vibrated itself onto the kitchen floor.

"Hello?" Megan cocked her head to hold the phone to her shoulder as she placed the toast on a plate and began to apply butter.

"Miss Stanford?" A young professional woman asked.

"Yes, how can I help you?"

"Hi. My name is Mindy. I work with Cape Shore Hospice."

"Good morning," Megan said as she bit into her warm, buttery toast.

"Good morning. The reason I'm calling is because our aide is in her car outside your house. She was supposed to start taking care of

Rose Stanford a few minutes ago, but she is having trouble getting into the house."

Megan finished chewing, wiped her mouth with a napkin. "Oh, that's my fault. I didn't unlock the door."

"Thank you, but apparently she can't get near the door. Either door, as a matter of fact. She tried the back of the house as well."

"I don't understand," Megan said as she walked toward the front of the house.

After a nervous pause, Mindy said, "This sounds strange, but apparently the aide says it looks like your house is being attacked by seagulls."

"What?" Megan sounded incredulous as she unlocked the front door and yanked on the handle. She took a step onto the porch and promptly slipped on something slimy. Her phone slid out of her hand as her butt hit the deck. "Crap," she yelled as she rolled over on her knees. A disembodied voice came from the phone which had slid under the closest window on the porch.

"Miss Stanford? Are you all right? Miss Stanford?"

Megan tried to stand, but had to hold onto the house. The porch was covered with a mixture of slimy bait and bloody chum. She tried to reach for her phone but screamed and jumped back as what seemed like hundreds of seagulls attacked the porch to grab a free piece of fish guts.

"Miss Stanford? I don't know what's going on, but I'm calling 911. Miss Stanford?"

Megan tried to run back toward the front door. Her heart pounding, her breaths coming in gasps, she threw her hands up around her head and hair as seagulls continued to swoop down and grab pieces of fish. Her feet continued to slip as she hurried toward the front door.

Reaching the door knob, Megan quickly pushed open the door and slipped inside before slamming the door shut. She held the door with her hands and leaned her head on the smooth surface. After a second, she realized she reeked of bloody fish guts and would also find bird poop if she looked hard enough. Disgusted, she quickly pulled off her clothes and ran up the stairs in her bra and panties.

Megan sprinted into the bathroom and threw on the hot water. She completely undressed, jumped into the shower and quickly rinsed off the slime and gross smell. Convinced she just set a new record for the shortest shower of the year, she toweled off and sprinted to her bedroom.

She had barely popped on a t-shirt and shorts when she heard more strange noises on the deck. She looked out her bedroom window and saw a police cruiser on the right side of the house. Seagulls continued to fly past the window and jet down for a tasty treat.

Megan ran down the large spiral staircase and went toward the back of the house. She looked out the window and spied the same scenario at the front. Slimy fish guts all over the porch and seagulls in a crazed pattern of swooping down, stealing a prize and flying away. She went back to the front of the house and checked the porch through the drawing room window.

Birds continued to circle and pay very close attention to the deck. Megan looked down and was rewarded with a glimpse of her phone where it had come to rest under the window. She had no idea if Mindy had ever hung up, but the police had arrived.

Taking a deep breath, Megan opened the window as little as possible, slid the screen to the side and tried to reach out the window and down to the porch to reach her phone. By the time her fingers circled the device, her belly was resting on the window frame with her feet kicking behind her.

Grabbing the phone, Megan used her free hand to push her body back up and flipped backwards into the window. The phone smelled putrid, was sticky and covered with slime. Megan quickly closed the window with her free hand and wrinkled her nose at the disgusting smell. She screamed as the phone began to vibrate in her hand. Not daring to place the disgusting device against her face, she hit the green button and speaker as fast as possible.

"Hello?"

"Megan? Are you okay?" Megan took a deep breath at the sound of Nick's voice. "What the hell is going on?"

"Nick, I have no idea." Megan trotted toward the kitchen as she spoke. She ripped off several sheets from a roll of paper towels which sat on the counter. Placing them on the counter, she dropped the phone on top and pulled the handle on the kitchen sink.

"Megan?" Nick yelled. "What are you doing? Are you okay?"

"I'm okay, I think," Megan said as she turned off the water and dried her hands. "I don't know what's happening. Are you here?"

"Yes, I'm sitting in the cruiser. We got a call from someone named Mindy. She said your house was under attack by birds."

"It is, Nick."

"There's another woman here, sitting in a car. It's the weirdest thing. You've got hundreds of seagulls diving in front of the doors."

Megan pulled out a chair and plopped down. She caught her breath. "Nick, Mindy told me the same thing so I went out the front door to check. Someone dumped what looks like a couple barrels of chum all around the first floor porch. I slipped and fell, my phone is covered in bloody slime and I have no clue what happened to Mindy. She told me the woman sitting outside in the car is the aide from the hospice."

"What the hell?" Nick sat and watched the birds continue to circle. "Do you have a hose connected somewhere?"

"Yes, it's on the back of the house, below the porch on the side of the back door."

"Is the water turned on?"

"I think so, but I haven't gone out back since your partner told me to stay away from that area."

"Okay, stay inside. Give me ten minutes. I'm going to try to grab the hose and start spraying off the porch. If I get the slime off your porch, the birds should start to thin out."

"I hope it works," Megan said, heart beating in her chest. "Nick, who the hell would throw chum on my porch?"

"I don't know, but you sure have someone's attention," Nick said. "Just calm down and stay where you are. I'll tell the aide to hang on for a bit more."

"Okay, be careful Nick. I hate when birds chase me."

"You'll be fine. Don't move until I get in there." Nick hit the disconnect button on his phone, dropped it into his pocket and opened the cruiser door.

Chapter Forty Eight

Twenty minutes later, Nick sat with Megan at the kitchen table and watched the hospice aide climb the stairs to check on Rose. Elbows propped on the table, hands balled into fists, Megan rested her chin on her fists. "Nick, what the hell is going on?"

"I haven't a clue," Nick said as he sniffed his sleeve and made a face. "Good thing the rest of the town is quiet this morning."

"I can't thank you enough for spraying the back porch," Megan said as she looked over at Nick. "At least the aide was able to get inside to take care of Rose."

"I'd help you do the rest, but I'm on duty."

"I know. I'm so thankful you stayed this long." Megan shook her head. "I'm frightened. Who would do something like this?"

"Not sure, but we're going to step up patrols in this area. Megan, think carefully. Has there been any other threats? Phone calls? Letters? Maybe something that didn't seem obvious at the time?"

"I don't think so, except for the car. There's been a lot of stress but nothing specific, except from Fran. That was weeks ago."

"I'll look into Fran Stiles. If she did anything like this, she'd need help."

"Agreed, but I have nothing else." Megan shrugged with palms open.

"What about your father?"

"What about him?"

"Do you know if he has any new enemies?"

"New enemies?"

"He's had scuffles around here now and then. When's the last time you spoke to him?" Nick pulled a pen from his pocket as well as a small pad.

"Honestly, he hasn't had the decency to call me since I got here. Not that I'm surprised. I handled the cottage destruction and you saw how well that worked out. Rose has care so he's not concerned with her health. He's enjoying his latest girlfriend in Europe."

"Are you sure he's in Europe?"

"I couldn't swear to it," Megan said, smoothing her hair back from her face.

"I don't know what's happening here," Nick said putting his pen and paper away. "But I want you to take precautions. Keep the doors locked. Don't go out alone. Let me know if anyone calls, even if it's dead air or a hang up. Something strange is happening."

Megan shook her head and looked at Nick. "It's been some time since the body was found. They must have preliminary results by now. Are you holding out on me?"

Nick's face reddened as he looked at Megan. "You know I'm not supposed to tell you anything."

Megan bristled for a moment. "I'm sure you have your orders. But I'm not asking for much and it's not your life on the line."

"No one said your life is on the line," Nick said with a grimace.

"That's the problem. We don't know anything official but you may have overheard something. I swear I won't tell anyone. Maybe it would help to know a little something. Maybe Rose will have a moment of clarity. Give me anything, please."

"Megan, if Davis finds out I told you anything, I could be fired."

"I swear I won't say a word, but I'd like to be able to sleep at night."

"Okay," Nick said, indecision written across his face. After a moment he said, "The initial exam indicates the skeleton is a male, approximately thirty years old. They have no idea how long the skeleton has been buried since decomposition depends on a lot of different factors."

"Do they know the cause of death?" Megan asked.

"Not yet. The local pathologist has called in forensic specialists from the state. They'll try to see if there's any bone marrow they can test or look at the dental pattern. Things like that."

Megan was quiet for several minutes. Nick reached out and held her hand. "Are you okay?"

"I don't know," Megan said with a nervous laugh. "I wanted to know, but I don't feel any better or have any clue who it could be."

"That's the reason why the police department doesn't release information. We don't want to jump to any conclusions. Identification may take a very long time, if at all."

Megan looked at Nick. "I wouldn't be so concerned if all these weird things weren't happening. I have no idea if the body has someone worried or if someone is just really pissed off I came back to town."

Nick paused and looked at Megan carefully. "Do you have any reason to be worried? Have you ever been threatened?"

"No, but...," Megan looked down at the table and played with a napkin.

"But what? Do you have any enemies?" Nick stayed silent until Megan felt compelled to speak.

"Not that I know of, Nick, but I worked for a virtual newspaper in Detroit. I dug up dirt on politicians, drug dealers, terrorists, you know, the usual."

"And I'll bet most of them knew each other well," Nick said with a sarcastic tone.

"You'd be right about that," Megan said with a shrug. "I can't imagine any of them followed me here. I threatened to sue the owner of the paper if they ever published anything."

"Really? And you think they care?"

"No, but I dug up some sensitive information and it established a link to the paper, so I doubt that information will ever see daylight," Megan explained. "As a matter of fact, I was fired about ten minutes before my father called and told me I had to come home to take care of Rose and the legal stuff. I didn't tell him I got fired. I was suspicious he knew somehow, but I doubt it. It was simply his narcissistic way of getting someone else to clean up his mess."

"Do you think your father could have ever killed someone?" Nick asked softly.

Megan was flustered. "How do I know? Rose was dedicated to keeping me out of my father's shadow. I know the police were called many times. Are there any records you could use?"

Nick shook his head. "We have some records, but they vary from paper sitting in a few dusty boxes in a warehouse to digital items. We've only computerized records in the last ten years. To make matters worse, part of the warehouse had considerable damage during Hurricane Sandy. Some of the paper records are gone forever."

Megan was silent for a moment. "Unbelievable, simply unbelievable."

"It's true. The department hired someone to attempt to scan some of the remaining records, but it's very slow work," Nick cautioned. "Nothing is going to happen fast, so live your life, but be careful. Stay aware of everything around you at all times."

"Is it safe to go outside and clean the porch?" Megan asked sarcastically.

"Yes, but wait a couple hours. The birds will get most of the fish pieces for you."

"Yes, except the porch will stink to high heaven and there will be a ton of bird poop littering the house."

"This house always had special features." Nick laughed as Megan wadded the paper napkin and threw it at him.

"Don't you have work to attend to?"

"Absolutely," Nick stood up and pushed in his chair. "Like I said, be careful and stay aware of what's going on around you. I'm going to start making some inquiries."

Megan stood. "C'mon, I'll walk you out." Holding the doorknob to the back door, Megan looked outside to check for birds. "There's a lot less than before. It seems the back porch now has a limited menu, so I guess it's safe."

Nick laughed and Megan turned to face him. In an unexpected motion, he pulled her close and brushed his lips against hers. He whispered in her ear, "I'll call you later." Letting her go, he opened the door and sped down to his car.

Cheeks bright red, Megan's stomach clenched as her body tingled. She continued to smell fish from Nick's uniform and feel the warmth of his lips as she mindlessly stared out at the backyard.

Chapter Forty Nine

Scrubbing the deck with a stiff broom, Megan poured another pail of sudsy water onto the wooden boards. She had spent the last three hours alternating between spraying off the deck, applying detergent and scrubbing it down. After several hours of work, Megan was rewarded with a clean wrap-around porch and total absence of seagulls.

Turning off the water, Megan wound the hose back onto the reel. She was wet, hot, and sweaty and smelled like fish. Her first goal was a long, clean shower. Megan opened the back door and was immediately greeted by the delicious aroma of Sunday dinner being prepared by Marie.

The hospice aide left long ago but Marie arrived to make dinner and continue watching over Rose for the afternoon. Megan was assigned the night shift, but she was lucky as her grandmother usually slept through the night, although, the number of nightmares and hallucinations were increasing for Rose, despite her medication.

Megan spent a few minutes explaining what had happened to Marie who immediately began to flit around the kitchen. "I hope you don't mind if I cook," Marie explained. "I like to work off stress that way."

On her way toward the stairs, Megan remembered the disgusting clothes she peeled off by the front door. She went to retrieve them for the wash and froze when she realized they were gone. She looked around the foyer, near the window and outside the front door. She needed her pants. Megan had finally found the attic key and shoved it in her pocket in anticipation of a complete search later that day. The last thing she expected was getting attacked by slime and seagulls.

Panic setting in, Megan raced over to the laundry room and searched the floor, the basket and the machine with no results. She needed that key.

Marie turned around as Megan ran into the kitchen. "What's up? You look like you're being chased by a monster and you smell." Marie scrunched her nose up.

Breathless, Megan leaned on the counter. "Did you see a pile of clothes by the front door?"

"See them? I almost tripped over them and then gagged from the odor. Why in the world would you leave them on the good floor? You're lucky the moisture didn't leave a water stain on the wood."

"I know," Megan said, sheepishly. "But where are they?"

"I was afraid to put them in the washer so I threw them in a box in the utility room."

Megan jumped away from the counter and ran to the utility room. Spying the box, she pulled out the pants and searched the pockets. She pulled them inside out, but no key. Anxiety gripped her as she threw all the clothes on the floor and searched all the flaps and corners of the box. There was no key. Megan muffled a yell, then jumped as the door was yanked open.

"What are you doing?" Marie asked as she looked around the room.

"I've lost something and I need to find it," Megan said with exasperation. "It was in the pocket of my jeans."

"Oh, you mean this?" Marie reached into the pocket of her apron and pulled out the large, shiny key.

Megan jumped up. "That's it. You're a lifesaver."

"Not really, I checked your pockets before I considered throwing your clothes out." Marie shrugged and handed over the key. "Force of habit. I don't know what that key belongs to but it's sure fancy."

Palming the key, Megan said, "I'm not sure yet, but I am definitely going to find out. Thank you, Marie. You're the best." Megan reached over and embraced Marie in a massive bear hug.

"Stop, you smell just as bad as the clothes on the floor," Marie said in mock disgust as she pushed Megan away. Megan let go and laughed all the way to another shower.

Chapter Fifty

"I know Megan's still in danger," Rose said as she looked toward the right side of her bed. The room was empty, yet Rose waited and nodded her head as if she were receiving a very logical response. "I can't leave this world until I know she's safe. Everything is coming to the surface now." Rose waited for a response as she picked at the sheet covering her frail body.

"I understand what you're saying completely," Rose nodded as she spoke. "I just hope it's enough. I've given her the key. The things she'll find in that attic will keep her busy for a long while and I trust her to cherish them while she unravels their history. Do you think Bill will tell her everything?"

After a few more moments of nodding and listening, Rose extended her hand into the air. "I can almost touch you. I can't wait to be with you again. All the pain and suffering, fear and anxiety will finally be gone." Rose heaved a small sigh. "Peace, tranquil peace, unlimited joy and happiness. I can't wait and I'll be there soon enough, but we have to make sure Megan is safe. I can't leave here until it's over. No one deserves the childhood she got."

Rose's face crumpled as tears formed in her eyes and she clutched the blanket to her chest. "I tried so hard to make things right, but what will be, will be. I just hope it's enough."

Chapter Fifty One

Stepping out of the second shower of the day, Megan threw on a pair of jeans, her favorite t-shirt and flip flops. She had intended to spend the next couple hours exploring the attic for clues as well as memories from her childhood, but as she dried her hair, Marie yelled up the stairs to let her know dinner was ready.

Whether from the hot shower or the strenuous day cleaning the porch, fatigue set in and Megan realized she was famished. She left her room and headed downstairs, stopping by her grandmother's door on the way. After several minutes of quiet observation, Megan was assured Rose was sleeping peacefully. Megan could not stop the disease or add years to her grandmother's life, but she was determined to make her final days full of comfort, dignity and love. It was the least she could do for the woman who raised her as a daughter instead of a grandchild.

Megan choked up as she descended the grand staircase. Guilt and remorse continued to creep in whenever she left the emotional door open, but her therapist, in Detroit, told her past events and feelings were lessons which helped mold the person she is today. Megan reviewed her prescribed mantra in her thoughts. Concentrate on today and move forward. Forgive yourself for everything and move on.

Before entering the dining room, Megan brushed her eyes with the heel of her hands and wiped them on her pants. She took a deep breath and turned the corner. Marie had set out dinnerware for one as well as a lovely spread of food. To start there was a Caesar salad with thick, creamy dressing and mounded shaved parmesan cheese, followed by a bowl of homemade minestrone soup. The main entrée was a steaming lasagna which smelled heavenly. Garlic bread rested on a small plate on the side.

Marie walked in with a wine glass and a bottle of White Merlot. She looked at Megan and knew she'd been crying. "I didn't realize you were down yet. Come, sit and eat."

"Thanks, Marie. Everything smells great. Why is there only one plate?"

"That's for you, honey. I made a tray for Rose. I thought I would feed her."

"I just checked on her and she's sound asleep. You worked so hard on this meal. Why don't you sit with me?"

Marie looked unsure for a moment. "Maybe I should check on Rose first. I chilled a bottle of wine for you. Would you like some?" Marie put the glass on the table and poured a generous amount for Megan. "You've been through so much since you returned to New Jersey. This may help you relax. This situation can't be easy for you."

"Thank you, Marie. Coming home has been much harder than I anticipated. Caring for Rose is one thing, but I certainly didn't expect dead bodies and threats. I don't know what's going on or why," Megan said as she shook her head. "But I do know, I'd be sunk if you weren't here to help me. So thank you from the bottom of my heart."

"It's my pleasure, honey. Rose has been wonderful to me over the years. I'm not sorry I didn't marry your father, but I am sorry not to have had Rose for a mother in-law. She is a terrific woman and it's the least I can do for her and you."

"Why don't you rest for a moment and have some wine with me?" Megan asked. "I'll get a glass for you."

Marie hesitated. "Are you sure Rose is sleeping?"

"I just checked her on the way down to dinner," Megan said with a smile. "It's okay."

"You stay where you are. I'll get the glass," Marie commanded as she pressed on Megan's shoulder. Marie left the dining room and returned a moment later with a small jelly glass.

Megan looked at the glass and smiled. "That's so funny. I remember Rose drinking out of glasses like that for years."

"Half the time, the only reason we bought the jelly was for the glass," Marie said as she poured a small amount of wine into the glass. She bought the glass to her lips and took a small sip of the wine. "Oh, this wine is better than I expected." Marie then poured a generous amount into her glass and took another sip while she watched Megan eat her meal.

"Have you given any thought to what you'll be doing after?" Marie asked when Megan swallowed a fork full of food.

"After?"

"Not to sound indelicate, but, you know, after Rose is gone," Marie said. "You've lived in Detroit for a long time. I have to be honest. People's tongues are wagging in town about everything."

"Like what?"

"They're worried. Most people don't like your father. They're worried about what will happen to Misty Manor and the property. No one wants to see a large complex of condominiums or houses go up and they feel your father will simply sell off to the highest bidder."

Megan sat for a moment and sipped her wine. "Sadly, that's true. My father has no attachments to Misty Manor and I don't know why. I have no clue what arrangements Rose made in her will and whatever it is will have to be. If she changed her will now, anyone can argue she wasn't in her right mind."

"What about you? Will you go back to Detroit and your job?"

Megan looked at Marie. "I don't have a job in Detroit anymore. I'll need a new job when things are settled for Rose and now that I'm back, I do believe I'll be staying in New Jersey. You adapt to wherever you are and don't realize how much you miss until you look back."

"Not to mention you may have another reason to stay here," Marie raised her glass toward Megan with a knowing look. "He's quite handsome."

Megan blushed at the thought. "Marie, I've barely been back a month. Nick is a great guy and rather easy on the eyes, but let's face it, he's probably living out his prom fantasy. At the moment, he's here a lot because of whatever's going on, but once everything is settled, he'll probably move on. You know how certain people bond in a crisis but there's nothing to sustain the relationship once it's over."

"I don't know," Marie said. "The gossip is all over about the two of you as well. Nick has been a fairly solitary guy. Many women have tried to attract his attention and failed. You waltz in and he becomes all jiggly in the knees. You haven't been here to know the history."

Megan chuckled at the thought. "I'll admit he makes me a bit jiggly in the knees. He's matured quite a bit from high school but deep down he has the same caring personality. He's a very decent, smart and responsible guy. I can see why ladies would be throwing themselves at him, but that's probably the reason he's been so helpful. He's just concerned and wants to help."

Marie almost choked on her wine. "Honey, the way he looks at you is not always decent." She then blushed and stood up. "I'm sorry. I should not have said that. It's certainly none of my business. It must be the wine."

Megan reached out and placed her hand on Marie's arm. "I have no idea what's in store for the future, but I'm in no position to start a relationship now. Tell the gossipmongers to look elsewhere for their daily fix. I'll be happy to accept status quo for a while and let things settle down."

"Of course and I didn't mean to suggest otherwise," Marie said with a small smile. "Finish your dinner. I'm going to bring a tray up to Rose and see if she's ready to eat." Marie turned and left the grand dining room.

Megan took a few more bites, then lost in thought, she spent the next ten minutes pushing delicious food around her plate.

Chapter Fifty Two

Although warm, Monday morning dawned gloomy, which was fine as the day matched Megan's mood. She had played with her food for a full fifteen minutes after Marie left the dining room the previous evening. As much as she wanted to believe Nick was attracted to her, and she felt a strange warmth in her belly when he was near her, Megan could barely hope for a relationship with Nick. Yet, she had cleared her place in the dining room and kept her cell phone close, waiting for his call. Several hours went by but the phone remained silent. After a quick visit with her grandmother, she finally went to bed, disappointed, and chiding herself for daring to dream.

Mentally scratching Nick off her list, Megan started her chores for the day. Preparing breakfast, she brought a tray to her grandmother's room. Rose was awake and Megan spent some time cleaning her, straightening her bed and making her comfortable. Torn between not wanting to burden her granddaughter and needing help, Rose protested throughout the process. Megan assured her she was fine and then sat with Rose for over thirty minutes trying to coax her to eat breakfast. Not having slept well the night before, Rose was quickly exhausted and fell back to sleep. Pulling the blankets up, Megan tucked her grandmother in, and carried the tray back to the kitchen.

After washing the dishes and pouring a cup of coffee, Megan called her landlady in Detroit. They exchanged pleasantries before Megan detailed her decision to stay in New Jersey. There was no fancy furniture or anything of high value in the apartment so her landlady was agreeable to keeping her things in order to rent a furnished apartment to the next tenant. If necessary, the landlady would make arrangements to donate any unwanted furniture to a charity and once everything was settled, Megan would receive the balance of her deposit in the form of a check.

Megan hung up the phone with a strange mixture of anxiety and excitement. She had closed the door on her past without having a plan for the future. The old Megan had everything planned, coordinated, and organized weeks in advance. The new Megan had a hard time planning past breakfast. Deep in her heart she was determined about one thing. She would stay at Misty Manor and do all she could to help Rose, and when the time came, she would fight her father every step of the way to keep Misty Manor from being sold and demolished. Megan had promised her grandmother she would keep the attic locked and not let anyone else inside, which brought her to the next task of the morning. She was determined to explore the attic, immediately.

Megan retrieved the key and climbed the final set of steps between the third floor and the attic room. When she got to the top of the stairs, she flipped on the small overhead light. Fishing the heavy key out of her pocket, Megan leaned toward the attic door. She saw the original mortise lock which was installed with the original attic door approximately one hundred years ago. For extra security, someone had secured a brand new steel hasp to the door jamb. Through the thick hook hung a heavy old fashioned padlock. Megan pulled the key out of her pocket and with sweaty palms, inserted it into the key hole. After a bit of resistance she was able to open the lock.

Nerves tingled down her arms as she reached out and removed the padlock from the hook. She pulled back the hasp and turned the glass knob. Megan did not have the original skeleton key, but the old lock appeared disabled and the door opened more easily than she expected.

Megan took a tentative step into the attic and reached around to find a light. It had been many years since she last visited this room and Megan couldn't remember if there was a switch on the wall or a pull chord. Sliding her fingers along the wall, she touched an old switch plate. Memories rushed in when she felt the push button switch and was rewarded with dim light.

Megan took a moment to look at the space. Dust and cobwebs were at a minimum which was interesting as she knew Rose did not have the strength to climb up the several flights of stairs necessary to reach the attic. The ceiling was low, but she was able to walk through without hitting her head. A tall person would have a much harder time.

Boxes and various items covered with sheets and paper were stacked or stood on end along the walls of the attic. Christmas decorations were piled in one corner and Megan smiled when she spied some of her favorite holiday ornaments and wreaths. She and her grandmother had a special collection of Christmas decorations sporting a beach theme. Wall hangings with Santa on a surf board, crabs wearing Santa hats, shells painted with themes of Christmas trees and candy canes filled a box to overflowing. Next to that stood a four foot lighthouse wrapped with green garland decorated by gold bullion and other pirate booty. Megan vowed she would decorate as much of Misty Manor as she could with her favorite decorations if she were still here at the holidays. Maybe Rose would want to see them now. Why wait for Christmas? Megan was sure there hadn't been any holiday decorating in years, especially after the Hurricane. Megan decided to bring some of their favorite things downstairs and decorate Rose's room now, if she wished.

Taking a deep breath, Megan inhaled the familiar smells of the attic. She was amazed to find the room smelled exactly as it had when she was a small girl. She had no idea if the unchanging odor was attributed to the contents or the wooden walls and floor, but it brought back happy memories of playing up here. On special days, she and Rose would take a few things out to the widow's walk and play outside.

Looking toward the end of the attic, Megan walked toward the far wall which held the door leading into the cupola. There was a second door on the right wall which led up to the widow's walk. Megan walked into the cupola and found another light switch. She walked to the end of the room and took in the view of the beach, ocean and lighthouse from the rounded wall of windows. Megan used to come to this room often, especially when it rained. She would bring her favorite books and a pillow, flop on a small divan and read for the day.

Megan opened as many windows as she could to allow the warm ocean breeze to freshen the attic. Leaving the door to the cupola opened, Megan walked back into the attic and opened the door on the right wall. There was a small hall with a staircase which led up to the roof and the widow's walk. Climbing the stairs, Megan reached the hatch, unhooked the door, pushed it open and stepped out onto the roof of Misty Manor.

For a moment, she remained frozen and a little unsteady as she looked out at the landscape from the high elevation and let the wind surround her. The floor was covered with seagull poop, but the small area was enclosed by a white fence, approximately two feet high. The original fencing had been replaced several times over the past hundred years due to harsh weather conditions and high winds. Apparently it had been replaced since Hurricane Sandy as well. Perhaps the same person who installed the lock.

Megan took a few tentative steps forward and looked down at the roof over the front of the house as well as the land leading toward the beach and ocean. She marveled at the natural beauty and was awed by the power of the water which spread out before her.

She tried to imagine her great grandmother, Mary Stanford, standing in this same spot, staring out to sea, hoping for a sign of her husband, John Stanford, and his ship returning to shore in the early 1900's. Although always pleased by the gifts her husband brought back with him, her greatest gift would be his safe return from sailing.

Megan stayed silent, standing at attention, letting the ocean breeze blow around her. Seagulls drifted over to see if there were any tasty treats leftover from the day before. Megan ignored the birds and kept her hands down by her side so as not to attract their attention. If a flock of seagulls suddenly descended on her, she could not run without potentially falling off the roof and most likely to her death. The birds drifted away and silence returned. Within a moment or so, Megan felt a presence behind her which she attributed to nerves. She tried to ignore it but suddenly turned when she heard a noise. Her heart thudding in her ears, she was sure someone followed her up to the roof, but when she turned she found no one there. Perhaps the wind was playing games with her.

After a few deep breaths, Megan crossed to the rear of the walk and looked down at the back roof and large property. She could see the newly turned dirt where the demolished cottages had been. A large yellow front loader stood silent on the side of the property. The bucket had been tested for presence of blood after pieces of the skeleton were found. The test had been negative as far as Megan knew. From this angle, the machinery appeared to be guarding the yard.

Yellow crime scene tape was wrapped around a series of poles pushed into the ground near the location of the corpse. As the investigation was ongoing, the police hadn't released the area so all would remain untouched until then. A pile of debris cluttered the yard and would need to be removed when clear. The crime scene techs had gone through the rubble, looking for additional clues. Pieces which were considered irrelevant formed the large pile where it currently remained.

Two of the cottages remained standing. Although scheduled for demolition, the work came to an immediate halt when the body was found. Megan would have to regroup when she was allowed to restart the demolition.

Megan looked to the distance. She studied the remaining acres of land, which held the undemolished two cottages, patches of trees, a small pond and the three car garage at the crest of the circular driveway. As she watched, Megan spied two cars drive down Ocean Blvd, enter the circular driveway and park near the garage. She immediately recognized the Cape Hospice aide and nurse manager, Nicole, emerge from separate cars. Realizing the front door was locked, Megan turned and headed back into the attic to run down several flights of stairs and let them into the house.

Chapter Fifty Three

"Hi, how are you today?" Nicole asked as the two women entered the house.

"Fine, just fine," Megan said as she smoothed back her hair which had flown all over from the wind.

"I hope you don't mind my coming along with my aide today," Nicole said. "I have to make sure she understands the care plan we put in place for your grandmother."

"Of course not." Megan closed the front door and stood to the side. "Rose was awake earlier so I cleaned her up and tried to feed her. She wasn't very interested in eating this morning."

Nicole smiled and softly said, "You might find she doesn't eat as much as you think she should. That's natural at this stage."

"I don't want her to lose her strength," Megan said.

"I realize that, but sometimes feeding our loved ones regular meals as they near the end of life can be worse for them. There's a risk of choking on food. It's called aspiration and you can get a serious pneumonia from that," Nicole explained. "Sometimes the body simply can't break down food as easily as before, which can result in bloating and swelling."

Megan's face fell as she listened to Nicole speak.

"It's okay," Nicole reassured her. "You'll know if she's hungry, but don't try to force her if she's not."

Megan swallowed. "Why don't we go upstairs?" She led them up the grand staircase and into her grandmother's bedroom. Rose was awake and was looking toward the windows when they walked in. She turned toward them.

"Megan?" Her voice was faint, barely a whisper this morning.

"Hi Grandma, how are you feeling?" Megan crossed the room and quickly knelt by the side of the bed. Rose reached out, cupped her chin and then smoothed her hair away from her face with shaky fingers.

After a few seconds, Rose whispered. "Were you in the attic? I had a dream you were up on the walk. Be careful, Megan. I don't want to see you get hurt."

Megan felt her arms cover with goose bumps. "Yes Grandma, you wanted me to check the attic, remember?"

"Yes, but only you. There are many things in the attic. Start under the stairs but be very careful, Megan. Promise me, no one but you." Rose's face appeared sunken, but her eyes were bright and intent on Megan.

Megan felt her stomach knot and she swallowed hard. How had Rose known she was in the attic? Maybe she heard footsteps through the ceiling. The widow's walk was two floors up. "I promise, no one, but me." She held Rose's hand while she leaned forward and kissed her on the cheek. Megan smiled at her grandmother once again. "I promise."

Rose simply looked at her, nodded and closed her eyes.

Nicole crossed to the bedside and put her hands on Megan's shoulders to draw her up from the floor. "Why don't you go rest and let us take care of Rose for now?" Megan allowed herself to be pulled upright. "Jessica, our social worker, will be coming here tomorrow with our chaplain, Anastasia. I hope you can spend a few minutes with them."

"Why?" Megan asked, perplexed.

"We want to make sure you're okay and whether you need any more support," the nurse said. "To be honest, we want to talk about what happened yesterday as well. We have to make sure your house is a safe environment for everyone."

Megan blanched. "Everything is fine. We just had to clean the porch." Nicole looked at her, doubt in her eyes, when they suddenly heard Rose snort.

Megan looked at Nicole and then anxiously back at her grandmother. "Is she okay?"

"Yes, she's breathing, but she's very weak. Let us do our job and make her comfortable."

Nicole walked Megan toward the door. Megan paused, took a long look at Rose, and left the room in tears. As she entered the hall, she realized she had left the windows in the cupola open as well as the remainder of the attic unlocked. Knowing Rose was safe, she slowly made her way back to the attic.

Chapter Fifty Four

Officer Nick Taylor walked into the small briefing room of the Misty Point Police Department. The room was packed with summer help. Junior officers, wearing bright yellow shirts with the word Police written across the back, were standing throughout the room and against the back wall.

Nick could feel the excitement as some of the officers waited for their morning briefing. The influx of the summer crowd caused the population to swell quickly. Misty Point needed the help to give out tickets for illegal parking, drinking on the beach, and to discourage drivers from running over sunbathers crossing Ocean Ave. for pizza, coffee and beer. Mostly, the junior police helped to keep a much needed eye on the town summer activity.

Nick smiled as he looked over the crowd of young officers. He had gotten his start the same way, right after high school. At first, he worked summers as extra help, then went on to graduate from the police academy and was lucky enough to land a job in Misty Point.

The fulltime police force in Misty Point was small. The town had a small year round population which tripled when summer beach lovers poured in. The standard crimes consisted of drunk and disorderly, parking tickets, petty theft, DWI, and lewd acts in public. Recently, they needed a traffic detail to concentrate on texting while driving and running over residents on the street and sidewalks. They had very few unidentified dead bodies in town.

The crowd quieted as Officer Davis approached the front of the room. "Okay, everyone listen up. In a few minutes, you'll all be meeting with Officer Peters who'll be going over your weekly assignments with you. You'll receive instructions on where to go and who you report to. If you see anything suspicious, you are to contact your superior immediately. Do not try to apprehend anyone. Do not discuss anything with anyone at any time. All reports remain confidential." Davis paused and looked around the room. His expression announced his sour stomach and bad mood. "As you may have heard, we did find a dead body in town. That is the only information you will get and it is not to be discussed. There are no further public details if anyone asks. If I hear that any of you discussed the case, you will be terminated immediately." Davis once again paused for effect and looked around the room, meeting the many eyes of the nervous crowd. "Any questions?" Several seconds went by, but the room remained silent. Davis shifted his feet and looked to his right. "Peters, come on up to the front." Davis then faced the crowd. "All right, everyone line up here. One at a time." As the nervous young officers scrambled to get in line, Davis walked to the door and motioned Nick to follow him out of the room.

Chapter Fifty Five

Officer Davis walked behind his scarred wooden desk and plopped into an old rolling chair. He started to flip through papers and threw a pile to the side as he searched for a specific document. He gestured for Nick to take a seat. "Make yourself comfortable."

Nick pulled a small wooden chair up to the desk and sat down. "What's up?"

Pulling a yellow envelope out of the mound, Davis sat back and sighed. "I got this report last night. The results are interesting." Davis opened the flap and pulled out the contents. "It's from the state forensic anthropology lab."

"Really? Did they get an ID?"

"Not exactly, but they have some conclusions."

"Which are?"

Davis flipped through the pages, then fumbled for his reading glasses. He placed them on his nose and looked for summary results. "Okay, let's see. According to this, the skeleton is a male, approximately thirty years old. The cause of death is listed as murder as they found what appears to be a bullet hole in the skull."

"That eliminates the father as a victim. He was fifty when he renewed his passport." Nick said, nodding his head.

"But it doesn't eliminate him as the shooter." Davis continued. "Apparently, the lab didn't have enough direct DNA for an identification, but they want to compare something with the DNA you collected from Megan Stanford." Davis looked directly at Nick. "If it matches, the result would indicate the body was related in some way to the Stanford family."

"Any idea who it could be?"

"No, but I think it's time to drag some of the domestic violence reports out of storage," Davis said. "There may be some interesting information in there."

Nick nodded his agreement. "How long was the body buried?"

"Not sure about that, but it's been awhile," Davis said while scratching the back of his head.

"Long enough to be the grandfather, George Stanford?" Nick asked, looking surprised.

"I'm not sure, but I think we're fairly positive something is not right with this family. I don't know if it's George or some other Stanford relative. I don't like Dean, never did. For all I know he could have iced one of his cousins years ago and dumped the body." Davis looked up at Nick. "You've been hanging around your friend, Megan, a bit more than I like. What's going on?"

"Nothing," Nick said defensively as he shook his head. "She's an old friend, that's it."

"Are you able to find out anything? Anyone talking over there?"

"Not about the body," Nick said. "I don't know if you got a chance to read the reports, but there is something going on. Megan's car was vandalized at the Clamshell Friday night. The windshield was shattered. The tires were punctured and there were also threats spray painted on the side of the car. On Sunday, someone trashed the front porch of Misty Manor. Dropped a load of fish guts near the doors so seagulls would be a nuisance for the family. Someone is not happy and sending a message."

"Any idea who?" Davis suddenly looked very interested.

"Not a clue."

"Okay, we have research to do. Let's get the old records on that family. Call the building department, too. I want plans and permits pulled for those cottages. Something doesn't smell right with this family and we're going to find out what it is."

Nick stood and began to leave the room. He turned back when he heard Davis call his name.

"Listen, be very careful how much you hang around Megan Stanford and what you tell her. If we do come up with a killer, I don't want any part of the case compromised. Understand?"

Nick reddened and nodded his head.

Chapter Fifty Six

Megan left her grandmother's bedroom and headed for the attic. She had left all the doors and windows open when she raced downstairs to let the hospice team in. She climbed the stairs to get back into the attic. The lighting had changed as the day wore on and the room looked different.

Megan strolled past boxes of old sheets and curtains which had been used years ago. Another box was filled with china and kitchenware. Someday she would find time to go through the boxes which were packed and stored with a loving hand.

The temperature in the cupola had dropped and the fresh breeze made the air feel damp. Megan crossed the room and closed each window, taking time to secure the locking mechanism in place. She took a moment to look at the water and then followed the boardwalk toward the shops. A bookcase, comfortable couch and a few pillows would make the cupola a great place to hide from the world.

Leaving the room, she headed for the stairs up to the widow's walk. Megan quickly popped her head out of the opening to make sure she had not left anything on the roof. Seeing nothing, she backed down the stairs, pulled the door closed and locked it securely.

Megan descended the steps and paused at the bottom. Rose had been insistent about looking under the stairs. Megan was standing at the base of the only set of stairs in the attic. She turned and looked at them carefully. There was nothing on the stairs or on the wall to the left of the stairs. To the right, there was a small passage, about two feet in width. Megan moved toward the narrow space and looked inside.

A faux wall had been built from the stairs to the floor. A quick peek revealed nothing more than a wall, but Megan persisted because of Rose. Now that the hatch was closed, the area was dark. Megan searched the attic and finally found a flashlight which had been left by the door. Squeezing into the passage she examined the wall with the flashlight. Megan was rewarded when she found a small door toward the back of the passage which would provide a way for her to get under the staircase. She opened the slim door and focused her flashlight inside.

Megan saw barrels, clothes hanging from a beam as well as trunks and a small wooden hope chest. Without windows, the air in the tiny space was dusty and stale. Squeezing into the tiny space, Megan shifted position until she was able to touch the fiber drum. As a child, she remembered her grandmother using the fifty five gallon barrels to store valuables in the attic. After tugging for a few minutes, she was able to lift the metal rim and lid off of the drum. Inside, there were many items, each wrapped in a linen cloth. Megan had enough room to lift one item at a time, but it was difficult to examine. The flashlight was perched on a beam to her side and she was not able to fully unwrap and study whatever was stored inside. Placing the metal lid back on the drum, Megan put the rim over the top and locked the lid in place. She would try to pull the drum out at a later time.

Walking sideways, Megan stopped in front of the hope chest. With a small amount of room, she was able to kneel in front of the chest and open it. She found a pile of newspapers inside the chest as well as photographs of her grandparents in beautiful gilded frames. Megan stared at a photo of her grandmother, who smiled radiantly at the camera. Rose was gorgeous. She was wearing an ivory wedding gown which appeared to be made of satin and silk. Pearls were sewn throughout the dress and with gloved hands, Rose was holding a gorgeous bouquet of flowers tied together with silk and satin ribbons. Her hair was rolled in waves and covered with a beautiful full length veil.

Megan was aware weddings were very simple during that time. Her grandparents were married in 1945 and WWII had just ended in May of that year. The fashion industry had been impacted by rationing during the war. Most weddings were quickly thrown together with borrowed dresses for the women and uniforms for the men. Bridesmaid's dresses usually never matched.

Rose and George Stanford were a couple who had substantial means. Megan's great grandfather, John Stanford, had collected many treasures during his travels as a sea captain. The wedding dress may have come from Europe during one of his voyages, to be worn years later by his future daughter-in-law. However, Rose's family also had some money. Megan was sorry she didn't know more details of her grandparents wedding, which was likely one of the grandest celebrations Misty Point had ever seen.

As Megan continued looking through the hope chest, she found packets of letters which George had written and sent to Rose before their wedding. The small envelopes were decorated with ornamental penmanship and held together with wide satin ribbons. When she had time, Megan planned to read through them all.

Under the letters, Megan found the gloves worn by Rose on her wedding day. She also found several hankies tucked away as well. In a box in the corner, she found a pair of satin shoes. The other side of the hope chest held a small box made of cedar which held a man's watch as well as cuff links and several tie pins. Megan was floored when she examined the watch and realized it was an antique Rolex. Obviously, the hope chest held very sentimental mementos of her grandparents wedding.

Megan replaced the contents and began to look through the newspapers. Viewing the old papers tickled her passion as a journalist. The papers were wide and had the irregular columns and typeface which was common back then. Megan lifted the papers and carried them into an area of the attic which offered more light. She opened them and slowly turned page by page.

Most of the papers had been published in 1955 and spanned the entire year. Megan read articles about the development of the drug Prednisone. President Eisenhower had suffered a coronary thrombosis. Elvis appeared at the Grand Ole Opry and Albert Einstein passed away. William Faulkner won a Pulitzer Prize and Lee Merriweather became Miss America. James Dean died in a car accident at the age of twenty six. The world celebrated the success of the vaccine developed by Jonas Salk to prevent Polio and Rosa Parks refused to give up her bus seat in Montgomery, Alabama. In sports, the Dodgers beat the Yankees in the World Series, 4 games to 3, and the Detroit Red Wings won the Stanley Cup. Between the articles she looked at advertisements posted by Heinz Vinegar, Hershey Chocolate Company, Maxwell House coffee and Barbasol Shave Cream.

One local newspaper, Misty Point Gazette, caught Megan's eye. There were several interesting articles and the headlines were bold.

George Stanford is Missing – *35 year old George Stanford, son of John Stanford, founder of Misty Point, NJ, has been missing for approximately one week. Mrs. Rose Stanford and son, Dean, recently returned from a trip to see her mother but Mr. Stanford was nowhere to be seen. The police were called and a search was conducted. Mr. Stanford's personal belongings were found in their proper place in his home. His beloved 1955 Lime Green Studebaker was in its normal place in the garage. Fearing he had drowned, police searched the ocean for several days with boats and volunteers in the water. No body was found. If you have any information on Mr. Stanford, please call the Misty Point police department immediately.*

Megan looked at the paper. There was a large photo of her grandfather above the small blurb detailing his disappearance. Several other articles filled the page. Stories about a recent storm and how it would affect the tides for the weekend. A photo of the winner of a fishing contest with several other men holding fish of various size and species. There were stories about a recent robbery of a royal family visiting Atlantic City where a very expensive necklace had been stolen. Another entry announced the Garden State Parkway had declared it reached full operation of 164 miles on July 1st, 1955, except for the Great Egg Harbor Bay crossing. The rest of the paper listed upcoming weddings as well as death notices and plenty of advertisements. Now she understood why Rose had kept the many newspapers.

Megan sat back on her heels. She did not have a grandfather as she grew up, but she had never put much thought into what had happened to him and no one ever discussed it. Gathering the papers, Megan leaned back into the small space under the stairs and placed them into the hope chest. She wanted to take the wedding photo as well as the hankie back to Rose, hoping it would provide some comfort. What did the social worker call it? Yes, life review, which would be fine as long as it did not cause Rose more stress to relive the nightmare she must have endured at the time.

Ruffling through the hope chest, Megan pulled out several of the framed photos of her grandparents. She closed the lid, backed out and stood up. Retrieving the flashlight, she made sure all doors and windows were latched tight, and left the attic.

Chapter Fifty Seven

Walking toward her bedroom, Megan felt her phone chime. She had wanted to wash her hands, but was afraid someone was trying to reach her about Rose and needed her right away. She jogged the last several steps and dropped the photos at the edge of the bed, while pulling the phone from her pocket.

"Hello?"

"Hey stranger, how are you?"

"Don't ask. Things are crazy around here and getting more stressful by the day."

"Really? I thought you were sequestering yourself with Nick." Georgie laughed into the phone.

"Apparently, you thought wrong," Megan said as her stomach knotted up. "I had a problem out here the other day. Someone threw a barrel of fish guts all over my porch."

"What?" Georgie exclaimed. "That's so bizarre."

"I know, right. Anyway, Nick helped me clean up the mess but he had to leave. I haven't heard from him since."

"Maybe he's busy. He is an active part of our police force."

"That's possible." Megan sighed as she sat on the edge of the bed. "Or maybe I made an assumption I shouldn't have."

"Such as?"

"I don't know." Megan fell backward on the bed. "I think I'm embarrassing myself."

"C'mon, don't stop now."

"Well, I kind of thought, Nick and I, well, you know."

"He was very protective of you at the Clamshell. But then, so was Tommy."

"That's Nick's job, as a police officer."

"Is it his job to drive you home? Megan, I saw the way he was looking at you. If he wasn't in public, his mouth would have been hanging open."

Megan laughed at the image. "What if he's simply reliving some weird prom fantasy? I can see the story now. Nick Taylor was stuck on the fact Megan Stanford refused to go to the prom with him. He was so crushed, he worked out and now he looks fantastic. Then, years later, he meets the prom date who rejected him. She immediately realizes her mistake and throws herself into his arms."

Georgie laughed so hard, she started to choke. "That's hysterical. I'd forgotten you were a writer."

Megan smiled as she realized her scenario was a bit foolish. "Ok, you win. It's not a prom fantasy, but I haven't heard from him recently."

"Maybe he's busy. So you need to be busy. Amber and I going out for pizza. Come meet us."

"I don't know," Megan said. "I need to check on Rose."

"Megan, you've secluded yourself in that house since you came home. You need to get out a little. Go check on Rose. Marie will watch her during dinner," Georgie said. "We're meeting at Antonio's in an hour."

"Oh, I don't know. Every time I leave, all hell breaks loose."

"No excuses, Megan."

"Ok, I'll try to make it, but if I don't show up, eat without me," Megan said with a laugh.

"Hurry, we'll be waiting. We've got summer plans to make."

"That sounds great." Megan laughed as she hung up the phone.

Chapter Fifty Eight

Megan peeked into her grandmother's room and found her staring out toward the ocean. Advancing into the room, she carried the pile of photographs to the bedside.

"Megan, is that you?" Rose smiled as she looked up.

"Yes, Grandma. How are you feeling?"

"I'm okay. I'm tired, but I'm okay." Rose reached out toward Megan. "I'm worried about you."

"I'm worried about you," Megan said with a smile.

Megan pulled up a chair and sat by the bedside. "Grandma, I finally had a chance to go into the attic." Rose's eyes widened with the news. "I found something for you." Megan pulled the first framed photograph from the pile. "Here's a photo of you and Grandpa on your wedding day." Megan gently held the photograph in front of Rose.

Fingers trembling, Rose reached out and touched the photo. "George," she whispered as a tear slid down her face. "I'll be seeing you soon." Rose then blew a kiss toward the photograph.

Megan teared up as soon as she saw her grandmother cry. Clearing her throat, she said, "Grandma, I have a few other photos as well." One by one she held the photos for Rose, who was pleased to revisit her memories. When Megan shifted the pile, an old unframed photo fell onto the bed. Megan picked it up and showed it to Rose who immediately stiffened.

"Grandma, are you okay?"

"That's not a good picture. You should throw that one away."

Megan looked at the photo. Four men leaned against her grandfather's Studebaker. They were smiling. There was also a younger boy standing off to the side. "I don't recognize any of these men. Can you tell me who they are?"

Rose grimaced as she looked at the photo once again. "Your grandfather was so damn proud of that Studebaker. This photo was taken soon after he bought it. The men would all gather round and talk him into giving them joyrides. It caused nothing but trouble."

"Do you know these men? I recognize Grandpa from your wedding photo, but I don't know the others."

"Nor should you want to," Rose said with a sigh. She pointed at the first man with a crooked finger. "That man's name is Fred Brown. Next to him is your grandfather looking so proud of himself. The next man is Henry Davenport. That would be Jeff Davenport's grandfather."

Megan was surprised. "I didn't know Grandpa was a friend of the Davenports."

"Just him. I never liked the man myself," Rose said with disgust.

"Do you know the other two?"

"Yes, on the end of the car is Robert Stiles."

"Fran's father? The woman who was taking care of you?"

"You mean the woman who tried to rob me blind and starve me to death?"

Megan placed her hand on Rose's shoulder. "I'm sorry, Grandma. I can't believe my father would have hired her if he knew."

Rose covered Megan's hand with her own. "It's not your fault or your responsibility. I'm sorry your father put this burden on your shoulders."

"It's not a burden. I love you, Grandma."

Rose swallowed and looked back at the photo. "The younger man off to the side is Billy Conklin. He's the man who lives in the lighthouse now. He adored your grandfather when he was growing up and he was heartbroken when George disappeared."

Megan wanted to cheer her grandmother up, not recall awful memories. She took the photograph and placed it out of sight, while she set up the wedding photo at the bedside. "While I was in the attic, I found your hankie too."

Rose took the hankie. She held it for a while and placed it against her face. "Your grandfather had these made for me. I always loved them."

"Good afternoon, Ladies," Marie said brightly as she walked into the bedroom holding a tray with Rose's dinner. "Rose, I have your favorite dinner tonight."

"I'm not very hungry," Rose said as she looked toward the windows.

"Well, let's try a little," Marie coaxed as she neared the bedside. "Megan, there's some dinner for you downstairs if you're hungry. Why don't you take a break?"

Megan stood up to get out of the way. "If you don't mind, I'd like to run out for a couple hours. Will you be here?"

"Of course, dear. You should take a little more time for yourself. I'll be here with Rose so go enjoy yourself."

"Is that okay with you, Grandma?"

Rose waved her hand to shoo Megan out the door. "I'll be fine. Stop fussing over me."

Megan leaned over and gave Rose a kiss on the forehead. "Okay, I'll be back soon. I promise."

Chapter Fifty Nine

Antonio's was crowded for a weeknight. Megan looked around and found Georgie and Amber waving from a table in the back corner. She waved back and started toward the table.

"Hey guys, it's great to see you." Megan pulled out a chair and sat down.

"Glad you could make it," Georgie said with a smile.

"Me too," Megan replied as a waitress hustled over and handed her a plastic menu. "Anything to drink?"

"Can I have diet soda? No lemon."

"You got it," she said as she put her pad in her pocket and walked away.

"Is Joanie here tonight?" Megan asked, looking around the room.

"She's off, I don't know this waitress," Georgie said.

Megan turned toward Amber. "Hi, how are you?"

"Doing ok. Work was a bear today."

"You look great," Megan said as she admired her designer clothes.

"For all the good it does me," Amber complained. Megan glanced toward Georgie who raised her eyebrows and made a face.

"So, how are you?" Georgie said as the waitress returned with Megan's soda. The three remained silent while she placed the drink on the table.

"Do you need a few more minutes?" The waitress asked.

"I think we're good," Georgie said, looking at her two friends for acknowledgement. When they nodded their heads in unison, Georgie ordered a large, thin crust, well done, cheese pie for the table with an individual side salad for each of them.

When the waitress left, they looked back toward Megan, who said, "First, I had to walk here tonight. I left my car at the Clamshell Friday night. On Saturday morning, Nick called to inform me someone had vandalized the car."

"Really?" Amber said, shock registering on her face.

"Really," Megan replied while nodding her head.

"That's odd, because this town is usually quiet. You've had your fair share of problems since you've been back," Amber pointed out.

"Tell me about it," Megan agreed. "Anyway, the windshield was smashed, someone spray painted the word *Die* on the side of the car and they punctured some of my tires."

"That sucks," Georgie said. "It certainly sounds like they knew it was your car."

"I would be so scared now, if I were you," Amber said.

"Nick didn't think there was enough of a threat to worry about anything else." Megan shrugged.

"It had to be Jeff Davenport," Georgie said as she sipped her water. "He was mad when Nick threw him out of the Clamshell."

"It seems obvious," Megan said. "Apparently, Foster had video monitors pointed toward the parking lot. Nick asked him to retrieve the images so they could identify the jerk who did it."

"So that's it," Amber said with a shrug. "Then Nick can officially arrest the jerk who will immediately call his daddy to bail him out."

"We're not done yet. On Sunday, someone dumped a couple of barrels of gross fish bait all over the wraparound porch."

"That's disgusting," Georgie said as the waitress arrived at the table with their salads and a pizza stand. The waitress apologized and looked at the food. Georgie laughed. "I'm sorry. I didn't mean the salad." Satisfied, the waitress walked away. "That doesn't sound like something Jeff Davenport would do. He doesn't like to get his hands dirty."

The girls ate their salad with gusto. After a few minutes, the waitress arrived with the pizza as well as a handful of paper plates. She placed the pie on the stand as Amber started to separate the plates so the fresh, hot slices could be passed.

"Well, there's more," Megan said as she looked toward Amber. "I'm going to tell you, but please don't get upset."

"Why would I get upset?" Amber asked as she served her friends.

"It's about Tommy."

Amber stiffened noticeably with clenched jaw. "Go on."

"I was reviewing the video tape I had to take for the insurance company before the demolition started. I did not see any bodies in the cottages or anything which looked amiss."

"So what's the problem?" Amber asked, waiting to eat her pizza.

"What I did see was Tommy in the woods behind the cottages. I have no idea what he was doing there."

"Maybe he was passing through," Amber said defensively.

"He was lurking," Megan said. "And he should not have been passing through private property."

"Come off it, Megan. People have been trespassing on your property forever to get to the lighthouse and the beach near the Point."

"He wasn't dressed for the beach," Megan pointed out as she seasoned her slice and took a bite. "No offense, but he does work on a fishing boat as well. He would have access to all the fish guts."

Georgie held up her plate for a second slice of pizza. "True, but Tommy really is the sweetest guy in the world which is why Amber is nuts about him."

"Not that he even notices," Amber pouted.

"Well, someone is deliberately harassing me and I want to know who."

"Why don't we simply ask Tommy?" Georgie said as she stared at the counter across the room. Amber and Megan followed her stare.

"Oh no, I don't have any makeup on." Amber looked down at the table. "Is he looking?"

"He is now," Megan said as Georgie caught his attention and waved him over to the table.

Tommy picked up his drink and plate and headed over toward the girls. As he approached the table, Megan quickly shifted chairs so he was forced to sit between her and Amber.

"Hi Tommy, what a surprise seeing you in here," Georgie said as she poured herself soda from a pitcher delivered by the waitress.

"Yea, just grabbing a slice after work. Thanks for calling me over."

"Amber loved your band the other night," Megan teased as Amber turned red with embarrassment.

"Really?" Tommy said as he started eating.

"I think you're band is great, mostly because of you," Amber said with a nervous laugh.

"Thanks, I appreciate that," he said with a grin.

Megan cleared her throat to regain Tommy's attention. "I have a direct question for you. I was reviewing video of the cottages from before they were demolished and I swear there was a guy in the trees who looked exactly like you. I was wondering if you remember seeing me out there with a camera."

Tommy stopped eating, turned bright red and turned to Megan.

"It was you, wasn't it?"

"Yes, it was me."

"So what were you doing in the woods?" Megan asked, leaving the rest of the pizza untouched on her plate.

Tommy did not immediately answer. "Megan's had a few problems at the house so she's looking for answers," Georgie explained.

"Really? I'd like to know about that. I was there, but it's not what you think."

"I'm all ears, Tommy." Megan said as she picked up her food.

Chapter Sixty

Andrew Davenport walked into the dining room carrying a silver tray. The table had been set earlier in the day by the housekeeper, who then prepared the evening meal for the three men. Henry's wife died many years ago. Although Henry had been the mayor and was well known to many people, he married late in life. He and his wife had one son, Andrew, and spent twenty wonderful years together until she was diagnosed with breast cancer at an advanced stage. The disease progressed rapidly and Henry was left a widower.

Andrew grew up and married young. He and his wife also had a son, Jeffrey Davenport. Andrew was popular but placed his career ahead of his wife and son. Andrew explained away the social events which required him to have a young female escort, and one evening he returned home to find his son with a babysitter. Andrew's wife had packed her clothes and favorite belongings and left town. Although she fought for custody, Andrew made sure she would never see her son before he turned eighteen. For many years, the three men had survived by caring for each other with the help of their housekeeper, Norma.

"Dad, can you move that glass?" Andrew asked as he placed the silver serving tray on the table. "Dinner smells pretty good, tonight. I think Norma made some sort of a crab salad for us."
Andrew walked toward the door and yelled upstairs. "Jeff, if you want food while it's fresh, you better haul your butt down here."

"What's that boy doing up there?" Henry asked. "When is he going to get a real job? He's either up in that room or out terrorizing the town."

"Dad, he's a young man," Andrew said. "I'm sure you were wild once."

Henry looked at his son. "I wasn't a saint but I never needed my daddy bailing me out or paying fancy lawyers to get me out of trouble. He's thirty years old. He needs to do something with his life and keep his mouth shut."

"He'll find himself sooner or later, Dad. Just leave him alone."

"Leave who alone?" Jeff asked as he walked into the room.

"No one," Andrew said. "The food's getting cold. Sit down and eat. What have you been up to all day?"

"Not much," Jeff shrugged.

"Spend any time looking for a job?" Andrew asked, hoping to prove his father wrong.

"No, there's nothing out there I like. Besides, do you think I could possibly work for any of the cretins in this town?" Jeff grimaced as he dug his fork into the serving tray. "We own this town. They should all work for us."

Henry put down his fork and looked over at his grandson. "Jeff, we don't own the town. It was originally settled by John Stanford and whatever hasn't been sold off is still owned by them."

"They own more than Misty Manor?" Jeff asked angrily.

"As far as I know," Henry said. "Rose Stanford is the wealthiest woman in this town. We've done well, but we do not have anywhere near the assets of the Stanfords."

"What happens when Rose dies?" Jeff asked as he greedily helped himself to potatoes without asking or leaving much for his father and grandfather.

"I imagine her son will inherit the estate as well as any other property currently owned by Rose."

"That loser?" Jeff said. "He hates this town. He's never around. Maybe he'll sell it off when the old woman dies."

Jeff jumped when his grandfather slammed his fist on the table. "Hush up, boy. Rose Stanford is a fine woman. She's spent the last sixty years taking care of Misty Point and Misty Manor with little help from anyone else. She's a strong woman."

"Excuse me," Jeff mocked angrily. "That family pisses me off. Someone should do the world a favor and take them all out."

"That's enough, Jeff," Andrew said staring at his son.

"We could have been royalty around here if it hadn't been for the Stanfords. I'm sick of them, especially that bitch, Megan. She was frigid on prom night and doesn't look like she's changed as far as I can see."

Andrew sighed heavily and put his fork down. "Please, leave the Stanfords alone. They're going under the microscope and I don't want any Davenports to be anywhere near that family right now."

"What's going on, son?" Henry asked, his face paling at the news.

Andrew looked at his Dad. He realized his father looked frail and was worse as each day passed. "It's nothing, Dad. Can you pass the vegetables?"

Henry picked up the broccoli dish and passed it over to his son. Leaving his plate untouched, Henry reached out and touched Andrew's arm. "Seriously, please tell me what's going on."

Andrew looked at his father and recognized the expression. He knew his Dad would not let the topic go until he was satisfied with the information he received. "Why is this so important to you?"

Henry cleared his throat. "Let's just say I've known the Stanfords for a very long time. We were acquainted before any politics came along. I need to know what's going on."

Andrew swallowed and nodded his head. Jeff kept eating but was listening to the conversation with interest.

"Okay, Dad. I truly don't know all the details but the police captain sent me a message. There's been a break in the investigation, some sort of lead and they've requested a search warrant for the whole estate. They've asked for blueprints and permits for the construction of the cottages. They want to search the garage too, but they're asking the judge to sign off on the whole property."

"Do you know what they're looking for?" Henry's hands were shaking as he placed them in his lap.

"No, not exactly, but I know they'll be looking for a gun. The coroner confirmed the victim was shot in the head mainly because the skull had a bullet hole in it. The police have officially changed it to a murder investigation."

Andrew looked at his father. Henry was trembling, pale and had a sheen lining his forehead. "Dad, are you okay?"

Henry did not answer right away. He remained frozen at the table, staring into space.

"Grandpa? Are you okay?" Jeff asked, trying to get his attention.

After a minute or two, Henry reached out and took his son's hand. He squeezed hard as he whispered. "Son, we need to talk."

Chapter Sixty One

"C'mon, Tommy, tell me why you were in the woods," Megan said as she stared at him over the pizza sitting on her plate.

"I was helping my uncle," Tommy said. "Actually, my great-uncle."

"I'm confused," Megan said. "Who is your great-uncle?"

"Bill Conklin," Tommy said. "The guy who takes care of the lighthouse."

"You're kidding," Georgie said. "You're related to Bill Conklin? How? Who?"

Tommy held his hand up as Georgie continued to register shock.

"I never knew that," Megan said.

"Really?" Amber said.

"Yes, my grandmother was Bill's sister. She passed a while ago. Uncle Billy never got married or had any kids, so I help him out and keep an eye on him."

"I've lived there most of my life, but I don't understand the whole lighthouse arrangement," Megan said. "I know Bill Conklin knew my grandfather when they were young."

"From what my uncle told me, he and George Stanford were pals back then," Tommy said. "George promised him a lifelong job working in the lighthouse as long as he promised to watch over Misty Manor and the Stanford family."

"And he's been there all these years?" Georgie asked.

"Yes, watching over the lighthouse and the family and I think he's had a lifelong crush on Rose as well."

"Get out," Megan said.

"Where does he sleep? How does he get paid?" Amber asked, still reeling from the revelation.

"He has a small bedroom in the keeper's living quarters, next to the lighthouse, with a tiny kitchen and a small office," Tommy explained. "I used to visit when I was in high school. He's always had a telescope in the lantern room and in the summer he'd let me take it out on the gallery deck and look at the ocean. As far as getting paid, I think there's some sort of trust fund set up by the Stanfords which covers his salary each year. Of course, he's been collecting social security for some time now."

"So what exactly did you do at the lighthouse?" Megan asked, realizing how little she knew about her own family.

"Initially, I would go and help him take care of the lantern room. He needed help keeping the glass and the lens clean, so I'd go after high school and earn a little money. I still clean and help him with anything else I can, like grocery shopping, doctor's visits and any maintenance which needs to be done."

"So why were you in the woods?" Megan asked again.

"Because I cut through the property all the time, but I don't like to make it obvious, especially since they found the body. I didn't want anyone to think I had anything to do with that mess." Tommy sheepishly looked down at his remaining cold pizza. "I'm sorry. I didn't mean it like that. I've been the one who fixes broken items on your property at night. I spend time replacing hoses, fixing the stone wall, windows or whatever. Bill never got permission, he just brought me on board because he wasn't sure what Rose would say."

"Why at night?"

"I have a day job with the fishing boat and I can't get there until night," Tommy said, annoyed at the inquisition.

"Speaking about that, I'm sorry, but I have one more question. Do you know anything about a couple barrels of fish bait being thrown on my deck overnight?"

Tommy reddened. "I don't, but Uncle Billy told me all about it. He saw the seagulls gather early in the morning. Then he saw the hospice people and Nick come over. Uncle Billy said you spent a good part of the day washing down the porch."

"But he didn't see who dumped it there?"

"No. It definitely wasn't me, Megan. By the time I talked to him, the deck was already washed and the seagulls gone. Otherwise, I would have helped you."

"So it seems, Uncle Billy sees quite a bit from the lighthouse," Georgie said. "I'll have to remember that next time I'm drinking on the beach." She giggled and picked up her drink.

"He's seen quite a bit over the years, but he's always kept his mouth shut," Tommy said defensively.

"Do you think he'd mind if I asked him a few questions about Misty Manor," Megan asked. "I think there's been something funny going on for a while and I want to get to the bottom of it."

"He's a loner and doesn't talk to people much, but I'm sure he'd be willing to talk to you," Tommy said. "I don't know if he can help you, but I'll talk to him."

Megan was silent for a moment as she bit into her pizza. She opened her purse, slipped out a photo and showed it to Tommy. "Does anyone in this photo look familiar to you?"

Tommy took the photo and eyed it for several minutes. "I'm not sure who these people are," he said nervously.

"According to Rose, the young man on the right is Uncle Billy when he was in his late teens or early twenties," Megan said as she watched Tommy closely.

Tommy looked at the photo again and seemed to come to a decision. "There is something strange about this photo. I wasn't going to say anything until I asked Uncle Billy. I honestly don't know who these men are, but my uncle has the same exact photo in the lighthouse. He keeps it in the bookcase, between two books. One day, I was straining to clean a window and I knocked the bookcase over. I found the photo when I was picking everything up off the floor."

"What aren't you're telling me?" Megan asked, watching his discomfort.

Tommy fidgeted before answering. "The weird thing is my uncle's photo has a red X over two of the faces."

"What?" Megan asked, shocked

"I'm not kidding," Tommy said, looking her in the eyes.

"Which faces?" Georgie asked, eyes wide with curiosity.

Tommy pointed to two men.

"The first man you pointed to is my missing grandfather," Megan said. "And according to my grandmother, the second man you're pointing to is Robert Stiles. He's the father of Fran Stiles, the witch who was starving my grandmother to death and left her home looking like a slum."

"No way," Amber said. "That's scary."

"What does that mean? The X?" Georgie asked.

"I have no idea," Tommy said. "We're going to have to ask Uncle Billy." Tommy looked at his watch. "It's a little late now, but we can go over tomorrow. Bring your copy of the photo."

"What if he doesn't admit he has a copy?" Megan asked.

"I don't know, we'll think of something," Tommy said. "There's definitely a story to that photo."

"Does your uncle stay up all night to run the lighthouse?" Amber asked.

"No, he sleeps like everyone else," Tommy said with a curious glance to see if she was being sarcastic.

"Who watches the lighthouse when he goes to sleep?" Amber asked, innocently placing her hand on Tommy's arm.

He looked toward her and smiled. He liked her much better without the makeup and corporate attire. "Most of the lighthouse is automated now, so he's able to get a good night's sleep."

"Oh," Amber replied, staring in his eyes. "I was wondering because of his age."

Georgie rolled her eyes and elbowed Megan in the ribs. Outside, a police siren cut through the night quickly followed by another. Megan looked at her watch. "I really should be getting home and checking on Rose. She's not doing very well."

"Okay, I'll talk to Uncle Billy tomorrow," Tommy said. "We'll get to the bottom of this. Sorry I wasn't honest with you from the beginning."

"Thanks, Tommy. It's hard enough with Rose being ill, this mischief doesn't help." Another siren cut across the front of the pizzeria. Megan looked out the window and frowned. "I'd better go."

Chapter Sixty Two

Megan half walked and half trotted back to the house. She was anxious when she was away from Rose. Approaching the house, she was happy there were no police cars in the driveway. The lights were on in Rose's bedroom, but Megan did not see anything else out of the ordinary.

Megan entered through the front door and heard noise upstairs. Now that she thought about it, there were a few extra cars in the driveway. She took the stairs two at a time and looked into her grandmother's bedroom. Marie was there ringing her hands as well as a woman Megan had never seen before.

"Hey, is everything okay?" Megan asked as she entered the room.

"I'm so glad you're home," Marie said as she crossed the room.

"What's going on?"

"I don't know but Rose has been very agitated all night," Marie said. "I couldn't get her to relax so I called the hospice and they sent the on-call nurse out."

"Is she better? Did they give her anything?"

"They tried medication to calm her down, but it's not working well." Marie turned to Megan. "I don't want to make you feel bad, but she keeps calling for you. Megan, Megan, I have to help Megan."

"Me? Wait, help me?"

The on-call nurse walked over to the pair. "Hi, my name is Tina. I'm the on-call nurse for Cape Shore Hospice."

"Hi, is she okay?" Megan asked.

"She's very agitated. She may be experiencing terminal agitation."

"What's that?"

"As the body shuts down, some patients become extremely agitated," Tina explained. "We try to comfort them with medicine, but sometimes the medicine has the opposite effect."

"Megan, I must see Megan," Rose yelled out.

"You'd better go to her," Tina said. "You may the only one who can calm her at this point."

"She took care of me when I was young," Megan said with tears in her eyes. "My parents weren't around much. Do you think she's having flashbacks?"

"It's possible," Tina said. "To be honest, I've seen so many unexplained things at end of life, I don't question much these days."

"Wow, that sounds ominous," Megan said, searching Tina's face.

"No, I wouldn't say that, but at times, there's an energy at the end of life which can't be explained. Why don't you go spend some time with her?"

Megan approached the bedside. She looked at her grandmother of ninety years. Her skin was ashen. She looked drawn and frail. Megan dropped to her knees at the bedside and took hold of her hand.

"Megan?" Rose asked as she turned her head in Megan's direction.

"Yes, Grandma, it's me, Megan. How are you?" Megan took a strand of Rose's hair and tucked it behind her ear.

Rose squeezed Megan's hand. "Megan, it's started. Things have started and it's not safe for you now." Rose pulled Megan's face toward her and whispered in her ear. "It's not safe. You mustn't leave the house. Promise me you won't leave the house until it's safe."

"Everything is okay, Grandma," Megan said with a small smile. "I'm okay."

"You're not safe," Rose kept repeating with renewed fervor. "Megan, promise me, you won't leave the house."

As Rose repeated her message, Megan's heart rate climbed and she felt slightly nauseous. "I promise, Grandma. I'll stay right here."

Rose sighed and let her head fall back against the pillow. Her eyes drifted close despite her struggle to stay awake. After a few minutes, the grip on Megan's hand loosened. Megan tucked Rose's hand over her belly and drew the sheet up to her chin. She then stood and went back to Marie and Tina.

"I feel bad she's so upset," Megan said.

"I don't know what's going on," Tina said. "She calmed down as soon as she spoke to you. This may not be terminal agitation. I'm not sure."

"I'll stay near her tonight, because she's so upset. I just want to change first. Marie, will you stay until I get back?"

"Of course, honey. As a matter of fact, I think I'll stay through the night," Marie said with a firm nod."

"Sure, that would be great," Megan said. "We have plenty of rooms. You have your choice."

Tina picked up her bag and slung it over her shoulder. "You know, I can try to get continuous care for Rose if you want."

"What is that?" Megan asked.

"When a patient is in pain or very restless, we can send a nurse to sit with her at bedside. It's allowed by insurance as long as she needs medication or some sort of supportive treatment every hour or so."

Megan took another look at Rose who was sleeping comfortably at the moment. "I don't know. I think we'll be fine. Marie and I should be able to take care of her tonight."

"You know if anything changes, you can call us anytime?"

"Yes, thank you," Megan said. "Thank you for coming out tonight."

"You're very welcome. I'm on all night so call me if you need me," Tina said as she turned to go.

"I'll walk you to the door," Megan said as she gestured toward the stairs.

"Megan, go change and make yourself comfortable before you come back. I'll be right here," Marie said as she pulled a Queen Anne chair up to the bedside.

"Thanks, Marie." Megan swallowed as she took one last look at her grandmother.

Chapter Sixty Three

She was crying. She walked along the beach, kicking the surf as she moved. She wasn't sure why she was crying. The day was beautiful but she felt a heavy pressure on her head. Her head hurt when she moved it. The seagulls were crying too, but she could not see them. She heard the birds, they were close by. She shivered as the cold wind blew around her. Something was wrong. She turned to the right and was shocked to see a bloated body floating in the ocean. Shocked, she jumped and felt a searing pain in her neck.

Megan gasped as she was startled out of her nightmare. Sitting in the Queen Anne chair, by her grandmother's bedside, she must have fallen asleep during the night. Megan reached up to rub away the spasm caused by the awkward position her head fell into during sleep. No wonder she was dreaming about a pressure on her head.

As the curtains billowed with the breeze, Megan could smell the welcome scent of the ocean. Beach sounds filtered in the room. Seagulls crying over the beach, surf pounding the shore, kids playing on the beach.

Megan's stomach clenched when she remembered her dream and the bloated body. *That was scary.*

A small snore escaped Rose as she slept in the bed. Megan had taken over for Marie last night. Rose had remained agitated, so they gave her another tranquilizer from the emergency kit after consulting with the on-call nurse. Finally, Rose calmed down and slept.

Megan stretched as she stood and heard a knock on the door. "Come in," she said looking toward the bedroom door. Seconds later, Marie entered the room with a tray bearing a pot of coffee, cream, sugar and a buttered toasted bagel.

"I brought you some coffee. I thought you could use it after last night."

"Thanks, Marie. It smells heavenly," Megan said as she accepted the cup handed to her.

"How did the rest of the night go?"

"She was much calmer. I feel bad she's so restless," Megan said.

"The hospice nurse warned us she may get restless. It can be common at the end of life," Marie said.

"I know. The on-call nurse said she'd let the case manager know what happened. They'll make a visit today. I want to make sure she isn't in pain or suffering." Both women jumped as the doorbell rang.

"Speaking of the devil," Marie said with a laugh. "You drink your coffee. I'll go let them in."

A minute later, Marie was back in the room. "Megan, you'd better go downstairs."

Megan saw the look on Marie's face and immediately was concerned. "Who is it? What's happened now?"

"It's Officer Nick. He says he needs to speak with you."

"So he finally shows up. Did he say it was serious?"

"No, but he looks official this morning," Marie said, her eyes reflecting her concern.

"Okay, I'll go. You stay with Rose and I'll be back as soon as I can." Megan placed her coffee cup on the tray. She took a moment to smooth her unruly hair and straighten her clothes. As she descended the grand staircase, she saw Nick standing in the foyer, with his back to the room. He was holding his hat and staring out the side window toward the beach. She reached the bottom of the staircase as he turned.

"Nick, how are you?"

"Fine, how are you this morning? How's Rose?"

"She had a rough night," Megan said. "We didn't get much sleep. I'm waiting for the hospice nurse to come and check her today."

"I'm sorry to hear that. I hope it goes well."

Megan shrugged and offered a small smile. "How do you define well when someone is on hospice?"

Nick shuffled and looked at his feet. "I guess it's different for everyone."

"So what's going on?" Megan asked, steeling herself. "I haven't seen you for a couple of days and now you show up looking very uncomfortable."

"I wanted to come by and visit, but I was given a talk about making sure I kept my personal and professional boundaries clear until this case is over."

Megan went still. "Something has happened, hasn't it?"

"There's a few things going on I wanted to talk to you about, but after this, I won't be able to say much until everything is sorted out."

Megan was not sure why but her heart started pounding in her chest. She felt a little short of breath and slightly dizzy.

"Are you okay?" Nick asked as he watched her face.

"Yes, but you're making me nervous."

"Let's sit in the parlor and talk," Nick said as he gestured toward the side room. They both walked into the parlor and settled themselves on the couch. Nick leaned forward and cleared his throat. "I wanted to let you know the investigation is taking a turn. Davis is pulling everything he can related to Misty Manor. He's looking at the original building permits for the cottages and digging up every police report ever filed."

"Why? What's he hoping to find?"

"Secrets. Something from your family history."

"Why?" Megan asked again, more forcibly. "Did they make a positive identification?"

"No, but when they do, Davis would be the one to make the official notification. Just know the heat is going to ramp up and I wanted to give you some warning. Remember, I could lose my job for telling you this. I'd appreciate it if you didn't mention this visit to Davis."

"Of course not," Megan said, uneasily. "I appreciate the notice, Nick."

"You have enough going on with Rose being sick, but things may get worse very quickly."

"You're still making me nervous," Megan said. "Do I need a lawyer or something?"

Nick noticed the strain on Megan's face. "No, I don't think so."

"You're obviously not telling me something. Davis wouldn't be getting crazy unless you've discovered something." Megan waited for an answer.

Nick came to a decision. "Megan, I shouldn't tell you this. We didn't identify the body yet, but we're expecting a result from the genetic testing very soon. At least we'll know if the body is a Stanford. What we do know is that whoever it is, was murdered."

Shock registered on Megan's face. "How?"

"I can't say too much, but it looks like it was a gun shot." Nick reached out and squeezed Megan's arm to help her focus. "Megan, this is important. Does Rose keep any guns around the house?"

"No, of course not," Megan said, shaking her head. "I've never seen a gun in this house."

"That will be one of the items listed in the search warrant." Nick grimaced. "I've said way too much already."

"Wait. When is Davis getting the search warrant? Are they coming today?"

Nick shrugged. "I don't think so. The genetic testing should be back this afternoon. Davis will wait for the results. Besides, the judge is busy with all the drama from last night."

Megan looked up at Nick. "What drama?"

Nick's facial expression did not change. "You haven't heard the news?"

"Obviously not, tell me."

Nick fell silent for a moment, considering what to say.

Megan continued her plea. "I was out with Georgie and Amber last night. We were at Antonio's eating pizza and suddenly there were a lot of sirens. What's going on?"

Nick took a breath. "Henry Davenport died last night. The sirens you heard were the first responders called to the house."

Megan's face paled with the news. Her heart sped up again. *The photo. Was there a red X over Henry's face now? She should tell Nick.* "What happened?" *Megan thought of her grandmother's agitation and warning that all was coming to the surface.*

"Not totally sure. We got an emergency call from the Davenport house. Andrew found Henry slumped over in the den. He called 911 and tried to revive him, but wasn't successful. Since Andrew is the current Mayor, everyone responded immediately."

"What killed him?" Megan asked as she noticed her hands were shaking.

"I don't know. We're waiting for the coroner's report. It could be natural causes. He had a bad heart."

"Nothing looked out of place or strange?"

"Not that I'm aware of, but the family is extremely upset," Nick answered, his face registering her question. "Why would you ask that?"

"I don't know," Megan lied. "It's strange another body has suddenly appeared."

"People do die, Megan," Nick said, cringing inwardly as he thought of Rose.

"Yes, I am well aware. I'm afraid it's becoming a trend in Misty Point."

Nick stood and was silent for a moment. "I'd better go."

Megan jumped up and led him to the door. "Thanks for coming, Nick," she said somberly. "I appreciate the warning. Rose is in a bad place. I don't want to upset her more than necessary."

Nick smiled and walked through the door. He paused and turned back to her. "Megan, take care of yourself. I don't think there's a problem, but be safe. Okay?"

Megan nodded. "I'll try."

Chapter Sixty Four

Once Megan was sure Nick had driven off the property, she grabbed her cell phone from her back pocket and dialed Georgie. She listened to it ring. "C'mon, C'mon. Pick up, Georgie." After another ring, Megan heard her voice and shouted, "Georgie!"

A recorded voice sounded. "Hey, it's me. If I'm not answering the phone, I'm probably on the beach. Come down and swim a lap with me. If not, leave a message and I'll get back to you."

"Damn," Megan swore softly.

"What's going on?" Marie asked as she walked down the stairs.

Megan turned to face her. "Henry Davenport is dead."

Marie's hand flew to her chest. "What? How?"

"I don't know. They found him slumped over in the den."

"Oh my," Marie said. "Bless his soul. Being an ex-mayor, everyone will make a big deal about this."

The conversation was interrupted by a knock on the door. Megan turned around and opened the door. She was about to ask Nick if he forgot something but her words died on her lips.

"Hi, may we come in?" The case manager and social worker from Cape Shore Hospice were standing on the porch.

Megan paused a second too long.

"Are you okay?" Jessica asked.

"Uh, sure," Megan said as she stepped back and held the door open. "Please, come in."

"How is Rose today?" Nicole smiled as she tilted her head.

"We had a rough night. We called the on-call nurse because she was agitated last evening."

"Yes, we got a message you opened the comfort kit," Nicole said.

"The night nurse told us to. We gave my grandmother a tranquilizer and she finally calmed down. Her breathing sounds okay but she was sweating an awful lot." Megan explained.

"Actually, she's starting to sound very congested today," Marie said.

Nicole cast a knowing glance at Jessica. "Why don't we go upstairs and look in on her?" She turned to Marie and Megan. "You both look exhausted. Why don't you relax for a bit while we check on Rose?"

Megan paused for a second. "Do I have time to run a really important errand?"

Jessica smiled. "Of course, it will be good for you to get out of the house for a while. The aide is on her way as well, so you probably have a couple of hours at least."

"Megan, take all the time you need," Marie said. "I'll be here. I was able to go to my room and sleep last night, so it's your turn to relax."

"Okay, thanks. I appreciate it. I have my phone if anything happens," Megan said as she slowly walked through the door, down the steps and over the lawn. The minute she hit the boardwalk, she ran like hell.

Chapter Sixty Five

Megan trotted down the boardwalk as fast as she could. She had not run in a long time and felt her lungs burn as she tried to hurry. Before she moved to Detroit, she had entered every 5K offered at the shore. Once she hit Detroit, the only running she did was away from annoyed people she was trying to get an exclusive from.

Years ago, Megan would love running down the boardwalk. The ocean breeze in her face, she would feel the warmth of the sun and imagine the cool sand between her toes. If she closed her eyes, she could smell the particular combination of suntan lotion, ocean, seaweed, grilled burgers, cold beer and pizza. She would run her hand over the metal railing on the boardwalk as she passed the various pavilions, some of which held shops which sold taffy, fudge, trinkets, beach supplies and ice cream.

In the past, she would get to the beach early on a Saturday and spend the whole day camped out at Georgie's life station. She helped set up the guard chair, life boat, and umbrellas. They would get something to eat on Georgie's breaks, spend the day with friends, spend money at their favorite amusement stands and then have a fire on the beach, drink cheap wine and relax. Nothing extravagant, yet those were the good old days. Time had moved on. Georgie was now in charge of the lifeguard program for the town and Megan was in a mess. Megan felt a pang as she wished she could return to a simpler life.

Megan took a deep breath and hoped Georgie was still at the same life station. She reached the right area on the boardwalk and ran past the gate attendant. He stood up and yelled after her. *Let him call the police. They're a bit busy and I need to see Georgie now.* Megan ran on the sand which became more difficult with each step but was eventually rewarded when she got to the life guard chair.

"Georgie, Georgie," Megan yelled as she doubled over to take a few breaths. Georgie jumped off the chair and down to the sand.

"Megan, are you okay? What the hell are you doing?"

"Trying to catch my breath," Megan said.

"What's wrong? Is Rose okay?"

"She's not great," Megan said. "She's getting closer every day and that scares me." Megan finally stood upright and her breathing evened. "Georgie, did you hear about Henry Davenport?"

Georgie grabbed her by the arm and pulled her away from the chair. "Yes, I heard he had a heart attack. I wanted to call you right away, but I couldn't get time alone. It's not something I wanted to discuss with everyone hanging all over the chair, if you know what I mean."

"I tried to call you, but I got your voice mail so I ran right down here. I blew by the gate attendant," Megan said as she lowered her voice and looked around nervously for police. "I'm dying to know if the photo Uncle Billy has in the lighthouse has another X over Henry Davenport's photo."

"Who knows?" Georgie said stretching as she spoke. "We need Tommy to check for us as soon as possible."

"How can we get hold of Tommy?" Megan asked.

"I'm not sure. He's out on the fishing boat and they don't have great reception. I don't know if I have the right cell phone number."

"What about Amber?"

"Ha, she's in the corporate world. She's probably at a meeting, the fourth of the day and hasn't even gotten to her desk yet."

"I'm so frustrated, Georgie. We have to do something right away," Megan pleaded. "Keep this a secret, but Rose was agitated all night. She said 'things have started happening and I'm in danger now.' She didn't know about Henry when she said it and she made me swear not to leave the house."

"That's weird. I'll call Amber's voicemail and leave a message to reach me as soon as she can, although I don't have great reception at the beach, either," Georgie said. "At any rate, she'll know where Tommy will be tonight. I don't know if he has a gig anywhere, but she'll know. We'll definitely find him and ask him if he spoke to Uncle Billy. He said he would try to take us there today. If not, maybe he can go over and check on that photo."

"Georgie, I'm nervous. Something is going to break soon. I heard a rumor they're coming to Misty Manor with a search warrant.

It's making me crazy and I want to find out all I can before it's too late."

"Why are they coming to Misty Manor?" Georgie asked.

Megan did not want to break Nick's trust. "They're looking for more evidence of something, but they won't tell me anything."

Georgie shook her head. "This is getting pretty serious. Why don't you hang out for a while?"

Megan shook her head. "I can't. Rose isn't feeling well and I promised I wouldn't leave. The hospice staff showed up so I was able to get out for a bit, but I've got to get back."

"Okay, I'll call you as soon as I'm off the beach," Georgie said. "We'll figure out what to do next. Don't do anything crazy until we get together, okay?"

"I won't," Megan said, holding her hand up.

"Keep your phone on," Georgie said as she started to climb up into the chair.

"Same to you," Megan said as she turned toward the boardwalk, but headed for a different gate.

Chapter Sixty Six

Arriving back at Misty Manor, Megan brushed sand off her clothes and shoes before entering the house. She headed upstairs to check on Grandma Rose and found Marie and the hospice aide in the bedroom. "How is she?" Megan sat down by the bedside. Rose was sleeping peacefully.

Picking up a pile of dirty linen, the aide turned to leave the room. "She's better and she's okay for now."

Marie walked up behind Megan and placed her hand on her shoulder. "I'm glad you're back, Megan. She asks for you when she wakes. You're her total focus."

Megan swallowed and held her grandmother's frail hand. "Saying goodbye is so hard."

"Yes, but at least she's resting now. The nurse said she would try to arrange continuous care if she gets worse again."

Megan whispered, "Hopefully, we won't need that."

Rose stirred in the bed and turned her head to look at Megan. "Hello, dear. How are you?"

"I'm fine, Grandma. I'm right here so you can relax."

"I'm worried about you. You must stay close tonight. You could be in danger."

Megan smiled. "I'm fine, Grandma. I'm right here and I promise I won't leave the property."

"Cross your heart?" Rose said as she raised a limp hand over her chest.

"Cross my heart," Megan said and squeezed her hand.

Rose looked at Megan and smiled. "Was that Nick I heard earlier?"

Megan tried not to show her surprise. One minute Rose seemed clearly delusional and the next she recognized someone's voice from another part of the house. "Yes, Grandma. He wanted to ask some questions for Officer Davis."

Rose looked at Megan with clear eyes and a pained expression. "Yes, it's all starting to unravel now isn't it?" Rose looked to see who else was in the room. "Your grandfather told me it's time."

"Grandma, please don't say that."

"It's okay, dear. I've been waiting a long time to see your grandfather again. But first, I have to make sure you're safe."

"I'm fine." Megan said as her stomach clenched with anxiety. Fatigue lined her face as she tried to encourage her grandmother. Megan wrestled with her conscious but then leaned over the bed and whispered to Rose. "Nick asked me if there was a gun in the house. You don't know anything about a gun, do you Rose?"

"Me? Oh no, I detest those things."

"That's what I told him," Megan said with a smile as she patted her grandmother's hand.

"All the problems started with the Studebaker," Rose said. "If you were going to worry about anything, it would be that darn car. I wish George had never bought it," she said as she started to tear up.

Megan felt bad she had upset her grandmother. "Please don't cry. Relax and try to fall back to sleep," she said as she smoothed her grandmother's hair. "Everything is fine. Go to sleep."

Rose mumbled as fatigue overcame her. "Promise you won't leave the property."

"I promise," Megan said as she continued to stroke her head.

Chapter Sixty Seven

Once Rose fell asleep, Marie followed Megan out of the room. "Poor Rose, she is so worried about you." The pair walked down the hall as they talked.

Megan choked on a laugh. "That's funny. I'm more worried about her. That's the way it should be. I can tell you who doesn't seem to be worried at all. Where the hell is my father?" Megan's anger grew as she expressed her thoughts. "He hasn't called to check on Rose or me. I don't mind being here to help Rose, because I love her, and after all she did to help raise me, it's the least I could do. But he has a lot of nerve. He called and basically dumped his whole legal problem with the cottages on me. Meanwhile, he stays away, doesn't get involved or deal with anything. Rose is his mother."

Marie reached out and hugged Megan as she shook. "Forgive me for saying, but your father has always been a narcissist and a jerk. Rose realized he had problems as a child and got worse as he aged. When you were born, she always worried about you and vowed to make sure you had someone in your life who offered nothing more than unconditional love."

Megan finally broke and let the tears flow. She stayed in Marie's embrace until she stopped shaking and could breathe. Marie pulled a clean tissue from her pocket and wiped Megan's face. "C'mon, let's go downstairs and I'll make you a cup of tea. The aide will be back in a moment so Rose will have someone with her."

The two descended the staircase and went to the kitchen. Marie pulled out a chair and turned to Megan. "Here, sit right here while I get the tea ready."

As Marie walked away to fill the kettle, Megan pulled out her cell phone and dialed her father. The past month had been a blur and it was easy to find his number as she had not had time to erase her call history. Music played in her ear as the phone company tried to reach her *party*. Megan softly cursed as a message then announced he could not be found, most likely because he was at a *party* or sleeping one off.

"Here you go," Marie said as she handed Megan a hot cup of tea and a plate with a few tea biscuits. "You haven't had a decent meal all day. Let me make a sandwich for you."

"No, please don't. I'm not hungry and I wouldn't want it to go to waste. Thank you for the tea."

"You're welcome. Sit and relax for a minute, then go take a nap. If anything changes, I promise we'll come find you," Marie said as she patted Megan on the shoulder and then left the room.

Megan sipped her tea as she organized her thoughts. Since coming back to Jersey, she found her grandmother and the house severely neglected. Fran Stiles had not surfaced but her father had been involved with George Stanford around the time of his disappearance. So had Henry Davenport, Uncle Billy Conklin, a stranger named Fred Brown and one lime-green Studebaker.

Megan stood up and carried her dishes to the sink. She was too wired to sleep and realized it was about time to visit the garage.

Chapter Sixty Eight

Pulling on the handle, Megan opened the old wooden door of the garage. It had been built many years ago and sported the old type barn doors. The clapboard was aging and had obvious areas of rot. Vines grew through the boards into the room. The building looked as if it had never been repainted past its original coat.

Megan had not spent much time here as a child. The side door was always locked and she was warned away from exploring inside.

She took a few moments to find a light switch. Finally, a weak bulb in the ceiling came to life. Stepping over the threshold, she looked around the area. There were various tools attached to hooks on the walls. Most looked to be as old as the garage. The damp smell of mold and mildew was unmistakable.

Megan stepped into the darkened area to explore the vehicle shrouded with a car cover in the center of the room. She moved forward and then jumped when she thought she saw a shadow pass behind her. Turning, she saw nothing except the fading daylight outside the door. Megan turned back toward the car. She reached out and touched the car cover. Years of moisture and temperature change had reduced the fibers to mere dust which collapsed in her hand as she tried to lift it.

Coughing and choking, she was able to pull most of the deteriorated material off the car. Underneath the dust, lurked the unused remains of the 1955 lime-green Studebaker Speedster. Megan scolded herself for not asking about keys to the car. The doors could be locked and who knew what years of sitting in a garage did to the engine and gas tank.

She gingerly circled the car and admired the style. It had a large front bumper and a huge chrome grille. Megan had written an article about cars from the 50's for the Detroit Virtual News and remembered some of the unique details of the design. Initially only twenty cars were manufactured for car shows, but the positive response caused the car to be put into production. She smiled as she looked at the whitewall tires and wheel covers.

Megan reached out, tried the door handle and was thrilled when the door opened with a squeak. She lowered herself and slipped into the driver's seat which had the genuine diamond-quilted leather made for that model. As she adjusted herself, she noted the front cushion was rather lumpy and uncomfortable. She felt around on the seat and realized there was a slit through which she could place her hand into the seat. She wondered if that had been there all along or if mice or other animals over the years had gotten into the car. Fearing excrement, she did not reach through the material.

Megan looked around and saw the carpeting in the front and rear and an old fashioned radio which required a button to be pushed to gain a station. It was amazing to think the last twenty years had revolutionized how music was listened to in a car. Megan looked for a glove box, but found none. The steering wheel felt gritty but she was surprised there was not a lot of dust inside the car. Perhaps, the closed windows limited exposure to particles.

Megan had no idea what she was looking for but tried to lift the carpet as well as she could and search underneath. She ran her hand over and under the dashboard and came up with nothing. Getting out of the car, she squatted and felt under the seats. Megan could not open the trunk as she had no key and chided herself once again for not asking but Rose would have been upset had she known Megan would be searching the garage so Megan was glad she did not ask.

She got out of the car and jumped when she heard a noise in the corner. Turning quickly to confront the source, she laughed when she noticed a cat slithering out the barn door. She was scaring herself and determined not to be so melodramatic.

She asked herself what she would be looking for without an answer. She was drawn to the car and knew there was an important clue here. Next, she concentrated on the bumpers. She traced her hand above and below the rear bumper without result. Megan then circled the car and did the same with the front bumper, but once again had no results.

Shrugging, she decided to lean forward and examine the grill of the car. After writing many articles about trace evidence in Detroit, she laughed as she turned on the flashlight of her iPhone and searched the grille. Perhaps someone had been hit by the car. Other than grit and grime, Megan found nothing unusual.

Just to be sure, Megan ran her hands around the inside of the large chrome grill and hit something metal. Not sure if it was part of the grill, she extended her fingers to see if she could dislodge it. As it moved, she became sure it was not part of the original grille and spent several minutes working the object out. Her mouth dropped as she held the object and realized she was looking at a Smith and Wesson .38 special. Again, thinking back to her Detroit research, she knew it was a Chief's Special. It had a three inch barrel and a nickel plated finish.

Her hands shook as she held the gun. *Nick had asked about a gun. Could this be the murder weapon? Crap, now my fingerprints are on it. I've got to call Nick immediately.*

"Congratulations. I came here to look for that. You saved me a lot of time. Now give it here."

Megan's flesh crawled as she heard the familiar voice. Steeling herself for confrontation, she slowly turned around and screamed when she saw the back of a shovel blade aimed for her head. Megan did not feel herself slam into the hood of the Studebaker and slide to the concrete floor of the garage. As she lay unconscious, her intruder picked up the gun and searched for a tarp and rope to dispose of her body as quickly as possible.

Chapter Sixty Nine

Fumbling for his glasses, Billy Conklin dialed his nephew Tommy. He had the number on a yellowed index card taped to the wall, near the phone. The phone rang four times and just as Billy was getting ready to hang up he heard Tommy's voice.

"Yah?"

"Tommy, this is Uncle Billy. I think we've got a big problem."

Tommy came to attention. "What's going on? Are you all right?"

"Yes, I'm fine, but I was watching the house tonight and something's wrong."

"Okay, tell me what's happening," Tommy said as he jumped off the fishing boat he was on as it reached the dock.

"I saw the granddaughter, Megan, go out to the garage about an hour ago. I kept watching because I knew there would be trouble as soon as she went out there. She hasn't come back out."

"That doesn't sound too bad," Tommy said as he pulled several fishing rods off the boat.

"I'm not done yet," Billy said. He continued to watch through the telescope as he talked to his nephew. "There was a black pickup truck parked at the end of the drive. I can't make out who it belongs to, but some guy. Anyway, a few minutes ago he jumped into the truck and backed it up to the garage. I don't know of anyone who's supposed to be hauling anything out of there right now, the police investigation isn't complete. I think you'd better call Megan. See if you can get her on the phone."

"Hold on a minute, Uncle Billy." Tommy put down his gear. He double tapped his phone and navigated to the text screen. He had Georgie's number and sent a text.

Need to get hold of Megan Stanford asap! If you have her number, call or text and get back to me right away. Uncle Billy says something's wrong at the Manor.

"I don't have Megan's number but I sent a text to Georgie. She has her number and will get right on it." Tommy's phone beeped in an instant.

Okay, she was here earlier. Heard Henry Davenport died last night. New information – she wanted to contact your uncle right away.

Damn, didn't know that. Text her and get back asap!

Ok.

Tommy navigated back to his phone. "Uncle Billy, are you there?"

"Yea, I'm here. Listen the guy just dumped something in the back of his pickup truck. It looked like a rug, but there ain't no rugs in that garage. I don't know if he's stealing something or hiding something but you'd better call Nick and have him check it out. It's hard to see with the storm clouds rolling in. Wind's picking up." Billy's speech was starting to speed up and he was getting agitated. "By the time I try to get down there, this guy will be long gone."

"Keep watching, call me back if something happens. Let me go and call Nick. I'll call you back as soon as I'm done."

"There's some damage on the back of the truck. Better hurry. I feel it in my bones," Billy said as he hung up the phone.

Tommy quickly checked the contacts in his phone but could not find Nick's cell. He gave up and called 911. After a few rings, dispatch answered the phone.

"911, what's your emergency?"

"Ah, this is Tommy McDonough. Something's going on at Misty Manor. I wanted to reach Nick Taylor, but I think you'd better send whoever you have out there to check."

"Are you at the house, sir?"

"No, I got a call from my uncle. He's watching from the lighthouse. He lives there and says something is wrong."

"What is your uncle's name and number?"

Tommy started to get frustrated. "Billy Conklin." Tommy looked at his phone as he heard beeps breaking into his conversation. Uncle Billy was calling back. Tommy put the phone back to his ear. "Can you hold a minute? My uncle is calling back."

"Please don't put me on hold, sir," the dispatcher said as Tommy hit the hold and then answer button on his phone.

"Tommy," Billy said breathlessly. "Did you call Nick?"

"I'm on the phone with the police now. What's going on?"

"The guy.. in the truck.. just drove away," Billy said, stopping to take breaths in between words.

"Why are you so short of breath?" Tommy asked as he listened to his uncle take deep ragged breaths.

"I was.. trying to get down here.. to catch the bastard, but I was too late."

"Are you nuts?" Tommy yelled into the phone.

"I'm going in the garage to see what I can find. I'll call you back." Billy's breathing had become more regular.

"No, that could be dangerous," Tommy said as he heard the phone click.

"Sir, are you there, sir?" The dispatcher was trying to reconnect.

"Hello? Yes, I'm here. My uncle said the guy in the pickup truck just drove off with something in the truck." Tommy's phone beeped again. He looked down to see Georgie was texting.

She's not answering. What's going on? Trouble?

Tommy texted back while he was talking. *Get Nick. Something not right. Megan in trouble?* He waited for a second.

Ok, let you know? What's the deal?

"Sir, are you there?" Tommy heard from the phone.

"Yes, I'm here," Tommy talked on speaker phone while he texted.

Someone with black pick up at garage. Hauling something out. Uncle Billy went to check. Said Megan went into garage and never came out.

Okay, calling Nick now!

"Sir," the dispatcher called.

"Yes, I'm here. Did you send anyone to the house?" Tommy's voice started to raise. "My uncle went to check the garage."

"The police are on the way. Please stay where you are."

"I'm on the docks," Tommy said as she shook his head in disbelief. "You don't need to send them here. Are you sending someone over to Misty Manor?"

"Help is on the way, sir." Tommy's phone had another call beep in.

"Hold on," Tommy said into the phone. He quickly hit the hold and answer button.

"Uncle Billy? Are you all right?"

"Yes, no one is in the garage, but there's blood on the floor and blood on the car."

"What car?"

"The Studebaker. Someone was searching the car. There's blood on the hood and there's a bloody shovel on the ground. The guy must have hit Megan with the shovel. Her cell phone is on the floor too. It keeps beeping and ringing, but I'm not going to touch it. Damn, there's a lot of blood." Billy was talking faster as he got more excited. "Where's the cops?"

Got Nick. He's heading over to the Manor.

Ok, tell him to call me asap. Give him my number.

"Uncle Billy, they're on their way. Don't touch anything. Go stand on the lawn." Tommy heard a siren coming across the phone. He tapped back to the dispatcher.

"Do not put me on hold, sir," she said, clearly upset.

"I think they're almost there," Tommy said. "I heard a siren while I was talking to my uncle."

"They should be arriving now, sir." Tommy's phone beeped again as a new call came through. He did not recognize the number but hoped it was Nick. He hit the answer button again.

"Hello?" It was difficult to hear as the wind was picking up.

"Tommy, it's Nick. What's going on?"

Tommy quickly ran through the story with Nick. "Uncle Billy called. He said Megan went into the garage and never came out. He said some dude was hanging out there with a black pickup truck. The dude threw something like a rug into the truck and took off. When Billy got to the garage, he said Megan was gone. There's blood on the Studebaker and a shovel on the ground."

"Damn," Nick said. "I don't want to make assumptions, but you know who has a black pickup?"

"Who?" Tommy asked as he racked his brain.

"Jeff Davenport," Nick said. "He just bought it about a month ago. He got into an accident within two days and messed up the rear fender."

"Something's not right here," Tommy said. "Are you at the house yet?"

"Not yet, but let me get a BOLO out." Nick hung up.

Tommy's phone switched back to the original call. "Hello?"

"Sir, please stop putting me on hold."

"Oh, I'm sorry," Tommy said. "I got a lot of people checking in here."

"Are you all right?"

"Yes, I'm fine. Nothing's going on here except everyone's calling me."

"Please stay on the line, sir."

Tommy stopped talking in time to hear the call in the background of the dispatcher. "Headquarters to All Units – be on the lookout for a black pickup truck with damaged rear passenger fender. Suspect vehicle is possibly involved in the abduction of Megan Stanford, 30 year old female, 5' 4", with light brown hair. The pickup truck was last seen in the vicinity of Misty Manor Estate, Misty Point." Static continued to break through, making it difficult to hear.

"That's it," Tommy said. "It's a small town, someone should see the truck." Tommy continued to hear squeals and noises in the background of the call with the dispatcher. By straining, he was barely able to hear the next call.

"Dispatch, this is Maureen Forsythe, Misty Island Taxi Service. I just saw a black pickup pealing out of Main, heading toward the marina. May be your guy."

Tommy looked up in time to see a black pick up pull into the marina parking lot and drive up to the docks clear at the other end. It was hard to see as it was getting dark and storm clouds were rolling in. What were the chances it was the same black pickup, except it looked fairly new and when the door opened, he saw Jeff Davenport step out.

Chapter Seventy

Rose was resting quietly as Marie sat in the bedside chair. Without warning, she screamed out. "Megan. Help Megan." Marie had been dozing and jumped up with her hand over her chest.

"Oh Lord, Rose are you all right?"

Rose turned her head toward Marie and caught her hand in a vise grip. "Megan, you have to help Megan. George says it's happening."

Marie gasped, her heart was pounding and her pupils dilated. She pulled her painful hand away from Rose's grasp. "Megan's fine. Calm down, you're going to upset yourself. Everything is fine." Marie took a few deep breaths and made her way to the bedroom door. She poked her head into the hall and yelled out. "Megan, Megan, can you come to Rose's room?"

"You've got to help her," Rose yelled out as she became more agitated. She tried to reach out and then was thrashing about in the bed.

Marie came back to the bedside but was unable to calm her. She kept looking at the door, hoping Megan would come running through. After several minutes, Marie pulled out her cell phone and tried to call Megan. The phone rang several times before Megan's voice mail picked up. "Megan, call me as soon as you can. Rose is very upset." Marie hung up her phone and stuck it back in her pocket.

Chapter Seventy One

"He's here. The black pickup is here, in the marina," Tommy yelled into the phone. "You need to send the police, here." Tommy hung up the phone, left his gear on the ground and started to jog over to the other end of the parking lot. He watched as Jeff opened the tailgate and pulled something out of the cargo area. The bundle looked heavy as Jeff struggled to lift it into the boat. He closed the tailgate, jumped into his boat, started the engine and took off faster than the posted dock speed.

Tommy reached the pickup truck a minute later. He stopped and leaned into the back to see if there were any clues as to what the cargo had been. "Damn," Tommy whispered as he saw a small pool of blood in the middle of the truck. He pulled his phone out and tried to call Nick.

"C'mon, C'mon, pick up," Tommy yelled into his phone as he jogged back toward his own boat which was an old fishing vessel. It could never match the speed of Jeff's boat. It did not matter, Tommy knew he had to try.

As he crossed the driveway, he stopped short when a car pulled in at high speed and almost hit him. He turned to yell and saw Nick in the driver's seat. Tommy ran over and placed his hands on the door frame. "Hey, Jeff was here and took off in the boat. I think he's got Megan with him. There was blood in the back of his pickup truck. My boat sucks, but it's all we got. Let's go."

Nick pulled over into the grass on the side of the driveway. He yelled to Tommy as he popped out the driver's side of the car. "Tommy, over here. We'll take the patrol boat." Tommy turned around and headed back toward the car. He was surprised to see Georgie pop out of the passenger seat. The three ran over to the slip where the patrol boat was docked. Nick had already untied the lines and had the motor running as Tommy and Georgie jumped into the boat.

"Where did you come from?" Tommy asked Georgie as they tried to get to a seat in the boat.

"After I texted Nick, I tried to text Megan. When she didn't answer, I tried calling her but still no answer. I was on the boardwalk, so I ran up to the house and I saw police cars by the garage. Then Nick was leaving for the marina and I jumped into the car in case I could be of help."

As Nick increased speed, the boat crashed off the waves. Rain pelted them as the wind picked up over the choppy waters. Nick turned around and yelled to his passengers. "I can't see his boat. Does anyone know which way they went?"

Tommy pulled out his phone and called Uncle Billy. He was hoping he had enough reception and, thankfully, Billy picked up the receiver on the second ring. Static filled his ear but he could still make out Tommy's words.

"Uncle Billy, Jeff Davenport took off in his boat. Are you back in the lighthouse? Can you hear me? Check the telescope. Can you see them?"

"Hold on Tommy. Let me look." Uncle Billy limped over to the telescope and tried to find the boats in the water. The rain and wind made visibility very difficult, but he spotted a boat heading northeast into the ocean. The patrol boat was leaving the harbor. "Head northeast. There's a speedboat heading northeast. It's hard to see but it could be Jeff's. There's no one else out there, so it has to be him."

Tommy listened to his phone and then tapped Nick on the shoulder. I think Uncle Billy said they're heading northeast. Tommy pointed as he spoke.

"You got it," Nick said as he turned the boat. Wind whipped through their hair while sea spray pelted their faces.

Georgie had tried to stand but lost her balance and dropped back into the side bench of the boat. "What is that bastard thinking?"

"I don't know," Nick said. "We'll ask him when we catch him unless I drown him first." Nick was standing as he steered and pointed. "I think I see the boat. Tommy, there's a pair of binoculars in the chest over there. Grab them and check it out."

Tommy tried not to fall as the patrol boat continued to bounce. He half crawled to the chest and pulled out the binoculars. After stabilizing himself against the seat and side of the vessel, he trained the binoculars toward the northeast. Rain slapped against the glass which made it very difficult to see anything. Tommy wiped the lens and looked again. "I think that's him. C'mon Nick, push it." The patrol boat hit its max speed, slamming the tops of the waves as the three of them were soaked with sea spray and rain. They braced themselves against the side so they would not be flung into the water as they gave chase.

Chapter Seventy Two

Megan's head bounced as she slowly came to consciousness. It was hard to breathe and her head was pounding. There was some material in front of her face and the side of her head felt warm and sticky. Her entire body seemed to be vibrating and bouncing up and down.

She tried to move her hands and realized there was something pulled tight around her middle, holding her arms to her sides. On one side, the restriction was low and on the other it was higher, near her elbow.

Her body continued to bounce as she shivered. Megan moved her right hand. She felt the resistance against her right wrist, but she had some room to wiggle her arm. By pulling her right shoulder up, she was able to lift her right arm above the restriction. The material was still wrapped around her, but she was able to push out and crawl her hand upwards, over her head. Megan was thrilled when she realized her fingers, now fully stretched over her head were free. She felt cold air and water splashing against her skin.

Megan took a breath and rolled back and forth to further loosen the material. She was successful except for the realization that her head was pounding and her nausea was growing. Megan tried to remain still for a minute or so, except for the vibration which continued to torment her body.

Once her nausea lessened she started to wiggle and was successful in loosening the tie around her body. She was able to pull her left hand up and extend it over her head where her fingers were free. Feeling the edge of the material, she grabbed and pulled it down to free her face. By wriggling upward and pulling in the opposite direction, she finally cleared her face and spent several minutes gulping big breaths of fresh, cold, salty air.

Megan blinked several times. Her vision was not perfectly clear, and she was not sure if it was from the vibration, the cold rain in her face or some other reason. It was now obvious she was lying on the floor of a boat. Each time they hit the top of a wave, her whole body bounced off the floor.

Turning her head to the right, Megan was able to see a man, standing in front of the steering wheel. Her mind was foggy, but she slowly felt terror creep in as she realized her last memory was seeing Jeff Davenport, wielding a shovel, in the garage.

As adrenaline shot through her body, she moved more quickly to free herself from the tarp and twine around her body. She kicked the material off her foot and rolled to her side. Jeff had not turned around and the noise of the boat engine as well as the cold water slapping against the sides, hid any clue of her movements.

Megan rolled over and tried to lift herself. Now on her hands and knees, she looked around for something she could use as a weapon. There were rods, fighting belts, and tackle on the floor. Crawling forward, she stretched her fingers and reached for one of the rods. As her fingers grasped the end of the pole, she tried to slowly pull it toward her as she watched Jeff out of the corner of her eye. Convinced he was not paying attention, she grasped the pole and transferred it to her right hand. She then sat up and braced herself against the back of the boat, holding the pole in front of her with both hands, waiting for Jeff Davenport to turn around.

Chapter Seventy Three

Lightning flashed as the storm grew stronger. Megan was splashed repeatedly as waves crashed over the side of the boat.

After one strong bolt of lightning, Jeff turned and for the first time noticed Megan sitting up. He immediately brought the boat to a stop and swung around. As he walked toward her, he shrugged and said, "What the hell?"

"Don't come any closer," Megan yelled as she jabbed the pole toward him. "I don't know what your problem is, but that's far enough."

The storm pitched the boat from side to side throwing Jeff's balance off. Megan remained seated to keep her position steady.

"What do you think you're going to do with that?" Jeff laughed as he continued to make his way toward her.

"Whatever I have to," Megan shouted into the wind and rain. She grimaced as she realized he had the gun stuck in the waist of his pants.

Jeff's face twisted into an evil grimace. He reached out, grabbed the pole and yanked it right out of her hands. Throwing it to the side, he shouted. "I'm tired of the Stanfords. My whole life, it's always been about the Stanfords," Jeff mocked. "As far as I'm concerned, worrying about the Stanfords killed my grandfather and now I'm returning the favor."

"I have no idea what happened to your grandfather, but it has nothing to do with us," Megan shouted as she half crouched in the back of the boat.

"I don't really give a damn," Jeff said as he lurched forward and grabbed Megan's shirt. She shrank away from him and pushed him off balance. As he fell on her side, she sprang up and ran toward the front of the boat, but he was quickly behind her and yanked her hair to pull her back towards him.

Jerked backwards, she heard ringing in her ears and had stars in her vision. Her head wound reopened and began to bleed. She turned and struggled, digging her nails into his face. He quickly pushed her away and then reached out and slapped her.

Megan fell to the floor of the boat. When Jeff approached she lifted her foot and kicked as hard as she could into his groin. Jeff yelled out and fell to the floor as she scrabbled to her side to escape him. The gun fell onto the floor and slid down toward the rear. Jeff turned, grabbed her arm and landed a punch to her ribs.

Breathless, she collapsed on her side as Jeff struggled to stand. He pulled her up by her hair and dragged her over to the side of the boat. In a swinging motion, he heaved her over the edge and she flew backwards into the ocean. "Die, you bitch. Let's see you survive that." Jeff watched as he saw her hand raise above the water. Her head briefly broke the surface and was forced under by a wave.

As intent as he was, watching for Megan to surface, he did not notice the patrol boat whip around the side until it was too late. He stood up and raced to start the motor.

As the patrol boat neared, Georgie jumped into the ocean and swam to where she had last seen Megan's body surface.

Tommy immediately turned the patrol vessel around allowing Nick to make a perfect jump into Jeff's boat. Nick knocked Jeff off balance and he fell to the floor. A wave tossed them to the side allowing Jeff to jump up and scramble away. He and Nick faced off, balancing themselves with the flow of the water. Jeff reached down and grabbed a large fishing hook, which he jabbed at Nick. Stabbing him in the chest, Nick fell onto the floor where he was able to pick up a heavy fishing reel. He dodged a sharp thrust of the hook as he slammed the reel into Jeff's knee, causing his leg to buckle. Nick was able to crawl over to Jeff. Bracing himself, he grabbed the front of Jeff's shirt with his left hand and pulled while he balled his right hand into a fist and smashed it into Jeff's face. "That was for trying to kill Megan." Dazed, Jeff fell onto the floor of the boat. Nick flipped Jeff over, stuck his knee in Jeff's back and grabbed his cuffs. "This is for being an absolute jerk." Nick secured Jeff's wrists behind him. "You are under arrest." Jeff continued to lie face down in the boat as puddles of water flowed over him.

Treading for a moment or so, Georgie saw Megan's body break the surface once more. Swimming over, she was able to secure Megan's arm and stabilize her as Tommy swung the patrol boat back toward them. He pulled as near as he could and threw out rope and life preserver. When Georgie latched on, he began to pull them towards the patrol boat until he was able to reach down and help lift them to safety.

Exhausted, the two women collapsed on the floor of the boat. Megan coughed and spit up water as Tommy reached toward the gear box, grabbed a flare gun and fired high into the stormy sky. Already en route, the Coast Guard was able to reach them within minutes.

Chapter Seventy Four

Looking through the telescope, Uncle Billy saw the flare fly high into the sky and heaved a sigh of relief. He had called the Coast Guard and alerted them to the situation so he knew a vessel was close by. Tommy was able to set off the flare and now everything would be okay.

In Misty Manor, Marie and a continuous care nurse sat at the bedside to care for Rose who had continued to yell out, thrash her arms and struggle in the bed.

Not able to find Megan, Marie called the hospice emergency number for help. As the triage nurse gave her instructions to administer medication, Marie saw the flashing lights of the police car. She excused herself and flew to the window where she saw police and strangers going in and out of the garage. When she went back to the triage nurse and explained there was some sort of emergency near the house and she could not find Rose's granddaughter, the hospice made arrangements to send a continuous care nurse to help watch Rose for the remainder of the evening. Unable to retire or rest, Marie stayed with Rose and the nurse until she could figure out what was happening. They had tried various doses of different medications but nothing worked up until this point.

Marie jumped as Rose suddenly shouted. "George, George, praise the Lord. Megan is safe." Rose clasped her hands together as if she was praying and looked up toward the ceiling. "My beloved, I'll be seeing you soon." Within seconds, her eyes closed and she slept peacefully.

Chapter Seventy Five

The funeral was beautiful. The entire church waited, in silence, as six pallbearers lifted Rose's cherry wood casket onto their shoulders and walk down the aisle of the church. Rose would be buried with her favorite hankies and photos of George.

Many friends had come forward and offered support as well as food and prayers. Megan had more than enough men willing to serve as pall bearers, but specifically accepted the offer of Nick Taylor and Tommy McDonough. Uncle Billy agreed to read one of the prayers as he was not strong enough to lift the casket. It seemed like thousands of people were at the wake and funeral. The whole town had been shocked by Rose's death as well as Henry Davenport's. The one person obviously missing was her father, Dean Stanford. After relentless efforts, he was finally reached and told of his mother's demise but declined to return to New Jersey from Europe for the funeral.

When prompted, Megan stood up and followed the small procession to the back of the church. After waiting a short time, she was escorted to a sleek, long black limousine and gently seated inside. She dabbed at her blackened eyes as she took a few moments to reflect back on the last week.

When the Coast Guard had arrived, they immediately transferred Georgie and Megan to their vessel. While the crew secured the other two boats, the women were given towels and robes and placed in a warm room with makeshift bunks. Once safe, only minutes went by before Megan fell into a deep sleep.

Eventually, Tommy, Nick, and Jeff were brought aboard and transported back to the harbor where police and an ambulance was waiting. Megan was brought to the emergency room and Jeff Davenport was read his rights and escorted to the Misty Point jail.

A forensic team recovered the gun, droplets of blood as well as the tarp and rope from the boat. Samples of blood were also recovered from the pickup truck as well as the garage and back of the shovel blade.

After spending a night in the hospital undergoing a CT scan of the head, various other x-rays and a neuro exam, Megan was released and allowed to return to Misty Manor.

Megan jumped as the door to the limo suddenly opened and Georgie and Amber climbed inside. "Hi, Megan. How are you holding up?"

"Okay, for now," Megan said as she reached for her friend's hands. "Thank you for coming today and helping me through this. I can't believe Rose is gone." Megan slowly shook her head side to side as a few tears began to slide down her cheeks.

"Of course, we're here for you," Amber said. "You've been through a horrible time since you returned to Misty Point."

Megan nodded her head. "Thank you, Amber." She turned toward Georgie and said, "And thank you, Georgie. You risked your life for me and I'll never forget it."

"No problem, Megan. I have to swim in the ocean every day, anyway." Georgie said with a smile as she tried to lighten the moment.

The back doors opened once again and Tommy and Nick stepped into the limo. Georgie, Tommy and Amber moved to the long side seat, allowing Nick to sit next to Megan in the back.

"You okay?" Nick said as he put his arm around Megan's shoulders and pulled her toward his side.

"As well as can be expected," Megan said with a small smile. "Are we still meeting with Davis, tomorrow?"

"Yes, we need to go over everything once again before we close this case," Nick explained. "After what happened, he didn't want to bother you until after the funeral."

Megan nodded and turned her head to look out the window as the limo followed the hearse toward the cemetery. Once again, Megan's thoughts turned to the last few days and Misty Manor.

Once Megan was medically cleared, Nick picked her up from the hospital and drove her home. Head still pounding, and more than slightly dizzy, Megan carefully walked up the steps onto the front porch and into the Grand Victorian home.

Megan walked up the grand staircase. She immediately went to her grandmother's room, sat at the bedside and held her hand.

"Grandma, it's Megan. I'm home."

Rose turned her head toward Megan and smiled. "I'm so happy to see you."

"I'm happy to see you, too," Megan said. "I hope you didn't worry about me."

"Oh, I did," Rose said as she nodded. "But your grandfather was watching over you and kept me informed. He told me as soon as you were safe."

Despite being warm and dry, Megan felt chilled as Rose spoke. "What else did he say, Grandma?"

"He's been singing our favorite wedding song to me," Rose said with a smile. "He said we'll have a wonderful dance when I see him again. He also said he was glad you found the gun in the car. You'll find the rest there, too."

Megan went still. Initially, only Jeff knew she had found the gun when he crept into the garage. It was in his waistband when they were on the boat and fell out when they struggled. She knew the forensics team had recovered it, but no one knew exactly where she had found it and Megan was unaware of anyone telling Rose about the gun at all.

"What do you mean by the rest?" Megan asked softly.

"I don't know exactly, dear. But your grandfather said once you find the rest, you'll understand everything. I'm happy knowing you're safe. I love you so much, Megan. You've always been a blessing, treasure and joy to me."

Megan started to cry as she held her hand. "Grandma, I love you too. Always."

"And I will always be with you, watching over you. Remember that," Rose said as she nodded her head for emphasis. Rose's eyes closed briefly. She looked so small and frail in the bed. Megan leaned over and kissed her on the forehead and when she did, Rose squeezed her fingers ever so slightly. Megan pulled a blanket over herself and sat with Rose in the dark. Somewhere in the middle of the night, Rose left to sing and dance with her beloved George, forever.

"Hey, what are you thinking about?" Nick asked her, drawing her attention back to the limo. The funeral procession had stopped at the entrance of the St. Francis cemetery and were waiting to be led to the grave.

"Something Rose said to me hours before she died," Megan said. "It was a message from my grandfather."

Her friends all looked at each other with wide eyes as a representative from the funeral parlor beckoned them all to the grave. With incredibly sad hearts and tear filled eyes, Rose was laid to rest on a beautiful hill overlooking the peaceful blue ocean.

Chapter Seventy Six

"Okay, everyone's here, so let's get started." Officer Davis commanded attention from the group seated in the parlor of Misty Manor. Although he had taken copious notes and interviewed everyone in the room separately, he wanted to have a conference to finalize the investigation. They were seated on couches and chairs in a semicircle around the room. Several trays of coffee and pastry were set up on a table for sustenance.

Everyone agreed to be present for the discussion. Georgie and Amber had come to support Megan as well as Tommy and Nick, except Nick was in uniform and maintained his distance in the presence of his commanding officer. Marie was present and Uncle Billy had come as well, by special request and command from Officer Davis.

When he heard about the death, Rose's lawyer had asked to attend as a representative of the estate of Rose Stanford and Misty Manor. On the way into the house, he whispered to Megan they should meet to discuss the estate the following week.

"Thank you, but you should probably be meeting with my father," Megan said with a dismissive shrug.

"As a very minor party, your father's presence will not be required. However, Miss Stanford, you and I have a lot to discuss." With that, he walked past her, poured himself a cup of coffee and took a seat.

Megan stared after him, eyes wide until she heard Officer Davis calling out.

"Gather round, let's get started," Davis said. "Everyone take a seat. First, let's understand this is a confidential meeting about an open criminal case. Any details discussed today are not to leave this room."

Everyone nodded their understanding and Davis continued. He drew a notebook as well as a pile of papers out of his briefcase. "We have most of the information, but there are a few pieces missing and I believe the answers lie somewhere in this room." Davis looked up and aimed a pointed glance to each member in the parlor. Several people squirmed when he looked at them. He then looked down, shuffled a series of papers and plucked one from the group. Adjusting his reading glasses, he cleared his throat and continued. "The results came in from the genetic analysis and it does appear as if the remains we found belong to George Stanford. The genetic material from the remains and Megan Stanford matched on many markers." Several people in the room murmured when they heard the news and looked at Megan. To avoid any shock or discomfort, Davis had informed her of the same fact early in the morning. They discussed when the remains would be released as Megan wanted to be sure they were interred beside Rose at the St. Francis cemetery.

Officer Davis continued. "The manner of death, however, was murder. It appears Mr. Stanford was shot in the head. The location of the bullet hole is inconsistent with a suicide and the fact the body was buried under a cement floor also indicates foul play was involved with cover up."

Marie O'Sullivan gasped from the corner of the room. Davis paused to look up at her as Amber raced over with a glass of water. After a few gulps and several minutes, Davis continued reading from his notes. "Since George Stanford disappeared in 1955, we assume the murder took place at that time. A missing person's report was filed. We pulled the building permits for the cottages. They had been approved several months before and construction was ongoing at the time of Mr. Stanford's disappearance. We assume he was shot in the head and then his body buried in the area which was scheduled to have a concrete floor poured."

Megan cleared her throat and leaned forward with shaky hands to clutch her cup of coffee. The others talked quietly as they needed a few minutes to let the information sink in. Nick walked over to Megan's side. "Are you okay?"

"As well as I could be, I suppose," Megan said. "It's not every day you hear about your grandfather's murder." Nick squeezed her shoulder and then rejoined Officer Davis in the front of the room.

Davis looked down at his notes, cleared his throat and started to speak. "Now, the next thing I asked myself is who was around in 1955 when the murder was committed?" Davis answered his own question. "Up until two weeks ago, Rose Stanford, Henry Davenport and Billy Conklin."

The crowd looked over at Uncle Billy who was seated in the corner of the room, with his arms crossed in front of him. He was deep in thought and staring down at his feet. Davis cleared his throat once again. "Mr. Conklin?" Uncle Billy looked up and realized everyone was looking at him. "Mr. Conklin, I have yet to figure out why George Stanford died and who was responsible. I was wondering if you had any more information to offer."

Uncle Billy shrugged his shoulders and looked at Tommy who silently pleaded with him to speak. Billy's facial expression was pained as he considered his options.

Megan looked over at Tommy and asked, "Did you ask Uncle Billy about the photo?" Tommy shook his head. "I didn't have time. Everything happened so fast."

"What photo?" Billy asked in a gruff voice.

Megan stood up, walked to the hallway and retrieved her copy of the photo from the mail desk and brought it to Uncle Billy. "We wanted to know about this photo and these men. I found it in the attic and I believe that's you on the side. Am I right?"

Uncle Billy grimaced as he nodded his head. "Yup, that's me. I was nineteen years old." He paused as his voice choked. He then swallowed and looked up towards Megan. "Your grandfather had just turned thirty and we were very good friends. He was excited because he bought himself a car for his birthday. It was the Studebaker Speedster."

"The same one that's in the garage?" Davis asked as he scribbled various notes, suppressing his anger at not being advised of the photo. He pointedly looked over at Nick who shrugged.

Billy nodded his head once again and answered softly. "Yes, that's the one. It was a big deal back then. Everyone wanted to ride in it and a lot of the guys who normally wouldn't give George the time of day started acting real friendly. They chatted him up and dropped hints about the car. George was happy to be center of attention so he fell for it all." Billy shook his head. "I tried to warn him they were up to no good, but he wouldn't listen."

"After a couple of weeks, driving them around, he disappeared for the weekend and when he came back he was nervous. He was acting funny so I kept asking him what was going on. Finally, one day he pulls me inside the garage and makes me promise to take care of

Rose if anything happened to him." Billy looked down and swallowed nervously. His hands were shaking as he used his handkerchief to wipe sweat off his brow. The room was silent as all eyes watched and waited for his next words.

"So I yelled at him. I said if you want me to make that promise you'd better tell me what was wrong. He said he didn't want to tell me so I'd be safe, but I promised I'd keep my mouth shut." Billy looked up at the guests. "And I did. I've been looking after Rose all these years, fixing problems with the house and watching out for her safety."

Officer Davis scratched his head and gestured at Uncle Billy. "Go ahead, sir. Please continue."

"Well, you know the Garden State Parkway?" Everyone nodded their heads in unison. "It was started around 1947 and a lot of it was built in the mid-50's." Billy looked down at the photo in his hands. "The guys in this picture are George, Robert Stiles, Fred Brown and Henry Davenport. Fred Brown came to the group and told them he could get a big job in Atlantic City, but would need a ride. He promised they could all get work if they convinced George to drive them and it would be a big deal if they could travel on the Garden State Parkway in the Studebaker Speedster. George agreed. He drove them down and they hung around for the weekend. George mostly stayed with the car while the other guys worked inside, but he never really knew what they were doing."

Billy accepted the glass of water Tommy brought to him and took a big gulp. After he swallowed, he continued. "Anyway, the last day, the guys come running toward the car and jump in. They told George they were finished and he should leave as soon as possible and that's what he did. When they got back to Misty Point, they were congratulating each other and bragging about their big job. They celebrated by drinking a lot of beer and then they pulled out a fancy necklace. George said it had diamonds and sapphires and was very expensive. One by one, the guys left or passed out, except George, because he wasn't drinking. The necklace was just sitting there so he took it and hid it."

"The next day, there was an article in the paper about a royal family visiting Atlantic City. They had gone to the police because they had been robbed and the piece of jewelry they described was the same necklace George had seen. He was real upset and wanted to return it to the police, but he didn't want to get arrested. Dean was small then, about five years old and George didn't want any trouble to come to him and Rose. He kept thinking on what he should do. He never told me his plan but he asked me to take care of Rose if anything ever happened and it did."

Uncle Billy sighed and sat back against his chair. Years of keeping the secret exhausted him as he exposed the details. He looked all of his eighty years as his shoulders drooped.

"I still don't understand what happened," Megan said as she shook her head.

"Neither do I," Officer Davis mimicked her as he turned to Billy. "You must remember something else. What happened when George disappeared?"

Billy took another sip of water. "Rose was gone that weekend. She had taken Dean to see her mother and she begged George to take her. He didn't want to go. He was nervous those days and acting a bit strange so Rose and Dean took the train to NY. When she got back, he was gone."

"But you were around at that time, weren't you?" Davis asked as he looked directly at Bill. "Did you see what happened?"

Uncle Billy fidgeted and swallowed hard as he nodded. His voice was soft when he spoke. "I was here that weekend. The night Rose left, the guys came over to Misty Manor to confront George. They accused him of taking the necklace and they were mad. They were also worried he would turn them in to the police and they got in a big argument. George swore he would keep his mouth shut and he didn't know where the necklace was, but they didn't believe him. They dragged him into the garage and beat him, but George didn't break. He was horrified when he realized he was part of a major robbery. He would have gone to the police eventually. I know he would of."

"What happened next?" Davis continued to press. "Were you in the garage?"

Uncle Billy shook his head. No, I was outside the building, but there was a hole I could watch through the back and not be seen. Anyway, when George didn't produce the necklace, Henry Davenport pulled out a gun."

"Oh Lord," Marie said, hands up to her face.

"He waved it around and pistol whipped George until he was bleeding and finally, George broke. He told them where he hid the necklace."

Megan sat on the couch, tears streaming down her face as she listened to Uncle Billy's story.

"And then?" Davis demanded.

"They left the garage to retrieve the necklace, but as they were walking across the back lawn, Robert Stiles fell back with Henry Davenport. He grabbed the gun out of Henry's hands and shot George right in the back of the head." Billy choked up and started crying as he told of the murder. After a few minutes and deep breaths, he continued. "They had a big fight about that. Henry made Fred Brown and Robert Stiles dig the hole to bury George in. The foundation area was already marked off for the new cottage so they buried him there. No one suspected the fresh dirt because they knew it had been recently dug up for construction. A few days later, the concrete floor was poured and that was that."

"Wow," Megan said as she pushed back her hair. "Did Rose know? Do you think she ever had any idea?"

Billy shook his head. "She never knew what happened, but she knew it was something bad. When the boys finished burying George, they ran off real quick. After that night, Fred Brown left town and was never seen again so he sort of disappeared too. Someone had seen him pack his car and leave, so they knew he wasn't dead. The other guys, especially, Henry Davenport, hung around a lot in the beginning. They kept asking Rose if George had left her any gifts or special jewelry before he disappeared. You see, Stiles shot George after he told them where he had hidden the necklace, but George lied about the location, so they never found it. They didn't realize they dropped the gun when they were digging the hole. I found it and hid it in the grill of the Studebaker, so they couldn't find that either. George was dead, and all for nothing. The hiding spot went to the grave with him."

Silence hung in the air like a lead weight as Billy finished. "Henry figured George was going to give the necklace to Rose, so he kept asking her about finding special jewelry. Rose was a smart women and she read the newspaper all the time. Stories about the royal family, the missing necklace and George's disappearance stayed in the paper for weeks."

Megan's head popped up. "I found a copy of the original article about a robbery in Atlantic City packed away with Rose's things but I didn't realize it was important at the time. I thought she kept the newspaper because there was an article about George."

"I think she figured it was related," Billy said. "Some people suggested George stole the necklace and ran away, but that was plain ridiculous. George owned almost everything in town at that time. Why would he steal a necklace and run away? I think Henry also realized Rose now owned a fortune and was hoping he could marry her and take that too, but Rose would have none of it. To be honest, I think he even had feelings for her. Rose was a wonderful lady."

"Why didn't you go to the police?" Georgie asked as she struggled with the details.

"What good would that have done? George made me promise to take care of Rose. He was dead, the necklace was missing, and if the police got involved it would have been worse for everyone. But I kept my promise. I stayed here and watched out for Rose. I warned her about Davenport being up to no good. He kept a vigil his whole life looking for that damn necklace."

"What happened to Robert Stiles?" Nick asked, more from curiosity than anything else.

Billy nodded. "He died in a tragic accident about two years later. Seems his car skidded into a pond and he drowned, but some thought it was awful funny. They tried to say he was drunk, but I'm not sure about that."

"I don't get it," Tommy said. "Why is all this coming out now? Why try to kill Megan?"

Davis cleared his throat. "I believe I have some of those answers. Nick had the video pulled of the Clamshell parking lot." Davis looked at Megan. "The person who vandalized your car was Fran Stiles."

"Fran?"

"That witch," Amber said from her side of the room. "What are you doing about that?" She asked as she stared at Officer Davis.

"We picked her up and charged her before we got here," Davis said. "She was angry she was thrown out of the house. When we searched her place, we found checks in Rose's name as well as some artifacts we believe she stole from Misty Manor. She had lots of plans. All will be returned when the investigation is complete."

"What about Jeff?" Georgie asked. "What the hell was his problem?"

"Apparently, he truly does have a deep hatred for the Stanfords. Andrew Davenport admitted his father was obsessed with Misty Manor and Rose Stanford. Whether Henry wanted the necklace, or felt guilty about George's death or was in love with Rose, I don't know," Davis explained.

"Jeff was the one who dumped all the fish," Nick added. "He wanted to make your life as miserable as possible. Jeff finally told us that Henry panicked when the construction crew found George's skeleton. He was worried the gun would show up, which had his fingerprints on it. He also worried the necklace would show up but was fascinated by the thought and obsessed about it. The night Henry Davenport died, he told his family he was partially responsible for George's murder. Jeff blamed the Stanfords for all the misery in his life and went after Megan."

"And I can't say 'thank you' any more than I have," Megan said, her face flushed as she looked at her friends gathered in the parlor. "If you didn't come after me, I wouldn't be here today."

"Uncle Billy is the guy," Tommy said. "He's the one who saw Jeff go into the garage and got the ball rolling."

Megan walked over to Uncle Billy and gave him a big hug. Billy returned an impassioned embrace. "I spent my whole life protecting you and Rose. I wasn't about to stop now."

"Hey guys," Amber said from across the room as she typed on her iPhone. "There's a story about your robbery and necklace on the internet. There's even a reward for the necklace if anyone finds it. Who would have guessed after all these years?"

"It's too bad we don't know where it is," Georgie said as she looked over at Megan and noticed her expression. "What are you thinking?"

Megan shrugged. "This is completely crazy, but I think I may know where the necklace is."

"What? Do tell," Amber said as she bounced over toward Megan.

"Yes, Ms. Stanford. If you have any information, please share." Officer Davis shifted his feet as he stared at her.

"I think it's in the garage, with the car."

"Did you see it when you were in there?" Davis asked. "The boys went over the place pretty well when you were abducted and we didn't come up with anything."

"No, I didn't actually see it and you'll think I'm crazy if I tell you why, but I'd like to go take a look if you want to come with me," Megan offered.

Davis put his pad and pen in his pocket and scratched the back of his head. He then gestured to the door. "Let's go."

Megan got up and walked through the main foyer toward the back door. Amber bounced along behind them. "I'm going too," she whispered to Georgie. Slowly, everyone followed to see if Megan was right.

Megan reached the large garage doors. Nick and Davis helped open them for her. She felt her stomach clench as she stared at the blood stain in the center of the garage. Silently, she asked Rose and George to help her find the necklace. She approached the Studebaker and trailed her fingers along the side as she rounded the car. Not quite sure how she knew, but she opened the driver's side door and sat in the driver's seat. In her mind, she quickly flashed back to her grandfather sitting in the same seat wondering what to do with the necklace as he quickly tried to hide it. With her arm resting down at her side, she once again felt the opening in the diamond quilted leather seat. To satisfy her curiosity, she reached her hand into the seat and stretched her fingers as far as she could. She felt something at the tips of her fingers which moved when she tried to grab it.

Stepping out of the car, she knelt at the side of the driver's seat, leaned over and dug into the front seat. Davis and a few others crowded behind her. She had to rip the tear in the seat wider, but by digging her hand in deeper, she was rewarded when she pulled out a shimmering necklace made of an exquisite array of sapphires and diamonds.

"I don't believe it," Amber squealed as she took a photo of Megan holding the necklace. "It's breathtaking."

"It really is," Megan said as she handed it to Officer Davis.

Uncle Billy crowded behind, shaking his head. "It's a shame such beauty could cause so much pain. Rose and George lost sixty years over that necklace."

Megan nodded her head and softly whispered. "Yes, but it's okay because they're together now, forever in each other's arms, dancing to their anniversary song and watching over me."

Two hours later, Megan sat on the front porch with Nick. He held her hand and said, "Are you sure you're going to be okay tonight?"

"Yes, I'll be fine," Megan said, shaking her head.

"I'm not sure it's a good idea to be alone," Nick argued. "Marie was willing to stay. Amber and Georgie said you're welcome to sleep at their place."

Megan turned and searched his eyes. "Trust me, I'm right where I need to be and I'm not alone, with you here."

Nick grinned and squeezed her shoulders. "I'd love to stay the night, but I have to work the late shift."

"It's okay, Nick. I'm not going anywhere and we have plenty of nights to look forward to. This may sound crazy, but I heard from Grandma Rose last night." Megan smiled as she turned and looked at the moonlight reflecting off the calm ocean. "I have a lot of work ahead of me. There are arrangements I need to make because we have big plans for Misty Manor."

About the Author:

Linda Rawlins is an American writer of mystery fiction best known for her Rocky Meadow mystery series, including The Bench, Fatal Breach and Sacred Gold. She loved to read as a child and started writing her first mystery novel in fifth grade. She then went on to study science, medicine and literature, eventually graduating medical school and establishing her career in medicine.

Misty Manor is the debut novel of her new beach series.

Linda Rawlins lives in New Jersey with her husband, her family and spoiled pets. She loves spending time at the beach as well as visiting the mountains of Vermont.

01 July 2016